Gillian laid her hand lightly on Bayard's arm, to offer what silent comfort she could.

Yet as she did she became achingly aware of the feel of his flesh and muscle beneath her fingertips. Of his proximity and the masculine scent of leather and wool attending him. Of his lips so close to hers.

He was her sister Adelaide's brother-in-law, sent to protect her. Not to woo her. Never to court or to kiss. Never to wed or to love. He drew her to him. She should stop him…protest…refuse…run…

She couldn't. Didn't want to. The moment their lips met the walls she'd erected around her heart broke into a thousand pieces, destroyed by his touch.

Desire, so long held in check, burst free from its restraints, and the longing she had tried to deny leaped into life.

She wanted to be in his arms, to feel and experience passion once again, and to be desired in return.

So she kissed him fervently, and with an almost despe　　　　　　　　　　n wanton with no m　　　　　　　　　　n warming a man

This

Praise for
Margaret Moore

THE NOTORIOUS KNIGHT

Margaret Moore

All the characters in this book have no existence outside the imagination of the author, and have no relation whatsoever to anyone bearing the same name or names. They are not even distantly inspired by any individual known or unknown to the author, and all the incidents are pure invention.

First published in Great Britain 2010
Harlequin Mills & Boon Limited,
Eton House, 18-24 Paradise Road, Richmond, Surrey TW9 1SR

© Margaret Wilkins 2007

ISBN: 978 0 263 88307 7

Harlequin Mills & Boon policy is to use papers that are natural, renewable and recyclable products and made from wood grown in sustainable forests. The logging and manufacturing process conform to the legal environmental regulations of the country of origin.

Printed and bound in Spain
by Litografia Rosés, S.A., Barcelona

Award-winning author **Margaret Moore** began her career at the age of eight, when she and a friend concocted stories featuring a lovely damsel and a handsome, misunderstood thief nicknamed 'The Red Sheik'. Unknowingly pursuing her destiny, Margaret graduated with distinction from the University of Toronto, Canada. She has been a Leading Wren in the Royal Canadian Naval Reserve, an award-winning public speaker, a member of an archery team, and a student of fencing and ballroom dancing. She has also worked for every major department store chain in Canada.

Margaret lives in Toronto, Ontario, with her husband of over twenty-five years. Her two children have grown up understanding that it's part of their mother's job to discuss non-existent people and their problems. When not writing, Margaret updates her blog and website at www.margaretmoore.com

Novels by Margaret Moore:

THE OVERLORD'S BRIDE
COMFORT AND JOY (in *The Christmas Visit*)
BRIDE OF LOCHBARR
LORD OF DUNKEATHE
THE VAGABOND KNIGHT (in *Yuletide Weddings*)
THE UNWILLING BRIDE
THE DUKE'S DESIRE
HERS TO COMMAND
HERS TO DESIRE
THE DUKE'S DILEMMA
MY LORD'S DESIRE

And as a Mills & Boon® Historical Undone eBook:

THE WELSH LORD'S MISTRESS

In memory of
Patricia Probert and Holly Stemmler

CHAPTER ONE

England, 1204

THE IRON RINGS of chain mail jingled as Sir Bayard de Boisbaston raised his right arm to halt his men.

"Well, Frederic, what do you make of Castle Averette?" he asked his young squire, pointing across the wooded valley.

Frederic de Sere squinted at the gray stone fortress on the low rise opposite and shifted nervously in his saddle. "Small, isn't it?"

"From what we can see, you'd think so," Bayard agreed, "but not every castle is built in a circle. It could be that the barbican and towers facing the main road are at the narrow end."

He gestured at the towers at either side of the gate. "Archers have a clear view of the portcullis and good angles to shoot anybody approaching or getting close to the gate."

He'd also noticed that the trees and bushes had been cut back from the sides of the road, leaving a swath of bracken-covered ground between the road and the wood that was at least ten feet wide on either side. No enemies or footpads could ambush travelers before they had time to draw their swords and defend themselves.

Frederic brushed a lock of light brown hair from his eyes. "Yes, I see, my lord."

"On to Averette," Bayard said as he nudged his horse into a walk.

Whatever else the late lord of Averette had been—and apparently he'd been a terrible man—he'd also been a man of some intelligence, at least when it came to defense, Bayard reflected as he and his men rode in silence along the river toward what looked to be a prosperous village. They passed a millpond and the mill, its wheel turning with a slow, steady motion. Cattle lowed from a nearby field, a few sheep scattered as they went past a meadow, and they could hear geese honking and chickens clucking in farmyards along the road.

The village itself was not large, but the buildings were in good repair and the people appeared well fed. A few ragged children, with mongrel dogs yapping at their heels, ran out of an alley between a chandler's stall and an inn sporting a sign depicting a stag's head to stare at them, openmouthed. At the inn's door stood an ample-bosomed wench who eyed Bayard and his men with avaricious calculation. If she thought she'd get any custom from him, however, she was sorely mistaken.

Around the green, merchants at their stalls, as well as their customers, stopped to watch them go by. So did the group of elderly men seated beneath the large oak by the smithy that belched smoke even on this summer day, and the girls and women standing by the well.

No doubt there would be the usual comments after he was gone, Bayard thought, about his body, and his bearing, and the scar that ran from his right eye to his chin. They'd wonder where he got it, and how, and who had done it. Some would say it marred his face; a few would declare they liked it.

He'd heard it all before. Too many times.

Soon enough somebody would remember they'd heard

of the notorious Sir Bayard de Boisbaston and recall the nickname he'd earned when he'd first arrived at court. He'd been sixteen, as well as spoiled, vain, and determined to make a name for himself.

He'd certainly done the latter.

Bayard slid a glance at fifteen-year-old Frederic, who was now sitting his horse with more lordly dignity and looking straight ahead as if completely unaware of the feminine attention directed their way.

Undoubtedly he was really enjoying every moment of that attention. The pride and folly of youth! One day he, too, would likely learn that not all attention was good, and not every woman who admired him was worthy of pursuit, or that winning his way into her bed such a great triumph.

A shout of warning came from the castle.

The sentries were alert, then. Given the news he had to deliver, Bayard decided it would be better to get the initial meeting over. He ordered his men to quicken their pace and lightly kicked his own horse into a canter.

As they neared the castle gates, a boy suddenly darted out from behind a farmer's cart filled with empty baskets, running toward the rickety gate in the fence opposite like a pheasant flushed from the underbrush.

Cursing, Bayard reined in his mount so hard, Danceur went back on his haunches and whinnied in protest. At nearly the same time, a woman appeared as if out of thin air in the cottage yard. She wrenched open the gate with such force she tore the top leather hinge clear off, scooped the child into her arms, and fled back to the well-kept yard. Clutching the child to her, she glared at Bayard as though he'd deliberately tried to murder the boy.

His heart pounding as if he'd been attacked, Bayard

glared right back. He hadn't harmed the child, and it wouldn't have been his fault if he had. The boy had run directly into his path.

He was about to remind this ungrateful peasant of that fact when he recalled his mission here. He was to offer help, not enmity, so he stifled his temper. Thinking a few coins would soothe any ill will caused by this near accident, he dismounted and walked through the broken gate toward the mother and her child.

The boy, who couldn't be more than six years old, stared at him with wide-eyed awe. His mother continued to glower.

She wore a simple peasant's gown of light-brown wool and her honey-brown hair was covered by a linen veil. She was no great beauty, however, and although she might be spirited—and Bayard usually liked women with spirit, at least in his bed—he didn't appreciate such vitality when it was directed against him.

A heavyset man clad in the rough homespun of a peasant appeared from behind the cottage. His stunned gaze went from Bayard to Frederic and the mounted soldiers on the road, then back to his wife, as if he'd never seen a nobleman with an escort before.

Or perhaps he was wondering why there was a knight standing in his yard.

The woman passed the little boy to her husband, crossed her arms—incidentally revealing that she had very fine breasts—and addressed Bayard without a particle of deference or respect. "What is your business here, sir knight?"

"Who are you to speak to a nobleman in that insolent fashion?" Frederic demanded.

"Easy, lad," Bayard warned, glancing over his shoulder at the disdainful youth.

Those had been no peasant's dulcet tones or accent; the woman had betrayed herself with the first word that passed those full and frowning lips.

Bayard removed his helmet, tucked it under his arm and bowed. "Greetings, my lady. I am Sir Bayard de Boisbaston and I bring you news from your sister."

Not unexpectedly, there was a flash of surprise in the woman's bright green eyes, but it was quickly gone. Nor did she try to deny who she was.

"What news might this be? And from which one of my sisters?" Lady Gillian d'Averette inquired as coolly as if she met knights in a farmer's yard every day while attired in peasant's garb.

Maybe she did, and maybe that was her usual mode of dress; Armand had warned him his bride's sister was rather unusual, although he hadn't gone into detail.

Maybe she discussed important news out in the open where anyone might hear, too, but he did not. "I don't think this is an appropriate place for you to read the letter I bring you, my lady."

She pursed her lips, and for a moment he thought she might actually refuse.

Fortunately, she didn't.

"Very well," she said as she marched past him with unladylike strides. "Come with me, if you will be so kind," she added over her shoulder.

Armand might also have mentioned that not only did his sister-in-law dress like a peasant, she issued orders like an empress, stomped like an irate merchant, and was nowhere near as beautiful as her sister, Adelaide. She hadn't given him a kiss of greeting, either.

God's blood, he'd had a friendlier welcome from the man who'd held him prisoner in France, Bayard thought as he followed her.

In spite of her discourtesy, however, he would say nothing and try to ignore her rudeness.

After all, he hadn't expected to be welcomed with open arms, so it shouldn't matter that she was less than thrilled by his arrival. Armand had asked him to bring a message to her, as well as stay to protect his wife's sister, and that he fully intended to do.

WHAT NEWS COULD this arrogant fellow be bringing from Adelaide and the king's court? Gillian wondered as she hurried toward the castle and the privacy of the solar.

She doubted it was good.

She and her sisters, Adelaide and Elizabeth—Lizette to those who knew her—were wards of the king. That meant John had complete power over them. He could marry them off as suited his purposes, without any regard at all for their happiness. He also gave guardianships of young male heirs to men who would strip the estates bare before the boys came of age. Indeed, he gave no thought at all to the welfare and safety of those for whom he was responsible, including the people of England.

Who could say what he might have done that could affect her, or the people of Averette?

And why had this knight been chosen to deliver her sister's message? If Adelaide were ill, a servant would have been dispatched.

Was it possible John had selected a husband for Adelaide, or Lizette, or even *her*—and this man was to be the groom?

Surely not. Please, God, she hoped not. Not for her, and not a man like this, an arrogant fellow who regarded her, and everyone else, with aggravating condescension.

Over the years she'd met many a man just like him. No doubt this Sir Bayard expected her to be impressed with his rank, his bearing, and his good looks. To be sure, he was handsome, despite the thin scar that went from the corner of his right eye to his chin, but she was no flighty, foolish girl to be so easily impressed.

Only once had she met a knight who had been generous, kind, and humble, and who had, surprisingly, been more interested in her than either of her sisters.

But that had been years ago, and James d'Ardenay was dead.

She glanced at Sir Bayard again. What was he seeing as he approached Averette? Tithes and income? Peasants who should be ready to fight in battles and die for their overlord's cause?

She saw her home and people who labored to keep it prosperous and safe, secure in times of trouble. She saw men and women with names, faces, families, hopes, and dreams—like Young Davy, who knew more about the history of this village and its folk than anyone else. Old Davy was like a grandfather to her, as his wife had been more of a mother to her than her own poor sickly mother had ever been.

She knew the miller and the baker with their constant conflict, Sam at the tavern and Peg, as well as the morose chandler, who barely said three words to anybody.

She saw people like Hale, the hayward, and father of little Teddy, whom Sir Bayard had nearly run down—not that he seemed troubled by that near accident, and of course he'd assumed a sum of money would be appropriate compensation.

There were many others, each one unique, some more likable than others, but all hers to protect, like this household, castle, and estate.

And she would. To the last breath in her body and regardless of who sat on the throne, she would.

AS THEY NEARED the barbican, ten soldiers of the garrison trotted out and blocked the entrance, their spears tipped forward like a spiked wall. The portcullis had been lowered and the inner gate closed. Several archers also lined the walls, which was no more than Bayard would expect.

"Your men are well trained," he noted in an attempt to achieve some sort of truce when he and the lady came to a halt.

She couldn't look prouder if she trained them herself. "They are," she replied. Then she announced, in a loud, clear voice, "All is well!"

He caught the expression that flashed across the soldiers' faces. That meant something, and it wasn't that all was truly well.

Likely it meant she saw no immediate danger but they should be prepared to fight.

The portcullis began to rise, and the soldiers wheeled back so that they lined the road. Bayard dutifully fell into step beside Lady Gillian as they passed through the large gatehouse and across the outer bailey, which contained a practice yard, a garden, a smithy, and a round stone dovecote. He'd been right to suggest to Frederic that the portion of the wall visible from the approaching road was no indication of the actual size of the fortress. This one had been built in a tear shape, with the barbican and gatehouse at the narrow end.

They entered the courtyard through thick, bossed oaken gates. He guessed this fortress was built within the last fifty years, although the round keep behind the long hall was clearly older. Judging by the black marks beneath some of the narrow loopholes in the keep, it had been fired more than once. That it was still standing was a silent testament to its builders' skill, as well as the quality of their mortar.

The main buildings within the inner wall included the hall, the chapel, storerooms, stables, and the kitchen that was attached to the hall by a corridor. The two-story building to the west of the hall was likely the family apartments and perhaps chambers for their guests. Otherwise, he supposed, he and Frederic would be bedding down in the hall with the soldiers and male servants.

There were no piles of barrels, casks, or baskets outside the buildings; no damaged wagons or other items left where they'd broken down until they could be attended to. Indeed, the courtyard was almost painfully neat, and he could only catch the slightest whiff of dung from the stables, which told him they must be cleaned often.

While the tidiness within the fortress might be impressive, he found the silence and the lack of servants—or at least the last of seeing the servants—unsettling. There wasn't a single person peering out a window or door, although their arrival had hardly been quiet. Either they were the least curious servants he'd ever encountered or this lady governed her castle with an iron hand.

Half the archers on the inner wall now faced inward, their notched arrows pointing at the cobbled space below. More soldiers stood lining the open area, and in the center stood a tall, barrel-chested man dressed in armor, save for his bare head. His expression was grim, his face clean-shaven, the black hair on his head shot through gray, and he faced the gate as if prepared to hold off an attack all by himself.

The garrison commander, Bayard assumed.

"My lady," the man said with a Scots accent while running a measuring gaze over Bayard.

A Scot. That was interesting. Bayard had developed a great deal of respect for the Scots during the fighting in France when John had tried to regain his lost possessions.

"Sir Bayard de Boisbaston, this is Iain Mac Kendren, the garrison commander responsible for my well-trained troops," Lady Gillian said with the merest hint of a smile.

She must like the Scot, which was also interesting. Many a lady treated the men who protected her as little more than hounds or hawks. "I'm honored."

The Scot's response was a dismissive snort—another reaction Bayard de Boisbaston was not accustomed to receiving.

"He brings news from Lady Adelaide," Lady Gillian announced, while Bayard struggled to control his annoyance.

Armand might have warned him about the garrison commander, too.

Mac Kendren cocked a bushy gray-and-black brow. "Does he, now?"

"I do," Bayard said, letting his tone convey some of his displeasure at being spoken to so insolently. "Your garrison commander is to be commended for continuing to hold such responsibility in spite of his poor eyesight, my lady."

"There's naught wrong with my eyes," the Scot declared with a slightly puzzled frown.

Bayard cocked a brow. "I thought there must be when I saw rust on the bottom of your hauberk."

The Scot glanced down, as did the lady. Bayard permitted himself a little smile of satisfaction when the

Scot's face turned scarlet, for there was indeed three spots of rust at the bottom of his hauberk.

More amusement and challenge came of Bayard's dark eyes. "I also note, my lady, that we haven't yet exchanged the kiss of greeting."

CHAPTER TWO

BAYARD WASN'T SURE WHAT to expect when he gently chastised Lady Gillian, but he wasn't completely surprised when her green eyes flashed with equal challenge and she boldly walked up to him, raised herself on her toes, and bussed him heartily on both cheeks.

There was more than a slight flush coloring her own round cheeks when she stepped back.

"Such enthusiasm," he remarked. "I may yet find myself delighted I was sent to Averette."

As her blush deepened and his gaze held hers, the door to the hall opened, and a man appeared. He was of an age with Bayard and wore a long tunic that brushed the ground. He could have been a priest, except he had no tonsure, and the look he gave the lady was not of priestly piety.

That was interesting, too. Between the hearty kiss and the young man's obvious affection, perhaps his first impression of Lady Gillian had been mistaken.

He'd been assuming she was the sort of noblewoman who would make a good nun.

Not that it mattered. He was here at Armand's behest, and for a serious purpose, not to amuse himself with defiant young ladies.

"Sir Bayard de Boisbaston, this is Dunstan de Corley, the steward of Averette," she said, introducing the young man. "Dunstan, Sir Bayard brings news from Adelaide. Please come with us to the solar."

She started toward the hall, then paused on the steps before turning back to the yard. "Iain," she called out. "I'd like you to come to the solar, too."

The Scot joined them, then the lady of Averette led Bayard, her steward, and her garrison commander through a hall that was equally empty of servants, their footfalls muffled by clean, herb-scented rushes on the floor. Hounds lumbered to their feet, as grim and wary as the soldiers in the yard.

One of the dogs started to growl; a brisk word from the lady silenced him.

Finally Bayard saw a servant. A young, red-haired, freckled wench peered out of the door that led to the kitchen. When she realized he'd spotted her, she ducked out of sight. Perhaps she was just shy, but he was beginning to think Lady Gillian's household was not a very merry place.

At the far end of the hall they went around a screen that hid another door, then up some steps leading to a narrow, covered wooden walkway. It went from the hall to the keep and was about fifteen feet above the ground.

One had only to set fire to the walkway to make the door to the keep unattainable save by ladders, supposing anyone was willing to risk a hail of arrows, or stones, or boiling water. If there was a well and food inside the keep, they could hold out there for weeks.

The lady unlocked the outer door, then waited while the others entered the building.

Once inside, Bayard surveyed the rough, gray stone walls. Stairs went up and around the inner wall to another level above, while others curved downward, probably leading to chambers used for storage and cells for prisoners.

Like the one in which Armand had been held captive for months, while he'd been treated more like a guest than a prisoner by the Duc d'Ormonde.

The room on the next level into which the lady led them wasn't precisely a solar, for there was no bed or anything else to indicate it was anyone's private chamber. Perhaps because it was so isolated from the rest of the castle, it appeared to have been turned into a place to keep accounts and the treasury of the estate, as evidenced by the heavy wooden chest bound with iron bands and a stout lock in one corner.

The sun lit the top of a table beneath an arched window. A holder bearing the remains of a candle sat near the right-hand edge of the table, and a few bits of quill littered the top, as if someone had tidied in a hurry. A chair waited beside the table, its cushion the only concession to personal comfort. A cupboard of the sort used to house records of tithes and other scrolls rested opposite the door.

Bayard reached into his belt and produced the letter Armand had entrusted to his care.

HIDING HER TREPIDATION, Gillian took the rolled parchment and went to the window. She trusted Dunstan and Iain, but she feared her face might betray too much emotion if she was close to them.

Mentally girding her loins, preparing for the worst, she broke the blue wax seal and began to read.

Adelaide hoped Gillian and everyone at Averette was well, as she was. Indeed, she was very happy, but she would explain more about that later. First, she had to warn Gillian.

Reading more quickly, Gillian discovered that Adelaide had helped to thwart a plot against the king that could have led to rebellion and civil war. Unfortunately, one of the conspirators had escaped and Adelaide feared her sisters were now in danger. Adelaide had written to Lizette, too, asking her to return to Averette at once.

Sir Bayard de Boisbaston, to whom Adelaide had entrusted this message, was a skilled knight and a champion of tournaments who had recently returned from the king's campaign in Normandy. He would be staying at Averette until all the traitors had been caught, imprisoned, or killed.

Gillian cut her eyes to Sir Bayard, who now stood with his hands clasped behind his back, calmly regarding them all like a conquering hero they should be glad to serve.

If he thought to overrule her here, in her home and among her people, he was sorely mistaken!

Grasping the letter tighter, Gillian read more quickly.

Sir Bayard was also the half brother of Lord Armand de Boisbaston, the finest, most honorable, bravest, best man in the world.

And Adelaide's husband.

Gillian stared, aghast, at the words on the parchment before her. Adelaide *married?* It couldn't be. It simply couldn't be.

Adelaide would *never* give herself to a husband, never let a man rule her and treat her as his chattel, with no rights or say in anything. Lizette, perhaps, would break their vow, but not Adelaide, who had proposed their vow in the first place and pointed out all the reasons a woman shouldn't marry.

Armand has agreed that Averette will still be your

home and your responsibility, Adelaide had written. *He has estates of his own in the north and says they are more than enough for him. Truly, Gillian, he is the best of men.*

Gillian didn't believe her. She knew the strength of infatuation, the power of love, and Adelaide sounded completely smitten. This Lord Armand de Boisbaston might merely be biding his time before swooping down upon Averette like a vulture—especially if he had his half brother already there to support him.

His features full of concern, Dunstan came a few steps closer. "What is it? Is Adelaide ill?"

She shook her head. "No, she's well." Or at least she wasn't sick the way he meant. Sick with love, perhaps.

Yet surely if the unthinkable *were* true and Adelaide had married, she would come here herself to tell them. She wouldn't send some stranger to do the deed, or to help protect Averette, either.

She thrust the letter at Dunstan. "Do you think this was written by my sister?"

"It looks like Adelaide's hand," he murmured as he started to read.

She knew the instant he saw the thing that had shocked her most, too. "She's *married?*" He stared at Sir Bayard. "To your brother?"

"Half brother."

Half or full, what did it matter?

"Who's married?" Iain demanded.

Sir Bayard's jaw clenched before he answered, but his voice was calm when he spoke. "Lady Adelaide has recently wed my half brother, Lord Armand de Boisbaston, a knight of the realm."

"When? How?"

"Four days ago," Sir Bayard replied with that same

damnable composure. "In the usual fashion. I myself was
not a witness to the nuptials, being newly returned from
France, but I assure you, they are wed and very much in
love—so much so that Armand has refused all rights to
Averette."

Something Sir Bayard obviously couldn't fathom, Gillian realized, and neither could she. "Whoever heard of
a lord who refuses more land?"

"Whatever you or I might think of it, that's the agreement he made with his wife," Sir Bayard replied. "As
a man of honor, he will abide by it. And I give you *my*
word as a knight of the realm that this letter *is* from your
sister and you *are* in danger."

"Danger?" Iain repeated. "What danger?"

Gillian quickly described what Adelaide had said
about a conspiracy, including the news that Sir Bayard
was expected to remain at Averette, something that
clearly upset Dunstan and Iain as much as it did her.

"For how long?" Iain demanded.

"Until my brother and his wife deem it safe for me to
go," Sir Bayard replied.

"Am I to have no say in this matter?" Gillian angrily
inquired.

"Rest assured, my lady, you're still in command of
Averette," Sir Bayard said. "I am to provide such advice
and assistance as you may require, and nothing more."

"We're more than capable of defending ourselves,"
Dunstan said, his hand on the hilt of the sword he'd only
ever wielded on a practice field.

Sir Bayard raised a brow and crossed his powerful
arms. "You've had experience commanding men in
battle? Or under siege?"

Iain threw back his shoulders. "I was in battle before
you left your mother's teat."

"That is *not* what I asked," the knight returned. "Have you *commanded* in battle, or under siege?"

Iain's answer was a stony silence. He'd been in battles, Gillian knew, but his appointment to garrison commander was recent, awarded by her father shortly before he died of apoplexy during yet another drunken rant about his lack of sons and abusing God for cursing him with useless daughters.

Dunstan had no battle experience of any kind. His skill was arithmetic and keeping accurate accounts.

"These enemies we face are determined men," Sir Bayard said to her, "and unless you'd put your pride above your people's welfare, you should welcome any aid I can provide."

What if this letter *was* true? she asked herself. What if these enemies Adelaide and Sir Bayard spoke of were dangerous and ruthless and coming to Averette? She had complete confidence in Iain's abilities, but she would be a fool to refuse the help of an experienced knight. "Very well, my lord, you may stay."

She held up her hand to silence Iain and Dunstan's protests and continued to address Sir Bayard. "Although I'm quite confident Iain and my men can defend the people of Averette against any enemy force, you and your soldiers may stay. However, I'm writing to my sister to confirm that you are who you claim to be and that what this letter says is true. Now, having delivered this message, my lord, you may go to the hall and avail yourself of refreshment."

The slight lowering of Sir Bayard's dark brows told her he realized he was being dismissed. Nevertheless, his voice betrayed no hint of anger when he said "Until later, then, my lady." Then he gave her an excuse of a bow and strolled out of the door.

"Hospitality or no, we should send that arrogant ass back out the gates right now," Iain declared the moment the door closed.

"That man should leave Averette today," Dunstan agreed. "Such impertinence!"

Gillian looked from one man to the other, appreciating their loyalty and concern, yet aware that Averette and its people were *her* responsibility. "What if he is related to me by marriage? Until we know for certain, we must treat him as a guest. If he *is* an enemy, it might be wiser to keep him here, where we can watch him."

"Aye, there is that," Iain conceded.

"What if he's a spy, trying to find out our garrison's strengths and weakness?" Dunstan demanded.

Gillian hadn't thought of that, and the notion sickened her. "Surely Averette has no weaknesses."

"There's *always* a weakness, my lady," Iain said, "no matter how hard we train the men or reinforce the walls."

Gillian knew he was right, but Adelaide's letter and her duty as chatelaine stopped her from ordering Sir Bayard to leave. There was a chance the letter was genuine and this knight had been sent by her sister to help them. She wasn't willing to run the risk of either offending a nobleman who was related to her by marriage or refusing his aid if Averette was in danger.

But she wasn't willing to allow a possible spy to wander at will about the estate, either.

"He and his men may stay," she decided, "*apparently* as honored guests. Tell the servants and soldiers to treat Sir Bayard, his squire, and his men with every courtesy until they hear otherwise. However, our guests aren't to leave the confines of the castle. If Sir Bayard or his men protest, they should be sent to me.

"Iain, have half the garrison billeted in the village to hide our true strength, and move the training and practices to the far meadows.

"I also want every soldier and servant told that if they see any suspicious behavior, we are to be informed at once."

She went to the tall cupboard and searched for an unused piece of parchment. "I shall write to Adelaide, ask her to confirm this letter we received, and put in some questions for her to answer that only she can. That way, we'll know if the letters are false or are being intercepted."

"A wise idea, my lady," Dunstan agreed.

She found a parchment and threw it onto the table, then turned back for a clay vessel holding ink, and a quill. "Until we know for certain that what this letter claims is true, we'll keep a careful watch on Sir Bayard de Boisbaston and his men."

"Aye, my lady," Dunstan said.

"Aye," Iain grimly seconded.

"So, WHAT'S YOUR name, then?" Peg coyly asked the merchant whose cartful of barrels and casks of wine stood outside the Stag's Head later that same day.

Not only was the merchant obviously well-to-do, to judge by his clothes, he was slender, young, and attractive—all qualities to make a girl eager to offer her company and her skills. He was clearly attempting to grow a beard and she didn't like beards, but she was willing to make an exception, if the price was right.

Also inside the tavern were several farmers and villagers drinking at the end of a busy day harvesting crops and tending livestock. The men liked to discuss the weather, the potential yield of grain and produce, and sometimes John and his laws. Most had their own accustomed places, like Geoffrey, the miller, who sat by the casks, his enemy, Felton the baker, who reclined on a bench on the opposite side of the low-ceilinged room, and Old Davy and his cronies by the hearth.

"I'm Charles de Fenelon," the wine merchant replied with a friendly smile. "From London."

"Really?" Peg replied, bending over to give him a good look at her breasts. "Are you coming or going?"

"I'm heading back to London on my way from Bristol," he replied. "First I hope to sell some of my wine at the castle yonder. How easy is it to meet with the steward?"

A jug of ale on her hip, the serving wench swayed from side to side and bit the end of a lock of hair. "Dunstan de Corley comes to the village all the time. I could introduce you, if you like."

"I'd make it worth your while," Charles said, patting the purse attached to his belt. "What's your name, lass?"

In view of that purse, she gave him an even broader smile. "Peg."

"Peg," he repeated, drawing out the name so that it seemed a promise in itself as he pulled her down onto his lap.

She glanced over her shoulder at the big beefy fellow manning the huge tapped cask.

"Your husband?" Charles asked, thinking that however much he might wish to assuage his cravings, he didn't want a fight on his hands.

"Not yet, he's not," she replied with a giggle, winding her arms around his neck. "Besides, Sam won't mind. The more I earn, the sooner we can marry."

"Ah," Charles murmured, nuzzling her neck, then

returning to more important business. "Does the castle steward drive a hard bargain?"

She giggled again. "He can get pretty hard."

"That's not what I meant."

She pouted a little when he didn't appreciate her jest. "He's a clever fellow, but it ain't him who finally decides. It'll be the lady."

"Lady Adelaide?"

"No, not her. She's with the king. Her sister, Lady Gillian—and she's even sharper than Dunstan, I can tell you! But they'll be needing more wine these days. A knight's just come and I've heard he's staying awhile."

The wine merchant's brows rose with interest. "A knight?"

"Aye, and his squire and a bunch of soldiers."

"A suitor for the lady? Perhaps they'll need wine for a wedding."

"Good luck to him, then, if that's his plan," Peg replied with a toss of her nut-brown hair. "Lady Gillian'll send him packin', I've no doubt—same way her sister did before her. Don't much like men, those ladies. Unnatural, I calls it."

Peg licked her lips, her tongue darting out in a very enticing manner. "Don't that seem unnatural to you, too?"

"Indeed," Charles replied. "I've heard Lady Adelaide is very beautiful. Is her sister, as well?"

"Lord love you, no!" Peg retorted with a snort of laughter. "She's pretty enough, I suppose, but compared to her sisters? Ugly as a hedgehog."

Peg gave a little wriggle that seemed very promising. "Are you going to have some of what we've got to offer, sir?" she asked, making it clear she wasn't thinking of ale.

"I certainly will." Charles moved again, letting her feel the effect she was having on him, while his hand traveled toward her breast. "I'll have some ale first, though."

Peg made absolutely no move to stop his wandering hand, or to pour his drink. "Not wine?"

"Ale is cheaper."

"Ale now, something else later…for two silver pennies," Peg replied as she leaned across his arm and re-filled his mug, pressing her breasts against him while he boldly caressed her some more.

God's blood, he could have anything he liked in London for half that. "That's expensive."

Her smile grew, exposing fine white teeth, and she squirmed a little more. "I'm worth it."

He slipped a hand into her loose bodice while simultaneously giving the big fellow by the cask a surreptitious look. Sure enough, the oaf grinned and looked as pleased as if his wife-to-be had given him a bag of gold. "All right. So, who's this knight come visiting, then?"

"A handsome fellow, although he's got a scar on his face. Bayard something."

"Bayard de Boisbaston?" Charles asked sharply.

"Why? What if he is this Bayard Boise—batton? What's he done?"

Charles shook his head and his expression grew grim. "Your lady had best have a care, if what I've heard of him is true. The women at court call him the 'Gyptian lover, saying he travels from bed to bed stealing hearts, just like those vagabonds who claim to be able to tell fortunes. They say he's had at least fifty lovers and that's just among the wives and daughters of the men at court."

"Fifty?" Peg breathed, her eyes wide. "How come he ain't been killed by some husband or father?"

"Because nobody dares to challenge him. He's won every tournament that he's ever been in, and they say he's so fierce when he fights, even the devil himself would flee his blade—if he chooses to use it. He doesn't always. Last year, he had charge of a castle in Normandy and surrendered after only three days. He was captured by the Duc d'Ormonde, whose wife was reputed to be a great beauty. Some at court say he surrendered just to have the chance to seduce her—and he did."

Peg drew in her breath. "He surrendered a castle just to be able to seduce a woman?"

The wine merchant nodded. "That's what they say, and now he's come here."

"If he's got any foul intentions toward Lady Gillian, she'll set him straight," Young Davy staunchly declared, interrupting their conversation as he handed his grandfather a piece of thick brown bread to go with his ale and cheese. "She's as fierce as the devil, too."

"Blasphemy!" the chandler muttered in the corner where he nursed his ale.

"You women are always thinking about marriage," Young Davy continued, ignoring him. "You had her married off to James d'Ardenay after the poor lad'd only been here a week."

"Well, *he* died," Peg said defensively.

"We wouldn't have to worry if she'd take a husband," Felton, the baker, noted from his place near the door.

"Would you have her take the first man who asked her?" the miller countered from across the room, as far from his enemy as he could get. "Would you want any of those fools who've come courting her to become the new lord? I wouldn't. God save us from arrogant idiots!"

"She probably don't want to marry 'cause o' that father o' hers," Old Davy piped up from beside the hearth.

"Cruel, vicious villain. He'd make any woman think death might be better than marriage."

The wine merchant shifted again, this time with impatience. "Perhaps if all you want to do is talk about the lady, I should retire alone."

Peg jumped to her feet and took his hand to lead him up to the second level of the tavern, where travelers slept and she plied her other trade. "Don't be angry, Charlie. We have to care about what goes on up at the castle, same as you have to worry about the king's taxes. Lady Gillian's a good woman, even if she is a lady, so nobody wants any harm to come to her."

Old Davy looked anxiously at the others after the merchant and Peg had disappeared up the stairs. "D'you suppose there's any truth in what that fellow said?"

"Not a bit," Young Davy said confidently. "Lady Gillian's too honorable and too clever to be fooled by any smooth-talking knight, no matter how good-looking he is. Why, remember that one knight that come, Sir Watersticks or whatever his name was? Didn't she send him packing quick enough?"

The men in the tap room chuckled and nodded.

"Set his hair on fire," Old Davy said between wheezes as he laughed. "She had to say it was an accident o'course, but it probably took a year for it to grow back. And oh, didn't he curse?"

"Ah, love! It's a grand thing," the miller said with a smirk in the baker's direction. Then he started to sing a ballad about a long-lost love, while the baker slammed down his mug and stormed out of the tavern.

CHAPTER THREE

TRYING TO CONTAIN HIS frustration, Bayard tossed his helmet onto the large, canopied and curtained bed in the extremely tidy chamber to which a male servant had brought him after he'd left the solar. Linen shutters covered the window, and a chest painted green and blue stood in the corner opposite the bed. There was a cot for his squire and another table with an ewer and basin, and plenty of clean linen. The floor had been recently swept and everything looked remarkably free of dust.

It was certainly an improvement over their accommodations on the road, which had tended to be cramped—except that here, instead of being welcomed, he'd been met with distrust, disrespect, and disdain.

Although his rational mind told him that Lady Gillian was right to be suspicious, for these were dangerous times and John the most untrustworthy of kings, he couldn't subdue his annoyance over his reception. You'd think *he* was the traitor, the way she'd treated him.

The garrison commander couldn't be more suspicious if he were Philip of France himself. And as for that steward...

He wondered if the lady had any idea that her steward was in love with her. She was a lady, a ward of the king, and he was an untitled commoner, but a marriage between then was not completely impossible. John needed money to mount another campaign to win back his lost lands in France—a lot of money. He would eagerly accept bribes and payments that would enable him to do so, even from untitled commoners and in exchange for the hand of a noblewoman.

Yet, he'd seen no little looks of intimacy exchanged, no apparent desire on the lady's part. Any tender concern had been in Dunstan's eyes alone, not hers.

No doubt she was too selfish and too determined to rule this estate on her own to fall in love, for it was now abundantly clear that she, and she alone, was in command of Averette.

The only other women he'd ever heard controlling an estate had been widows and even then, not many and not for long. Then again, he'd never heard of a young woman like Lady Gillian, who might dress like a peasant, but was as arrogantly confident as any man he'd ever met. And stubborn.

Shaking his head, Bayard strode over to the table beside the bed and ran his finger along the top, skirting the beeswax candle in a bronze holder. No dust there, either.

The door crashed against the wall, heralding his squire's entrance. Frederic carried the leather pouch containing their clothing over his shoulder and, with a weary sigh, heaved it onto the bed beside Bayard's helmet.

Bayard was used to Frederic's theatrics by now. "I didn't realize a few items of wool and linen would be so taxing. Perhaps you should lie down."

Grinning, for he was likewise getting used to his master's sense of humor, Frederic pushed on the cot, making the ropes creak. "I would, if you think this'll hold me."

"If it doesn't, try not to wake me when you land on the floor. But before you take a nap or unpack our clothes, get me out of my hauberk."

It took a few moments to remove Bayard's surcoat and to get the heavy mail hauberk over his head.

After Frederic helped him remove them, Bayard rotated his neck and stretched his arms over his head. He untied his mail hosen that protected his legs and gave them to Frederic to put away, then removed his padded gambeson and likewise handed it to his squire.

Clad in his loose shirt, breeches, and boots, he went to wash. There was a lump of soap that smelled of lavender beside the linen, as well as plenty of water in the ewer. He poured some into the basin until it was half full and felt his face, deciding he need not scrape the whiskers away until tomorrow.

"Did you see that pretty serving wench?" Frederic asked as he started to close the lid of the chest. "The one with red hair and freckles?"

"Yes," Bayard replied, recalling the one female servant who'd been bold enough to show herself while he was on the way to the keep with Lady Gillian. She was pretty, he supposed, and slender, and about fifteen years old.

His squire got a look on his face that Bayard easily recognized. He'd encountered many jealous or envious men in his life, starting when he was younger even than Frederic, and including the Duc d'Ormonde—although that had actually proven to be a beneficial thing, or he might be in Normandy yet. The duke had feared that his captive was far too attractive to his wife and so had let him go on the payment of a very small ransom.

He'd seen it earlier today, too, on the steward's face.

Unfortunately, he inspired jealousy wherever there were women, and whether there was cause or not.

In this instance, definitely not, and aside from the fact that Lady Gillian was Armand's sister-in-law. She might be spirited—and a woman without spirit was like food without spice—but otherwise? Not at all appealing.

Her hair was a dull brown, straight, and drawn back tightly from her heart-shaped face. There were no charming little curls, no cunning little wisps escaping to give a man the opportunity for a surreptitious caress under the guise of tucking in a stray one. Lady Gillian's nose was a pert little button, and a splash of freckles crossed the bridge and dotted her cheeks, marring her complexion. To be sure, her green eyes were bright and vibrant, but they weren't particularly alluring. She was too thin, too, even though her breasts were full and round and her hips had a certain seductive sway when she walked...far too quickly.

"My conquests have been greatly exaggerated," he reminded his squire. "And I assure you, that servant's too young for me."

His lips curved up into a wry little smile. "I'm not particularly fond of red hair, either."

As his squire grinned with relief and set to work unpacking, Bayard inwardly, and sourly, added, "Nor am I fond of shrews."

BAYARD WAS PLEASED TO NOTE that despite Lady Gillian's less-than-enthusiastic reception, she'd had the courtesy to give him the seat to her right at the evening meal.

The jealous steward sat on her left-hand side. Frederic was on Bayard's right, as was the priest, a Father Matthew who ate as if he'd been fasting for days. His own soldiers were seated immediately below the dais with the garrison commander and more of Averette's men.

The food was good, thank God. Since he had to stay here, he was grateful for that as he speared another piece of veal dressed with vinegar with his eating knife. Meanwhile, his hostess continued to ignore him and talk to the steward.

Lady Gillian had rather nice hands, he noticed, although they were browned by the sun. Ladies were supposed to sit inside doing nothing more strenuous than sewing or, if they were particularly active, engaging in a hunt, wearing gloves. If they went outside, they were supposed to sit demurely in the shade. Clearly she did little that other ladies did, or in the way they did it.

Determined to concentrate on something other than the chatelaine of Averette, Bayard studied the hall and the soldiers gathered there. The garrison appeared well trained, as far as mustering in the yard went, anyway. It remained to be seen how good they'd be in battle or during a siege.

"Oh, not again!" Lady Gillian suddenly—and loudly—exclaimed.

When Bayard turned to look at her, she was regarding the steward with dismay, although there was laughter lurking in her eyes.

"It's true, I'm afraid," Dunstan replied, shaking his head and smiling. "He's charged Geoffrey with false measuring again. I truly think Felton would rise from his death bed if he thought he could shame Geoffrey."

Lady Gillian laughed—an amazing, throaty, hearty laugh completely unlike the decorous little titters most ladies made in company. It was the sort of laugh one might hear in bed after a joyous bout of lovemaking, a laugh to make a man want to laugh, too, and he was astonished at the difference it made to Lady Gillian's appearance. She looked years younger, and prettier.

Her full lips were very appealing, he realized, especially the charming dent in the top of her upper lip, and he was suddenly tempted to touch it. With his tongue.

Which was ridiculous. The journey here, so soon after his return from Normandy, must have been more taxing than he thought.

"Will there never be an end to this squabbling?" Lady Gillian asked when she stopped laughing. "Father Matthew, can you not speak to them? This feuding must cease!"

"Alas, my lady, I have tried," the priest replied, "but they will not turn the other cheek."

"There's a feud?" Frederic asked eagerly, despite the arrival of baked apples—his favorite—for the final course.

"It's a conflict of long, long standing," she said, smiling at the lad.

Bayard wished she'd smiled that way at him when they'd first arrived. If she had, he would have been slower to take offense at her manner and swifter to forgive and forget the lack of a kiss of greeting.

Not that he regretted reminding her about that. Although at the time she'd held no great attraction for him, he'd been acutely aware of the sensation of her warm breath on his cheek and the knowledge that her body was a hair's breadth from his own. Now, after hearing her delightful laugh and seeing her lovely smile—

"How did the feud start? An insult?" Frederic asked interrupting Bayard's musing as the red-haired serving maid set down the spiced apple before him.

"A woman," Lady Gillian replied. "The miller and the baker both wanted to marry the same one, and she chose the miller."

"Ahh!" Frederic cried, giving Bayard a knowing grin.

Bayard clenched his jaw and stayed silent. He wasn't going to say a word about jealous men, or women making choices, or anything to do with marriage.

"The baker brings a charge of false measure against the miller every hall moot, or so it seems," the steward explained. "In two days' time, they'll stand before us again, arguing."

That got Bayard's full attention. "You're having a hall moot?"

"Yes, in two days," the lady answered as if he were dim.

"I don't think that would be wise."

Her brows lowered. "Why not?"

"Because it's too public, and puts you in danger."

"It's to be held in my courtyard," she protested. "Surely I'll be perfectly safe there."

"I don't think so," Bayard firmly replied. "An assassin could easily slip in with the villagers. It only takes one well-aimed arrow or knife throw to kill."

Lady Gillian shook her head and spoke with most unfeminine certainty. "The hall moot cannot be delayed. The people have been expecting it. There are several quarrels to be decided and fines to be assessed."

"I can appreciate that you require income, but your safety must come first."

Her green eyes flashed with stubborn determination. "Hall moots are necessary for the peace of the estate. What can begin as a small disagreement, easily dealt with in a hall moot, can become much more serious if left to fester."

She raised her pointed chin and got a remarkably defiant expression on her face. "I am still in command of Averette, am I not? If I am—and unless you know for certain I'm in immediate danger—the hall moot will be held as planned."

"I'm sure she'll be perfectly safe, Bayard," Frederic seconded, although nobody had asked him. "You're an even better swordsman than your brother." He looked past Bayard to Lady Gillian. "He told you about the trial, didn't he? That Lord Armand won?"

The lady frowned. "Sir Bayard has said nothing about a trial."

Frederic grinned from ear to ear, looking more like an excited puppy than ever. "He's too modest to brag about his brother, but you should be very proud of your brother-in-law, Lord Armand, my lady. It was an amazing victory."

"I would never have suspected modesty to be one of Sir Bayard's virtues," Lady Gillian remarked.

Bayard's grip tightened around the stem of the goblet. She had to be one of the most aggravating women in England. "I saw no need to speak of it," he said, "since Armand was proven innocent and the real traitor exposed."

"The man who has wed Lady Adelaide, was accused of *treason?*" the steward asked as if that was the most disturbing thing he'd ever heard in his life.

"*Falsely* accused and proven innocent," Bayard said, wishing Frederic had kept quiet about Armand's recent troubles, especially since everyone else in the hall had fallen silent, as well they might.

The lady abruptly rose from her chair. "I was planning to announce this at the hall moot," she said in a clear voice that easily reached the far end of the hall, "but the news has already been revealed here tonight. I have recently been informed that my sister, Lady Adelaide, may have wed Lord Armand de Boisbaston."

As Lady Gillian's servants and soldiers exchanged surprised looks, a murmur of wonder, disbelief, and excitement filled the hall. Over by the door leading to the kitchen corridor, the red-haired maidservant and another young woman whispered behind their hands, and so did several others seated at the tables or standing in clusters around the hall.

"This knight, Sir Bayard de Boisbaston, is his brother."

Another mutter went through the hall, this time less excited and more suspicious. Bayard's own men shifted uncomfortably, aware of the sudden tension in the hall. It was as if an ill wind had blown through, chilling all it touched except Bayard, who smiled as if all was well with the world, and he was delighted to find himself related to this termagant.

"I'm sure some of you fear that there will be a new lord of Averette," Lady Gillian continued, balling her napkin in her hand. "That is not so. Lady Adelaide has given me her word Averette will always be mine to govern. She assures me this is still so, despite her marriage."

However odd that might be, Bayard thought grimly.

A collective sigh filled the hall. Apparently the men of Averette didn't share his reservations about having a woman in command of a castle.

Perhaps it was different here because of what Armand had told him about the late lord of Averette. Lady Gillian's father had been vicious, cruel and unjust. Under those circumstances, perhaps any new lord would be met with dread and suspicion. Nevertheless, and despite the evidence of his own eyes—for seeing Armand and Adelaide together, no one could doubt but that they were deeply in love—Bayard still couldn't accept that Armand was willing to leave this castle and estate in a woman's

control. To be sure, Lady Gillian was not the most feminine female he'd ever encountered, but she was still a
woman.

"Now, my lord," she said, returning to her seat and
turning the full force of her vibrant green eyes onto him,
"tell me about this trial."

Since Bayard had no choice but to answer, he did,
repeating the bare facts. "My half brother was falsely
accused of treason and proved his innocence in a trial
by combat against one of the men who denounced him
to the king."

"I'll say he proved it!" Frederic cried, fairly bouncing
in his chair. "He ran his sword right through Sir Francis's
face!"

The lady gasped, the priest paled, and the steward
looked rather queasy.

"That was the traitor's choice," Bayard explained, not
wanting them to think Armand was some kind of savage.
"Francis ran into Armand's sword rather than suffer a
slow execution."

"I wish I'd seen it!" Frederic exclaimed.

"A true knight takes no pleasure in death, however it
comes about," Bayard said swiftly, and sincerely. "When
he has a duty to do, he does it, but he should never relish
the taking of a life."

He turned back to Lady Gillian, whose face bore an
expression he couldn't quite decipher. But he didn't care
what she thought. He'd had enough of her unladylike
demeanor and behavior, her envious steward, her orders
and refusals.

"If you'll excuse me, my lady," he said, getting to his
feet, "it's been a long day, so I'll give you good night."

No doubt just as happy to see the last of him for the

day, she regally inclined her head. "Good night, Sir Bayard."

"May I stay?" Frederic asked.

Since he didn't require his squire's help to prepare for bed, Bayard nodded. Then he bid his men a restful night and marched from the hall.

WHILE SUPPOSEDLY LISTENING to Dunstan relate the cases expected to come before for judgment at the hall moot, Gillian watched Sir Bayard cross the hall with long, purposeful strides. He paused to have a word or exchange greetings with his men, and they replied with seemingly genuine good humor, as if he were their friend as well as commander.

Interesting, and quite different from Iain's method of command. He would no sooner jest with his men than he'd strip naked in the courtyard.

Sir Bayard would likely be only too willing to do such a thing if he lost a wager or for some other silly reason. With such a body he'd probably be *glad* to.

She could just imagine him standing there, smiling with arrogant vanity, taking off his clothing one piece at a time….

"My lady?" Dunstan said, laying his hand on her arm. "Did you hear me?"

As embarrassed as if Dunstan had read her thoughts, she swiftly pulled away. "Yes. If the chandler's daughter wishes to marry the cooper's son, I have no objections."

Unable to prevent a blush, she took a drink of wine while Dunstan slowly and deliberately folded his hands upon his lap.

CHAPTER FOUR

THE NEXT DAY, GILLIAN ROSE from her seat at the table in the solar where she'd been reviewing the tithe rolls and lists of foodstuffs she'd recently purchased. She had to be aware of estate income and expenses, but sitting and staring at rows of figures was not how she preferred to spend her time.

Walking to the window, she looked out over the land she loved—the fields, meadows and woods, the village, and especially the people she cared about as if they were her family. She could see the mill and its wheel slowly turning, suggesting a peace she knew was absent from the miller's household. Boats plied the river, and on the banks, several women did their washing, spreading their linen on bushes to dry and bleach in the sun. A few children swam a short distance away, splashing each other, their shouts and laughter inaudible above the bustle of the servants, and wagons, and merchants delivering goods in the yard below.

Smoke rose from the smithy in gray wisps and she could easily imagine Old Davy holding court with his fellows, talking about the news of the day, speculating about what the king might do next to try to retrieve his lands in France, and what he might tax to raise the money to do it.

She could see the open space of the green, and the wagons of some peddlers drawn up there, no doubt to the chagrin of those merchants whose stalls bordered the green. In the yard belonging to the widowed alewife, the cooper was unloading barrels. She was likely complaining, albeit in a good-natured way, about the price he'd charged her to make them. When he was finished, they'd probably retire to her brewery and sample her latest, then finish the day in bed together, for it was no secret that their relationship went beyond the bounds of business.

If she were to marry, Gillian reflected, she'd have to leave her home, and her friends, and the people she cherished to go to her husband's estate. She would be a stranger among strangers, and surely very lonely.

Even when James was alive and they'd talked of a life together, she'd been troubled by that possibility.

To think it had been less than a year since her father's death and she'd become the chatelaine of Averette, with Adelaide's blessing and promise that it would always be so. Less than a year since Adelaide had gone to court. Less than a year since Lizette had gone north to visit friends and make more, for as Gillian never wanted to leave Averette, Lizette hated the notion of being tied to one place.

Would a man like Sir Bayard ever understand how she felt about her home and her desire to ensure that everyone here was safe and secure, at least as much as she could? That she would forego the things women were supposed to crave—a husband and even the joy of children—to make it so? And that she didn't want to be under the power of any man?

Probably not. Indeed, she could easily imagine his disbelief and scorn if he ever learned of her vow never to marry, and that she had taken it willingly—nay, eagerly, since James had died.

"My lady?"

She turned to find Dunstan, dressed as usual in a long, dark tunic, standing on the threshold with a parchment in his hand. He wasn't alone, however. There was a man standing beside him whom she'd never seen before. He was about the same age as Dunstan, and well dressed. He was well groomed, too, except for his rather unkempt beard.

"My lady, this is Charles de Fenelon," Dunstan said as he stepped into the room. "He's a wine merchant from London, with most excellent wares."

Judging by his clothes, the merchant's business must be a prosperous one. She guessed from the slight scent of wine about Dunstan that he'd recently tasted samples of some of the aforementioned wares.

"It's a pleasure to meet you, my lady," de Fenelon said with a bow and an ingratiating smile. "I've heard nothing but praise of you in the town."

Dunstan, who knew how she felt about flattery, held out a small scroll. "Here's a list of his prices."

As she took it, their hands touched for a moment. Trying to ignore the unwelcome sensation, she moved toward the window.

"Our stores are rather low," Dunstan noted. "Of course, we wouldn't need so much wine if our guests would take their leave."

Gillian wasn't pleased that Dunstan had said such a thing in front of the merchant, but she wasn't going to chastise her steward, not when she knew that more than concern for the wine stores had prompted his remark. He was jealous of Sir Bayard, although he had no reason to be. She didn't care about Sir Bayard that way.

But neither did she harbor any desire for Dunstan.

She'd always thought of him as a brother, for his gentle, kindly father had been the steward here before him. Recently, however, and much to her dismay, she'd realized Dunstan's feelings for her had changed into something more than brotherly affection. Unfortunately, while she could be blunt and direct about many things, she couldn't bring herself to speak to Dunstan about his feelings for her, or tell him that she did not, and never would, reciprocate them.

Instead, she hoped the difference in their rank would prevent him from speaking to her of love. She was, after all, a lord's daughter and he the untitled son of a Norman knight's bastard. Although that difference didn't influence either her affection or her trust in him, many would tell him to look for love elsewhere because of that alone. There were plenty of young women of lesser rank in and around Averette who would gladly consider marriage to the kind-hearted, competent steward.

But not her.

Focusing on the list, she read it quickly and said to de Fenelon, "Your prices seem a bit high."

His face fell. "That is the best I can do, if I'm to make any profit at all."

He probably thought that because she was a woman, he could play on her sympathy and thus charge her more. "We shall either take them at the prices you have written here, or not at all."

"Very well, my lady," he agreed, thankfully without trying to haggle.

Because his prices were satisfactory, she said, "If your wine is as good as Dunstan claims, we'll be happy to do business with you again."

"Thank you, my lady," Charles replied, beaming with delight.

"Charles knows Sir Bayard de Boisbaston," Dunstan said with a significant look.

"Not personally," Charles added hastily. "I sell wine to many of the nobles who are friends of the king and his court."

"Then you've seen him?" Gillian asked, trying not to betray any overt interest to de Fenelon.

She would also prefer that this wine merchant, whom she'd never met before, not be privy to any suspicions they might have about their supposedly noble guest.

"Many times, most recently when I came through your hall. He's playing chess with a young man your steward says is his squire."

So that knight really was who he claimed to be.

Gillian walked to her chair and slowly lowered herself onto it. That made it more likely that the letter she'd received was really from Adelaide, too, and therefore everything in it was true, as well.

If so, Adelaide *had* broken her vow and married, and Lord Armand de Boisbaston could be the master of Averette. Therefore, and regardless of whatever Adelaide had promised, Gillian had no legal right to govern Averette. Lord Armand did, if he would lay claim to the estate.

God help her, he could take command of Averette and do whatever he liked. He could even send her away.

Dunstan cleared his throat and she realized the wine merchant was still there, watching her. She wanted to tell him to go, and Dunstan, too. She wanted to weep, and rant, and wail, but she managed to control that impulse.

Dunstan took a step closer and clasped his long fingers together, shaking his hands to emphasize his point as he always did when he had something important to say. "Unfortunately, my lady, there's more. Charles tells me Sir Bayard is notorious for his seductions, and is a coward, as well. He's reputed to have seduced over fifty women at court, and he surrendered the castle he was charged to hold in Normandy after a siege of less than a week. They also say he seduced his captor's young wife."

Gillian's eyes narrowed. Sir Bayard didn't appear to be a coward, but how could one tell that except in battle? As for being a lustful rogue…he was handsome enough that she could believe he would be successful at seduction. Her maidservants certainly acted like addle-pated ninnies when he was nearby.

On the other hand, he hadn't behaved like some of the lustful noblemen who'd come to Averette claiming to be interested only in the lord's daughters while chasing every serving wench who crossed their paths.

If the merchant was merely repeating gossip, she knew how little faith she should have in his information. Adelaide had once told her some of the stories being spread about the ladies of Averette. "Is that so, Charles?"

"I'm sorry to say it is, my lady," the wine merchant reluctantly replied. "At court, they call him the 'Gyptian lover because he travels from bed to bed, stealing women's hearts."

That shouldn't surprise or disappoint her; what did she know of Sir Bayard de Boisbaston, after all? But she was disappointed nonetheless—perhaps because there was a chance she was related to him by marriage.

"His squire's also putting it about that Sir Bayard once came upon a troubador entertaining some ladies before a tourney," Dunstan said. "The troubador, aware of Sir Bayard's alleged prowess in the melee, asked him to reward his song with a horse. Sir Bayard agreed, spotted an approaching knight, immediately unhorsed the fellow and returned to present the singer with the horse before his song was done."

Gillian had heard this story before, but not about Sir Bayard de Boisbaston. "The Earl of Pembroke did that."

"So at the very least, the man takes credit he doesn't deserve," Dunstan averred.

If this was true, Sir Bayard did not sound like a man she wished to be related to. She wondered if Adelaide knew what he was like—or if she really knew the man she'd married, either. The wedding had apparently happened with rather remarkable haste.

"Are you likewise familiar with his brother, Lord Armand de Boisbaston?" she asked Charles.

"Indeed, my lady," he replied with more confidence. "What happened to him at Marchant was a bad business. The king should have sent reinforcements."

Instantly wondering why Charles felt he could criticize the king to her, she said, "It's not for us to question the king's actions."

"No, no, certainly not," Charles quickly replied. "I was only thinking of Lord Armand's unfortunate capture."

He gave her another obsequious smile. "His luck has certainly changed since he returned. The very day he arrived at court, he won your sister's heart."

Had it really happened as quickly as that? Or was this another tale embellished in the repeating?

"I see that beauty runs in your family, my lady."

It was all Gillian could do not to roll her eyes. She was no beauty and never would be. Adelaide and Lizette took after their poor, pretty mother. She looked like her father's late sister. "The image of that ugly sow Ermentrude," he would shout at her.

Dunstan shifted his weight from his right foot to his left, drawing her attention. "Perhaps, my lady, you should—"

She rose before he could offer her advice, or try to tell her what to do. She already knew what that would be—that Sir Bayard should go.

But if everything in Adelaide's letter was true, then Averette was in danger from unknown enemies and she should not be keen to rid herself of a man who could help protect them. "I wish you a safe journey back to London, Charles."

The wine merchant bowed. "It's been a pleasure, my lady. I hope this is adieu and not farewell."

She gave him a smile for an answer as she started for the door. "Dunstan, pay Charles and see to the unloading of the wine. I am going to the kitchen to talk to Umbert about the evening meal."

"Yes, my lady," Dunstan replied.

When she was gone, Charles regarded the steward with raised brows. "What do you think she'll do? About Sir Bayard, I mean?"

Dunstan shook his head as he pulled the key to the strongbox from his belt. "I don't know."

He wished he did, almost as much as he wished Sir Bayard on the far side of the world.

Or dead, like James d'Ardenay.

AFTER LEAVING THE SOLAR, Gillian entered the hall, heading for the corridor leading to the kitchen. As the wine merchant had noted, Sir Bayard and his squire were seated at the trestle table on the dais, the chessboard between them. Several of his soldiers were in other parts of the hall. One with close-cropped hair was talking to Dena and saying something that made her laugh. Others were cleaning their mail with sand and vinegar, or sharpening their weapons. A few of her own men were doing the same, as well as keeping an eye on Bayard's men.

Two servants replaced torches in the sconces and they, too, watched the visitors with wary eyes.

Twisting a lock of his brown hair around his finger, Sir Bayard's squire frowned as he studied the board, the few pieces no longer in play at his elbow. Sir Bayard leaned back in his chair, one leg casually thrown over the arm, as if this were *his* hall. Clearly he was used to making himself comfortable wherever he happened to be.

Although that annoyed her, she noticed a tension in his body that was distinctly at odds with his seemingly negligent attitude. She realized he was really paying close attention to his squire and the board, as if calculating every possible move, and every repercussion of every possible move, his squire might make.

No doubt there lurked a sharp intelligence in that man's mind, and she wondered if his lovers had appreciated that about him, or if they thought only of his handsome face and powerfully built body.

His squire made a move, and even from where she stood, she could tell it was the wrong one.

"Checkmate," Sir Bayard said matter-of-factly.

She got the impression that he was consciously making light of his victory, perhaps to spare his squire embarrassment.

Frederic swore and scowled anyway. "How could I not have seen that? I'll do better next time. Another game?"

"I think not," Sir Bayard replied, glancing away from the board—to her. "My lady!"

It would be too obviously rude to ignore him now, when he was also getting to his feet. "Yes, my lord? Is there anything you require?"

"I was wondering if you'd care to indulge in a game of chess?"

She suspected he was merely being polite and she had much to do; even so, she was tempted to accept. She and Adelaide had played chess often, for it was something they could do that wouldn't disturb their father.

Lizette never played chess; she had not the patience.

"Thank you, my lord, but no," she said. "I have too many other demands upon my time."

"I'm not very good. You can probably beat me," he cajoled with a smile that reminded her of a man who'd once tried to sell her bogus jewels, and she wondered if he thought her that stupid or vain.

"I probably could," she agreed, hiding her annoyance, "but not today."

Aggravation flashed in his eyes, yet it was gone nearly at once. "Another time, then."

"Perhaps," she said with a nod of farewell as she again started toward the kitchen.

"You shouldn't have asked her," she heard his squire say. "She would be upset when you won."

Did Frederic think she was afraid to lose? Or that she couldn't possibly win?

Gillian spun on her heel and marched back to the dais.

CHAPTER FIVE

SIR BAYARD AND HIS SQUIRE scrambled to their feet when they realized Gillian was returning, Frederic nearly knocking the chessboard off the table in his haste.

"Have you changed your mind?" Sir Bayard inquired with every appearance of good humor as Frederic shoved the board back from the edge.

She darted the squire a look that made him blush, then addressed his master. "I've heard a very interesting story about you, Sir Bayard."

Frederic's cheeks started to redden, and he slowly inched his way from the dais to join the soldiers.

She ignored the young man's departure to concentrate on Sir Bayard. "I've been told that you once met a troubador who begged a horse of you in return for a song. You saw a knight, beat him in an unplanned joust, took his horse and brought it to the troubador before he'd finished his ballad. It was my understanding William Marshal, Earl of Pembroke, did that, *not* Sir Bayard de Boisbaston."

Sir Bayard didn't look the least bit nonplused. "William Marshal *did* do that."

He must be truly shameless.

"But so did I," he continued, crossing his arms and leaning his weight on one leg. "I'd heard that tale, you see. I think my mother told it to me even as I suckled. She thought the Earl of Pembroke quite the finest man in the world—certainly finer than her husband, as she never tired of telling him.

"One day, as I was nearing Salisbury to take part in a melee, I came upon a troubador entertaining some ladies as they waited for fresh horses at an inn. He was telling the ladies that story and, braggart that I was, I said that I could do it, too, if ever the opportunity presented itself. At nearly that same moment, another knight, obviously headed for the same tourney, appeared on the road. The troubador immediately challenged me to prove my boast.

"I accepted the challenge and ordered him to start singing as I rode out to meet my foe. I beat the knight in the first pass, took his horse and returned in triumph to give it to the troubador before he ended his song."

That might be true, or he might be a very glib liar. "I hope the knight you defeated was a worthy foe and not an old man or poor youth hoping to make a name for himself."

"I regret to say it was my half brother, Armand," he admitted with a wry little self-deprecating smile that could explain how he'd managed to seduce so many women. "Not the best way to ensure family harmony, especially since I knew it was Armand the moment I saw him. Fortunately, I won some prizes the next day and bought him another horse.

"And then he wrestled me to the ground, gave me a set of bruises the like of which I never hope to have again and made me promise I would never challenge him again, which I very gladly did."

What sort of family had her sister married into? "You compete and even come to blows, yet you still feel obliged to do whatever he asks of you?"

"We're brothers, and we've been through much

together," Sir Bayard answered. "Don't you ever quarrel with your sisters?"

"Not with Adelaide," she replied as she started to put the white pieces back into place on the chessboard.

"Because she's the oldest?"

"Because she's been like a mother to us. Our mother was often ill before she died."

"And Lizette?" he prompted, replacing the black pieces on his side of the board.

She wondered if he could sympathize with her inability to get along with her younger sister. Even she could overlook the reasons Lizette could be so aggravating—when she wasn't there. "I prefer order and she seems to enjoy chaos."

"It's been my experience that those who create disorder are never the ones charged with maintaining it," he replied. "They don't care about the disruption they cause, thinking only of their own wishes and desires."

Apparently he *could* understand.

"Young people can change, my lady, if they're treated with patience and kindness. I was no paragon in my youth, but I'm better than I was, thanks to Armand's tutelage."

As she lined up the pawns, Gillian wondered if that was really true, and what he meant by *better*. "I do *try* to be patient. Unfortunately, my patience doesn't seem to last very long when I'm with Lizette."

"Because she doesn't take anything seriously and laughs in your face."

Gillian glanced away from his long, slender fingers that moved with such delicate precision to his face, and the scar that ran down his cheek. "How did you know?"

His lips jerked up in another little smile. "Ask Armand."

All her chess pieces in their proper order, she straightened and regarded him quizzically. "Were you such a holy terror?"

"Indeed, I was," he admitted as he put his last piece—the king—in its place on the board. "I was spoiled, and selfish, and rash. I suspect I'd have made your sister look like a model of all the virtues."

Again he gave her that wry little smile, like a good friend sharing a confidence.

She didn't want him to be her good friend. She already had plenty of friends, ones who didn't make her feel as if she was fifteen years old again and seeing James smile at her for the first time. She was older now, and wiser, and love had come and gone for her.

Besides, Umbert was waiting to hear what she wanted for the evening meal. "If you'll excuse me, my lord, the cook is waiting."

"Of course," he said, bowing, before she hurried from the dais.

"By all means, we mustn't upset the cook," he muttered as he watched her go, her slender back as straight as a lance and her hips swaying like a reed in the breeze.

GILLIAN WAS STILL in the kitchen when Dunstan appeared on the threshold, a scroll in his hand.

She raised her brows in silent query.

"From the court, my lady," he replied.

She hurried toward him and, as they proceeded to the hall, broke the wax seal.

When they reached the larger chamber, and before she'd had a chance to read the contents, she halted. Something was…different.

And it wasn't just Sir Bayard standing expectantly on the dais.

"Why are there so many of our soldiers in the hall? It's not nearly time for the evening meal."

Dunstan answered quietly. "If that letter should show that the last one supposedly from Adelaide was full of lies—"

"I see," she interrupted, opening the letter and reading it quickly.

The writing was the same and revealed that Adelaide had indeed written and sent her message in the care of Sir Bayard de Boisbaston. This letter was undoubtedly from Adelaide, for the writer gave answers to Gillian's questions that only her older sister would know.

In spite of that reassurance, and for the first time since she'd taken charge of Averette, she felt afraid. If everything Adelaide had written was true, she could be in grave danger. Her heart raced, until—and unaccountably—her gaze fell on Sir Bayard de Boisbaston, champion of tournaments, standing on the dais.

As she grew calmer, she forced her attention back to the anxious Dunstan, who was watching her intently. "Everything in the other letter was true," she whispered. "Adelaide is married, Sir Bayard is her brother-in-law, and there's a conspiracy against the king that's put us in danger, too. Dismiss the soldiers. Send them back to their duties."

His lips thinned, but Dunstan didn't protest, or say anything to her. He moved away and quietly issued an order to the men, who began to go.

Taking a deep breath and rolling up the scroll, she approached Sir Bayard. "It seems, my lord, that we were wrong to doubt you."

His shoulders relaxed and a smile slowly blossomed

on his face. "So now you believe I am who I claim to be."

She nodded and took a seat, regarding him gravely. "Which means I must also believe we're in danger here."

"Yes," he agreed, clasping his hands behind his back. "But less than before, now that I am here."

She tried not to reveal her displeasure at his arrogant remark.

Unsuccessfully, apparently, for he gave her a rueful grin and said, "Not because I'm such a fearsome warrior, my lady. Because I'm an experienced one—and so I still think it would be a mistake to have a hall moot."

She rose abruptly. "I do not, my lord. Now, if you'll excuse me, I have much to do!"

THE NEXT MORNING, after a very restless night that she ascribed to anticipation of the hall moot, Gillian rose from her bed and wrapped her light bedrobe around herself. She went to the narrow window of her bedchamber and looked out at the eastern sky now lighting with the first pink flush of dawn. There were only wisps of cloud in the sky, their undersides orange and rose and a bevy of tints in between, and promising a fine day for the hall moot.

Which they must and would have today, in spite of Sir Bayard's disapproval.

Disapproval he'd still harbored at the evening meal, no matter how genially he'd behaved last night. She had seen it in his face and his dark, intense eyes, eyes whose regard made her feel so...so...

She wouldn't think about Sir Bayard's eyes, and his notion to cancel the hall moot only offered further proof that he had little experience running an estate.

Otherwise, he would understand that disputes between tenants should be settled as quickly as possible, before the conflict worsened.

The door to her chamber opened and Dena came bustling in with a jug of warm water. "Oh, it's nice and cool in here this morning!" she exclaimed brightly as she poured the warm water from the jug into the basin on the washstand. "I'm thinking it's going to be a hot day, though, my lady. Are you sure you want to wear the gold gown?"

"Yes," Gillian replied before she started to wash. She should look her best when she sat in judgment; her gold damask gown was the finest one she possessed.

"At least the silk veil's light," Dena noted as she started to make the wide, curtained bed.

Gillian sat on the stool and started to run her comb through her long, straight hair. Sometimes she envied Adelaide her bountiful curls and waves, but not in the summer months. She well remembered the tears that came to Adelaide's eyes when she tried to get a comb through the thick, curly riot of her hair on a summer's morn.

Gillian deftly began to braid her hair. After she had done so, Dena would pin the braids around her head.

"I hear Geoffrey and Felton are at it again," Dena said as she glanced over her shoulder at her mistress.

"Apparently."

"Do you suppose Sir Bayard will attend the moot?"

"I don't know why he would," Gillian replied. "It's nothing to do with him."

On the other hand, there was little enough for him to do in Averette, so he might attend, if only to be entertained.

"Are you quite well, my lady?" Dena asked, her brow

furrowing as she came to finish Gillian's hair. "Your hands are shaking."

"It's nothing," she said as she clasped them together. "I'm always a little anxious before a hall moot. You can never be sure how someone will react to a judgment."

That wasn't a lie, exactly. But she would *not* admit her state had anything to do with the possibility of Sir Bayard watching the proceedings.

Besides, even if he did come, she could ignore him.

By the time she was attired in her gown, with its long cuffed sleeves lined with scarlet sarcenet, her veil held in place by a slender gold coronet, and wearing gilded slippers that belonged to Adelaide, Gillian was confident that she would be able to conduct the hall moot with perfect ease even if King John himself appeared to witness it.

As she proceeded to the courtyard where a dais had been erected and one of her father's chairs placed for her, she felt very much the chatelaine of Averette, as her own mother had never been. Her mother had been a timid creature, terrified of her husband and his rages, and ill from the constant struggle to give him the son he demanded.

Dunstan waited on the dais, likewise dressed in his best—a black tunic that swept the ground. He held the scroll containing the list of all those who sought justice and those against whom they had complaints. It was a long one, in no small part because the Lady of Averette was known to be just, as her father had not.

As she surveyed the crowd, several people exchanged wary glances and shifted uneasily. Even Old Davy, in his usual place by the stable doors, looked far from comfortable.

It was as if her father had returned to rule Averette.

She looked out over the gathering and found a possible

explanation for the people's anxiety. Several soldiers were now stationed around the dais where she would sit in judgment. More lined the wall walk and extra guards manned the gates. Iain stood, feet planted, fully armed, beside the dais.

One would think a trial of the utmost importance was about to take place, not a simple village hall moot.

This was Sir Bayard's idea of suitable precautions, no doubt, but it seemed far more threatening than comforting.

She was tempted to dismiss the extra soldiers, but what if she *was* in danger? There were always a few unfamiliar faces at a hall moot—visitors seeking entertainment, petitioners' relatives from other towns, merchants, and tinkers, and others who traveled to sell their goods. She couldn't be certain that there were no enemies with other goals among them.

Taking her seat, she nodded at Dunstan, who unrolled the scroll and read out those named in the first case.

Just as he finished, a startled murmur went through the crowd and the people seemed transfixed by something—or someone—coming toward the dais from behind her.

She looked over her shoulder to see Sir Bayard de Boisbaston, dressed in chain-mail hauberk, coif, gauntlet gloves, mail hosen, and surcoat, march toward the dais. Without a word, he stepped onto the platform and stood behind her chair, resting one hand on the hilt of his broadsword as if he intended to remain there the entire day.

Or as if he were the lord of Averette.

She'd accepted that they might need extra guards, but this was too much. Some of her tenants were clearly frightened; all of them looked uncertain and confused.

Only little Teddy, holding tight to his father's hand, smiled with unreserved happiness. He waved at Bayard and as Gillian glanced over her shoulder again, she was surprised to see the knight raise his hand in a small salute. Yet even that gesture couldn't lessen the impact of his dramatic—and intimidating—arrival.

Dunstan didn't look pleased at all, nor did Iain. Both men glared at Bayard as she would have liked to. However, dignity, decorum, and a need to appear united was more important than registering her dismay at this particular time. She could wait until they weren't in full view of everyone in the yard to tell Sir Bayard precisely what she thought of his unnecessary presence.

Instead, she turned to Dunstan. "Summon the first petitioners."

First was Felton bringing his charge of false measure against the miller. Many a miller was accused of using false weights, but such a charge had never been proven against Geoffrey.

Unfortunately, Geoffrey never ceased to act the gloating victor over the matter of his wife's choice, even if he and his spouse often quarreled. Perhaps goading the baker was some compensation for his less-than-blissful marriage.

Whatever the cause of their squabbling, Gillian tried to maintain an appearance of impartial serenity as the baker declared his grievances, and the miller, smug as always, defended himself.

"Has anyone else ever complained about my weights?" Geoffrey concluded. "No! Because everyone knows I don't cheat and never have! I'm an honest, God-fearing fellow."

"Honest?" Felton sneered, his round belly quivering with indignation. "How honest is it to have hollowed-out weights? To put your finger on the scales? To charge more than—"

"Enough!" Gillian had to say, or they would go on forever. "Dunstan will check the measures *again,* Felton. If they're found to be false, Geoffrey will be punished according to the king's laws."

"But, my lady," Felton protested, "that's what you always say!"

Behind her, she heard the soft clink of metal, as if Sir Bayard had moved. She didn't want to acknowledge his presence, yet she couldn't resist the urge to see what had made that sound.

Sir Bayard stood in the same place, but now his arms were crossed and it was quite obvious that beneath his helmet, he was frowning with displeasure.

Felton blanched. "I—I beg your pardon, my lady," he stammered, backing away. "I meant no harm. I just think Geoffrey's… I thought that maybe…never mind!" he cried before he rushed away through the crowd.

Leaving an even more smug Geoffrey. And an even more annoyed Gillian. "Geoffrey, you had best hope your measures are utterly accurate, and if I were you, I would cease behaving as if you've won a crown, not a wife. Otherwise, I might be tempted to rescind my permission for you to operate the mill and give it to someone more humble."

Now it was the miller's turn to blanch. "Yes, my lady."

"Next, please, Dunstan," she ordered, once again trying to ignore the presence of the knight behind her.

Which proved impossible.

As the day wore on, Sir Bayard never moved from behind her chair. She didn't look at him, yet she was always aware of when he frowned, crossed his arms, or shifted his weight, because of the reactions of the people coming forward for judgment and permissions. In spite of the rulings she made, she felt more like a doll dressed up and put on the dais for show than the chatelaine of Averette.

The moment Dunstan declared the hall moot concluded, she rose and faced Sir Bayard. She didn't raise her voice, but each word was an icicle, sharp and cold. "Sir Bayard, to the solar. *Now!*"

CHAPTER SIX

WHEN THEY REACHED the chamber in the keep, Gillian splayed her hands on her hips and her whole body quivered with the rage she'd been fighting to suppress. "Just who the devil do you think you are?"

"I am Sir Bayard de Boisbaston," he answered with aggravating calm as he removed his helmet. He set it on the table and untied the ventail, the flap of mail that protected his throat. He just as calmly shoved his coif back, baring his head and revealing his tousled hair.

"Are you the lord and master of Averette?"

"No," he replied.

He actually had the gall to smile at her! "I have no wish to try to command you, my lady."

"Then by what right did you stand on that dais and act the part?"

He slowly and deliberately took off his gauntleted gloves. "I have no wish to be the master of Averette," he replied, regarding her steadily with those deep brown eyes of his. "I was doing what I was sent here to do. I was protecting you."

"Iain and the men of my garrison can do that," she retorted, barely resisting the urge to knock his helmet from the table and send it crashing to the floor. "I thought I'd made that very clear. But no! The bold, the mighty, the notorious Sir Bayard de Boisbaston must come and stand behind me like a one-man praetorian guard, to frighten and intimidate my tenants, or to grant his august approval of my judgments!"

"I did no such thing. I simply stood there, keeping watch."

Still glaring, she crossed her arms over her heaving chest. "Oh, yes, keeping watch, as if I'm a little girl who needs a great big man to help me!"

His lips thinned and she could see anger in his eyes. Let him be enraged. *He'd* enraged *her.* He'd treated her like a weak and helpless child!

"I played no part at all in your decisions, nor did I try to," he said.

"Oh, no," she scornfully replied. "You didn't terrify Felton into silence with your stares or make the alewife start to cry, or frighten the chandler's daughter half to death."

"I was on guard, my lady, but I'm not a statue, nor deaf nor blind. I'm sorry if my reactions offended you, but I was not attempting to influence the proceedings."

"Nevertheless, you did—by your very presence and especially in your armor with your sword at your side!"

"Then that could not be helped."

She went to stand nose-to-chin with him. "Never, *ever,* presume to do that again!"

He regarded her quizzically and, to her further aggravation, she saw amusement lurking in those brown eyes. "What, stand behind you?"

"You know full well what I mean!" she charged, more annoyed than ever because he didn't appreciate the enormity of what he'd done, the humiliation he'd caused her, the embarrassment she felt. "Don't *ever* try to act the lord here!"

"I assure you *again,* my lady, that is not in my plans."

"Don't smirk at me, you...you *man!*" she exclaimed, her hands balling into fists. "With your chain mail, and your sword, and your handsome face! Don't think I'm like every other foolish woman who's fallen under your spell. That I'll simply bow down before you and let you do what you will. I will *never* let any man rule me—or Averette!"

"Including the king?"

He was purposefully goading her, the cur. "You know I don't include the king. But I won't let *you* tell me what to do, or order me or my men about, or try to take control of what is mine to rule! I've waited years for this chance, to stand in my own light and not in the shadow of Adelaide's beauty or Lizette's charm. To show everyone what *I* can do. To be *seen* at last. But no, you must come here and take that away from me, too."

"I watched as Armand vied for recognition from our father," he answered slowly, an inscrutable expression on his face. "Attention that should have been Armand's, but that came to me instead. I won't do that to you."

"So you *say,* but words are cheap!" she retorted. "You're just like all men. I *hate* what you did today! I hate *you!*"

She raised her hand, wanting to hit something...anything...perhaps him. He grabbed her wrist, his long, strong fingers wrapping around her arm and holding her still. His gaze held hers just as strongly, as if challenging her to try to look away.

She couldn't. She wouldn't. She would stand there forever with his hand holding her, standing so close, his broad chest rising and falling as he breathed heavily, his face close.

His lips close, too. His whole body near, closer to her than she'd been to a man in a very long time.

Touching her. His eyes looking into hers as if seeking...what?

Her breathing quickened and grew shallow. She felt the pressure of his grasp and much more now. A desire, a need, long suppressed, almost forgotten.

Almost. Until now.

And he...what was he feeling, as he looked at her that way?

His Adam's apple bobbed with a swallow. His breathing, too, had grown shallow and fast. His grip loosened, but he didn't let go.

He didn't let go.

He started to draw her forward. Pulling her toward him, as if he wanted to...was going to....

She wrenched her arm free and stepped back, gasping for air as if she'd been held under water. "What are you doing?"

His surprised expression hardened. "Stopping you from striking me. I already have one scar on my face and don't wish another."

If he wasn't going to acknowledge what had just passed between them, neither was she. "Do you understand your place here?"

"Better, perhaps, than you," he had the gall to reply.

"Then stay in it!" she snapped, before she strode from the solar.

BAYARD SCOWLED AS SHE slammed the door behind her. God's blood, what a witch! As if he *wanted* to stand on a dais all day and listen to the petty complaints and conflicts of merchants, tradesmen, and peasants! He'd only gone out of duty, because he'd promised Armand he'd keep his sister-in-law safe, so his brother would have one less worry at court.

He owed Armand that much, and more. If it hadn't been for Armand's guidance and counsel, if Armand hadn't sought him out and told him he was garnering a reputation that would only do him harm, if his half brother hadn't shown him, by word and deed and manner, how to be a better man, who could say where he might be now?

Bayard picked up his leather gloves and, slapping them against his palm, strode to the window. His gaze flew over Averette, and he wondered if Armand had any idea what he'd given up when he'd refused to take this estate.

Bayard had rarely seen such a prosperous, well-run estate, or a happier group of peasants and townspeople. Even the ones who'd come forth with complaints had seemed confident that justice would be done. There could be no mistaking the effect of that security.

Yet according to Armand, the late lord of Averette had been a terrible, vicious, mean man who'd abused his wife and ignored his daughters, except to chastise them for not being sons and threatening to marry them off to increase his wealth and power.

The sense of security he'd felt today must be due to Lady Gillian's governance. Having seen her dispense justice, he could believe that. She'd listened carefully to the complaints—even the incredibly ridiculous ones— and given everyone her full attention. He was impressed with her decisions that were based not on emotion, as one would expect from a woman, but on the facts and evidence provided and, he suspected, a very deep understanding of the people involved.

Yet the fact still remained that she was a woman and while women certainly had *their place*, to use her words, governing an estate was not one of them, not even if the woman was intelligent and perceptive and just.

Such a woman should certainly be in charge of a noble household, though, and Lady Gillian would no doubt make some lord an excellent wife. She'd surely be a better mother to her children than his own had ever been.

But then, most women would be a better mother than his own had ever been.

And it wasn't as if he was in need of such a wife, or any wife at all. He was in no great rush to tie himself down to domesticity and the responsibilities that adhered to it.

There would be time enough to take a wife later and when he did, she would be pretty and pleasant, merry and sweet, amenable and charming, with just a touch of spirit to make life interesting.

She wouldn't stand before him like an enraged empress, her eyes gleaming, her whole shapely body vibrant, her full lips quivering with emotion.

Why, then, had he felt a nearly overwhelming urge to kiss Lady Gillian d'Averette?

BAYARD FOUND FREDERIC in their chamber polishing his armor and decided, once he had his mail off, that Frederic could do with some practice with a lance. He'd noticed a quintain dummy in the outer bailey, and since the wooden replica of a man with a bag of sand tied to one outstretched arm and a shield on the other wasn't in use, Frederic might as well take a few passes. Instructing Frederic would occupy his wayward mind, too.

Surely they wouldn't have to ask permission for that; The practice area was still within the castle walls, after all.

Whether he was supposed to or not, he wouldn't. He

was tired of feeling more like a prisoner here than he had in the Duc d'Ormonde's castle.

He told Frederic his decision, and the lad's eager grin stretched from ear to ear. "Truly?"

"Truly."

"It's not too late in the day?"

"I don't think so."

Bayard almost regretted his suggestion as he helped the lad into his hauberk. It was like trying to get clothes on a wiggling fish.

When the lad was finally attired in his armor, surcoat, and swordbelt, and with his shield over his left arm, Bayard said, "Go to the armory and get a tipped lance. I'll have your horse saddled and waiting in the outer bailey."

"Yes, my lord," Frederic said as he proudly—and unnecessarily—straightened his swordbelt.

After Frederic hurried from the chamber, Bayard followed more slowly and permitted himself a chuckle. God's blood, to be so young and carefree again!

That red-haired serving wench whose name he could never remember passed him on the stairs leading to the yard. She squeezed against the wall, lowering her eyes and blushing as if he were about to make her a lewd offer.

Obviously rumors about his past had reached the household. Lady Gillian had likely heard them, too, although she was acting no worse than she had before. No better, either.

When he reached the stable and his eyes adjusted to the dimmer light, he spotted the senior groom, a tall, broad older man. "I'd like my squire's destrier saddled."

The groom shuffled his feet and didn't meet his gaze. "Where, um, where might you be off to, my lord?"

Bayard clenched his jaw and cursed silently. The poor fellow obviously feared he'd have to tell a knight he couldn't leave the confines of Averette.

"To practice lance charges in the bailey," Bayard replied, barely resisting the urge to lie and say he was planning on riding all around the castle walls to find out where undermining might be the most effective.

The groom grinned, tugged his forelock and hurried to obey while Bayard turned over a bucket by the door and sat down.

For a big man, Ned could move quickly. He would have made a good soldier, Bayard reflected as he watched the groom prepare Frederic's tan destrier.

"Thank you, Ned," he said, taking the reins of the horse to lead it from the stable when he was finished.

As he headed for the gate, he wondered if the sentries were going to challenge him. They didn't, but one did head for the hall the moment he went past.

To report his whereabouts to the lady, probably.

That was another galling thought, but his ill humor lessened when he saw Frederic waiting, a broad grin on his young face and fairly jumping from side to side in his excitement.

Bayard could remember how excited he'd been on similar occasions, until his father began his litany of instructions and cautions, often using Armand as an example of what *not* to do.

Then Armand won his first ten jousts in a tournament, finally silencing their father.

The practice area wasn't the largest Bayard had ever seen, but it would do. The dirt wasn't too hard-packed, and the grass had been left long to cushion falls.

After Frederic mounted, he was so anxious to begin, he could hardly hold the tournament lance steady.

"Remember what I've told you," Bayard cautioned, determined to instruct Frederic not like his father, with criticism and scorn, but like Armand, with patience and encouragement.

"I will!" Frederic cried, lowering his visor.

Bayard let go of the horse's reins and got out of the way. "Whenever you're ready."

Frederic took a deep breath and punched his horse's sides with his heels. The beast leapt into a gallop, gaining speed as it moved down the bailey. The lad's lance wobbled precariously until Frederic managed to get control of it and aim for...the dummy's head?

Not again! Not the head *again!*

Not surprisingly, Frederic missed completely.

As Frederic brought his horse to a halt, Bayard jogged down the field toward him. "That wasn't bad, but you've got to stop aiming for the head. Go for the shield. It's larger and you want to knock your opponent off his horse, not kill him."

"Isn't the object to win the battle?" Frederic grumbled as he doffed his helmet and tucked it under his arm, revealing his sweat-streaked face.

"Capture and ransom is the aim, not death," Bayard reminded his squire as he grabbed the horse's reins and started walking back to the opposite end of the bailey so Frederic could try again. "Wars require money, too, for men, and arms, and ships. Catch a knight and ransom him, and you weaken your enemies. Catch a man and be merciful, and he might think twice about attacking you again. Kill a man, and all you've got is a dead knight and a family who will hate you forever."

His squire obviously didn't agree. "If you let your enemy live, he might kill you the next time."

"Indeed, he might. That's one reason wars should be avoided."

Seeing the look of scorn on Frederic's face, Bayard tried a different tack. "How popular do you think you'll be at tournaments if you always go for your opponent's head?"

The lad sniffed contemptuously. "Men will learn to stay away from me."

"Indeed, they will," Bayard concurred, "and then one day, you'll find yourself without friends or allies."

That gave Frederic pause, as if he was finally beginning to comprehend that letting an opponent live might have some merit, and Bayard pressed on.

"The main thing is," Bayard continued, "a man's head is a much smaller target and if you don't get your opponent off his horse, he can charge you again. Now, take another pass and this time, aim for the shield."

"The shield, then," Frederic confirmed as he turned his horse and couched his lance.

He did indeed aim for the shield, striking it nearly dead center. Bayard let out a whoop of triumph as the lighter lance splintered and broke on the heavier shield, the resounding crash filling the air.

Then, as the dummy spun around, Frederic swayed left to avoid the bag of sand. As Bayard watch with dismay, he tried to regain his balance and leaned too far to the right. Although the heavy bag missed the youth, he fell out of the saddle, hit the ground with a sickening thud and lay still.

Cursing, Bayard broke into a run. If Frederic was seriously injured…or dead…

Reaching him, Bayard threw himself onto his knees beside the boy, whose face was pale, his eyes closed. "Frederic!"

The lad's eyelids fluttered open. Alive, thank God, although he might still be seriously hurt.

"Am I dead?" he asked groggily.

With relief that the boy was conscious at least, Bayard sat back and looked for any sign of blood or broken bones. "Are you in pain?"

Frederic struggled to sit up. "No, I don't...." He blinked as he frowned at the walls of Averette. "Why is the castle moving?"

"You're dizzy."

"Oh, yes, that's it," the boy agreed. "Dizzy. It's slowing down now."

Bayard removed the boy's helmet, dropped it on the ground and helped Frederic to his feet, then he picked him up as he would a child.

"Let me down!" Frederic protested with more vitality. "I'm not a baby!"

"Stay still," Bayard ordered.

He had to find Lady Gillian. As chatelaine, she should have some knowledge of medicine; if not, she would know where they would find a physician.

GILLIAN FROWNED AS SHE crossed the yard. She should have been thinking about the evening meal, but she was still disgruntled about the hall moot and distracted by what had happened in the solar.

It was difficult to concentrate on peas, and lentils, and ham when she kept wondering what would have happened if she hadn't pulled away from Sir Bayard. Would he really have kissed her? Or was he trying to intimidate her?

Surely he wouldn't have embraced her. She was hardly the sort of woman to arouse a man's passion. If he felt anything at all for her, it was likely anger and frustration, and he wouldn't want to kiss her if that was what he was feeling.

As for what *she'd* been feeling…. He was an attractive man and his actions had caused her blood to heat. She'd let her emotions get the better of her. She hadn't been thinking clearly.

And if *he* had not been thinking clearly?

Such speculation was surely ridiculous. If there'd been a moment of mutual desire between them, it had been fleeting, aroused by their overwrought emotions, and wouldn't happen again.

A woman shrieked.

Coming to a startled halt, Gillian turned to see Dena standing as if frozen beside the well, a broken bucket and puddle of water at her feet. The distraught girl's shaking arm pointed toward the gates.

Gillian followed that gesture, to see Sir Bayard striding toward her, with his squire in his arms.

As if he were dead. Or seriously hurt.

"Good God!" she cried, aghast, before she hurried to meet them. "What's happened?"

The youth raised his head, his expression more peeved than pained. "It's nothing. Really."

He certainly wasn't dead, or even seriously hurt, she didn't think.

"He was hit by the quintain," Bayard explained. "He was dizzy and disoriented. He may have hurt his head."

"I'm fine!" Frederic cried, struggling to get down. "Really! I was a little dizzy, but I'm quite well now."

He struggled in vain, for it was clear Sir Bayard wasn't going to set him on his feet.

Which was just as well, for if he'd been dizzy, the less he moved, the better, until she could examine him.

"He can have my bed," Bayard said, his voice a rough growl that told her how upset he was as he ignored his squire's squirming.

"Take him there," she said. "I'll follow."

She called out to Dena, who was still standing by the well, her face a little less pale than it had been before. "Go to Seltha in the kitchen and have her bring me hot water, as well as a bucket of cold, then fetch some clean linen and bring it to Sir Bayard's chamber. At once, Dena!"

The girl started as if she'd been asleep, then hurried to do as she was ordered.

CHAPTER SEVEN

As LADY GILLIAN tended to Frederic, Bayard stood outside the door to the bedchamber. He wasn't going to go to the hall, or anywhere else, until he knew if the lad was seriously hurt or not. He was prepared to wait as long as necessary. Thanks to his father's training, he could stand motionless for hours.

At last the door to the chamber opened, but it wasn't Gillian who came out. It was the weeping Dena and Bayard's stomach clenched with dread.

"How's Frederic?" he asked as Dena pulled the door closed. She answered, although sobs and hiccups garbled her voice. "He's...going...he's going...to be fine...my lady says. I'm to...fetch him...something...to drink and to...call... Robb to stay with him."

Relief washed over Bayard. Lady Gillian was an intelligent woman; he could have faith in her estimation of Frederic's state. And she had wisely called for one of his own men to stay with him, a man *he* could trust to do as he was ordered, regardless of Frederic's complaints or demands.

Then Dunstan—one of the last people Bayard wanted to see—appeared on the stairs and spoke with a condescension that set Bayard's teeth on edge.

"I hear your squire's met with an accident. You need not have any worries about his care. Lady Gillian is very skilled, as good as any physician. My father saw to her education in such arts when he was steward here."

"I'm glad," Bayard said, and he *was* glad that she'd been taught such skills. Still, it wasn't as if Dunstan himself had taught her, although he was acting as if he had.

Suddenly weary, Bayard wished Dunstan would just go away. "What brings you here, Dunstan? Estate business, or have you come to give me your best wishes for my squire's speedy recovery?"

"I've come to see if my lady wishes us to hold the evening meal for her or not," the steward replied as he stepped up to the door and knocked.

In a few moments it opened to reveal Gillian. Behind her, Bayard could see Frederic sitting in the bed, pale but conscious, and more relief flooded through him.

"My lady," the steward began.

She held up her hand to silence him, then smiled at Bayard with genuine pleasure in her green eyes. "I don't believe your squire is badly injured. His pride appears to be hurt more than his body. Nevertheless, I think it would be better if he rested tonight, and stayed off his horse for a few days. He might not be so lucky if he has another fall."

Bayard stepped forward. Dunstan didn't move aside until he caught Bayard's eye. Then he shifted one step to the left.

"Frederic's not going to happy about that," Bayard said.

"No, probably not," she agreed. "However, I think it's better to be cautious. Tonight, he should be awakened at every change of the watch. I've sent for one of your soldiers to sit with him."

Her eyes sparkled with what looked like amusement.

"Soldiers may not be the most gentle of nursemaids, but they can be counted on to follow orders and not be duped by comely young men who don't wish to do as they're told."

Bayard nodded his agreement, although that would mean a night of discomfort and disrupted sleep for him on Frederic's cot, unless he found someplace else to lay his head. "You have my thanks for all your care and concern, my lady."

"There's no more we can do for Frederic now," she replied. "So there's no need for you to stay."

"I'd like to sit with the lad until my man gets here."

"Very well, my lord," she replied. "Tell him what I said about waking Frederic at every change of the watch. If he won't wake easily, I'm to be sent for at once."

"I will, my lady," he replied, "and again, I thank you."

As BAYARD ENTERED THE bedchamber, Frederic struggled to a more upright position. "There's no need for me to stay abed," he said, his tone somewhere between indignant and imploring. "I'm quite well. Really."

He certainly sounded fit enough, and yet orders were orders, whether they came from a lord or a lady. "Unless you've been hiding the fact that you're a physician, you'll do as Lady Gillian tells you," Bayard said as he sat on a stool beside the bed. "Head hurt much?"

"A little."

A knock sounded at the door, and at Bayard's invitation, Robb ambled into the room. He was a tall Yorkshireman, with close-cropped hair and a stocky build. Rumor had it that he'd been a poacher in his youth. Bayard could believe it, for he was able to follow a trail better than most men.

He was also, Bayard had noted, quite taken with that red-headed wench.

"I've been asked to play nursemaid for a bit, my lord," Robb announced with a grin.

Frederic frowned and whispered to Bayard, who got up to go. "If I must have a nurse, ask Lady Gillian to send Dena, will you?"

Bayard couldn't fault the lad for wanting a pretty girl instead of the six-foot Robb, but as Lady Gillian had said, Robb would do as he was told, regardless of any threats or entreaties on Frederic's part. "You can learn something from Robb. Ask him to tell you about the time he took on three outlaws on the London road. He was unarmed and they all had swords, but they wound up dead and he came away with barely a scratch."

Robb's grin widened. "Oh, that was a day, that was!"

Bayard ruffled Frederic's brown curls. "So rest as my lady says, and learn from Robb."

AFTER A VERY CHILLY and uncomfortable night in the hayloft—where at least he didn't have to listen to the snorts and snores of other soldiers and male servants as he would if he slept in the hall—Bayard woke up sneezing, and with straw poking through his shirt.

He shoved off the equally scratchy blanket Seltha had provided him, rolled onto his hands and knees, and peered through a crack in the wattle and daub wall of the stable. It was barely light and the guards on the walk stamped their feet to keep warm in the early-morning chill.

The cook and the kitchen servants were also awake and at work, judging by the smoke rising from the louvered opening in the kitchen roof.

Wrapping the blanket around himself, Bayard thought of the weeks and months Armand had spent in a dank, frigid dungeon. He would probably have considered this pile of clean straw luxurious by comparison.

While Armand had been suffering, he'd been sleeping on clean sheets, in a chamber warmed by a brazier, and never—regardless of the rumors spread about him—with the wife of the Duc d'Ormonde.

He couldn't deny he'd been tempted by the duke's pretty bride. What virile man would not, when she kept telling him how lonely she was, looking at him so piteously with her coquettish eyes? But he'd been the duke's guest as much as his captive and he was determined to live up to the ideals of chivalry as best he could.

There had been other women before that, though, whose husbands had not been his host. Pretty wenches, lovely ladies…. He had made love with at least a score, if not nearly the number attributed to him. Yet how many women had touched his heart? How many had seen *him* as nothing more than a fleeting pleasure, a lover for a few nights of exciting passion to enliven their dull days? How many would have stood up to the king for him, as Adelaide had for Armand?

Not a one, he suspected, which was a distressing thought.

If he had to have a feminine advocate, who would he want? Marion, with her fair hair and dimpled cheeks? Amelie, who'd giggled with every caress? Jocelyn, who was the prettiest, but who thought only of clothes, and jewels, and gossip?

If he were in serious trouble, if he required a woman of sense—shrewd, brave, and competent—there was only one who came to mind: Lady Gillian of Averette.

And if he wanted a lover who didn't giggle with every

touch or look at him as if he were a piece of livestock on display, and with whom he could actually have a conversation that wasn't about the salacious intrigues of the court?

Lady Gillian…perhaps.

What would she do if he kissed her? Slap his face, or return passion for passion with the same bold spirit with which she ruled her home? Eagerly throw herself into his arms, push him down and—

Good God in Heaven!

He must be coming unhinged. Or been far, far too long without a woman if he was getting aroused imagining making love with Lady Gillian.

Cursing himself for a frustrated, fatigued fool—for surely last night's restless slumbers must also be to blame for his wandering mind—and keeping his head bent so that he didn't hit the beams, Bayard swiftly folded the blanket, brushed bits of chaff from his clothes as best he could and climbed down from the loft.

As he strode through the courtyard, he glanced at some of the women gathered around the well. More than one smiled when they saw him, yet not a one appealed to him.

It was like he was bewitched, unexpectedly drawn to the one woman in the castle he should not desire.

Lady Gillian was probably already in the hall.

That thought had nothing to do with his decision to check on Frederic before he went there, he told himself. Frederic was his responsibility; he should be thinking of his squire before his hunger, even if his stomach growled.

He took the stairs to his bedchamber two at a time, shoved open his bedchamber door—and got one of the greatest shocks of his life.

As Bayard stared in stunned disbelief, an earthy curse burst from Frederic's lips. He scrambled out of the bed, grabbing the top blanket to hide his nakedness.

While Dena, her face as red as poppies, clutched a sheet to her bare breasts.

Appalled, Bayard slammed the door shut behind him. "Where the devil's Robb?"

Stupid question.

"Dena took his place." Frederic answered, attempting to sound dignified as he wrapped the blanket around his narrow waist.

Bayard glanced at the cowering servant. "Not exactly."

Still holding the sheet, Dena started to cry. "I'm sorry, my lord. I could do what Robb was supposed to do—I *did* do what Robb was supposed to do. I woke Freddy up every change of the watch."

Freddy? "Did you indeed?"

"I—I love him, my lord," she stammered, "and I wanted to make sure he was all right and being taken proper care of."

She couldn't see Frederic's face, but Bayard could. The boy looked annoyed and impatient, as if he was upset that they'd been discovered, but not guilty or remorseful.

Nor did he come to Dena's defense, which told Bayard Frederic didn't really care about the girl or her fate. He'd used Dena to assuage his lust; she meant nothing more to him than that. And yet she believed he loved her.

Poor, naive, gullible girl. Even at his youthful, selfish worst, he had never been so careless of a woman's virtue, even if she were just a servant. "Get dressed, Dena, and leave us."

Her gaze flew from Bayard to Frederic and back again, and she raised the sheets a little higher. "Freddy?"

"I think you'd better go, Dena," his squire said, dismissing her with a cold arrogance that turned Bayard's stomach.

Damn Frederic for taking advantage of her. And damn *him* for not telling Frederic to stay away from the women of this household where they were guests. He'd failed in that duty and he must try to make it right.

Sniffling, the girl started to get out of the bed, then paused and, blushing, glanced uncertainly at Bayard.

Although she could possess nothing he hadn't seen before, Bayard dutifully turned his back, allowing her a little dignity. Standing with his arms folded, he heard her dressing and the sounds of Frederic putting on his clothes, as well.

"I'm sorry, I'm sorry," the weeping girl whispered over and over to Frederic. "I love you."

His squire didn't answer.

"Don't you love me?" she pleaded, her words full of pain.

"I might have said something like that, in the heat of the moment," Frederic muttered.

To get what he wanted, like many men before him.

Bayard could remember another woman crying nearly the same thing as his father had whipped her out his castle gates. "You told me you loved me!" the woman had wailed long ago, her thin arms around the boy she tried to shield from the strong blows. "You said you loved me!"

Which is why he had never, ever told a woman he loved her, no matter how much he desired her.

Sobbing, Dena fled the room, her clothes loosely fastened, her dishevelled red hair flying behind her like a banner.

Bayard turned to face his squire, now dressed in breeches, boots, and unbelted tunic. "What did you think you were doing?"

Frederic shrugged his shoulders.

"We are guests here."

Frederic didn't answer.

"Was she a virgin the first time you took her?"

The youth muttered something under his breath.

Bayard's teeth clenched and his hands balled into fists. "Was she or wasn't she? Couldn't you tell, or are you a *complete* dolt?"

"What's it matter if she was?" Frederic muttered defiantly, still not meeting Bayard's gaze. "She's not a child."

"Thank God for that! And if she gets with child? What will you do then?"

"Might not be mine."

"Do you expect me to believe that after having given her virginity to you, she began bedding any man who asked her? God's blood, boy! Having taken her maidenhead, will you besmirch her honor, too?"

His squire gave another petulant shrug. "She's only a peasant."

It was all Bayard could do not to strike him to the ground. "If she bears a child in about nine months' time, you will take no responsibility for it, or her?"

Frederic raised defiant, accusing eyes. "Why should I? I'm a nobleman's son. Surely you can't expect me to marry the wench?"

"No," Bayard retorted, for that was true enough, "but I *can* expect you to behave with generosity and honor."

"You have women all the time," Frederic retorted.

He straightened his slender shoulders. "How dare you chastise *me?*"

His ire exploding, Bayard grabbed Frederic by the tunic and pushed him against the bedpost. "Dena put her fate in your hands when she put her body in your bed and, by God, you'll treat her well, or so help me, I'll drag you back to your father and tell him I won't have such a dishonorable lout for a squire!"

Frederic flailed helplessly. "Let me go!"

"Do you think you're suffering now, boy?" Bayard charged. "Have you ever seen a woman in labor? Ever heard her cries of pain? Ever listened to a woman called a cheap whore and seen her whipped because a man sweet-talked his way between her legs?"

A woman's sun-browned hand grabbed his arm and pulled him away. "Stop!"

He found himself facing a pale, thin-lipped Gillian. Sobbing so that her whole body shook, her hands covering her face, Dena stood on the threshold of the chamber behind her glaring mistress.

Frederic rubbed his throat and raised a shaking arm to point at Bayard. "He...he tried to kill me!"

Bayard regarded him coldly. "If I wanted you dead, you'd be dead."

"My lord," Gillian said, her tone commanding, "Frederic is my guest, too, and you will *not* lay hands on him again!"

The knight planted his feet. "I regret, my lady, that my squire has callously and cruelly seduced your maidservant."

"I didn't seduce her," Frederic hoarsely protested. "She wanted me. Tell them, Dena. I didn't force you, did I? You gave yourself willingly."

Dena lowered her hands. "Yes," she whispered, her face puffy and tear-streaked. "I was willing."

"You see!" Frederic crowed. "I did nothing wrong."

"I—I thought he loved me, my lady," the girl explained, wiping her eyes as more tears slid down her cheeks. "He said he did. I—I believed him."

"Is that true?" Gillian demanded.

"I might have," Frederic grudgingly admitted. He puffed out his chest like an indignant rooster. "Sir Bayard's had plenty of women and so have most knights. There's nothing wrong with that. She's only a serving wench, after all."

"I've never callously seduced any woman, be she lady or maidservant, with talk of love," Bayard retorted. "And if a woman I bedded got with child, I would provide for them and ensure they didn't suffer for our sport."

After giving Frederic a look that could have frozen the millpond in high summer, Gillian went to the distraught Dena and gently put her arm around her.

"Go to my chamber and wait for me," she said, her voice comforting and kind, softer than Bayard had ever heard before. Gentle, like the sweetest of women, and a far cry from the commanding tones she'd used at the hall moot, or when she'd confronted him in the solar afterward.

It was as if there were two Lady Gillians, the termagant and the matron who cared about her people as if they were family.

Sniffling and wiping her nose, Dena hurried away.

"My lady," Bayard said, his own tone more subdued, "you have my word that if the girl gets with child, she and the babe will be provided for. I will see to it myself if Frederic won't."

The youth dug his toe into the floor. "Are you dismissing me from your service, my lord?"

He was trying to sound brave, but there was a tremor in his voice and Bayard could guess where it came from.

Frederic's father was a harsh, stern, and very proud man, as his own had been. That was one reason Bayard had chosen Frederic to be his squire, to show the youth that a man could be both respected and benevolent, as Armand was and as he tried to be. If Frederic were sent home in disgrace, the least he could expect from his father would be a beating.

And how then would Frederic treat women in the future? Kindly, respectfully—or would he hold Dena, and all women, responsible for his disgrace?

Frederic had acted as many another would in his place, and he would probably continue to treat women as objects for his amusement unless he was shown a more honorable way.

Yet if the lad wanted to go, he should go. "Are you willing to stay?" he asked his squire.

Clearly taken aback by the question, Frederic stammered his answer. "Y—yes."

"My lord," Gillian said, her voice firm and her expression determined. "This is *my* castle—"

"Yes, it is," he interrupted before she got any angrier. "And because it is, the decision as to whether Frederic stays or goes is yours."

She relaxed—a little. "Since Dena's going to suffer most for their folly, I think Dena should decide if he stays or goes. If she wants him to leave, he'll leave."

Bayard nodded his agreement, then fixed his steadfast gaze on the youth. "While Lady Gillian speaks to Dena, I'm going to wait in the hall. Since you seem to have recovered completely from your fall yesterday, you'll stay here, alone, to contemplate the responsibilities that come with being a knight. If you stir from this chamber until I give you leave, it won't matter what Lady Gillian decides. *I'll* send you home. Do you understand?"

"Yes, my lord," the youth answered so quietly, Bayard could hardly hear him.

"My lady," Bayard said with careful politeness, offering her his arm.

She took it and allowed him to escort her from the chamber, while Frederic sat heavily on the bed and watched Bayard close the door.

CHAPTER EIGHT

"I TRULY REGRET WHAT'S happened, my lady," Bayard said as they walked down the corridor toward Lady Gillian's chamber, which was at the opposite end of the family apartments from the one given to Bayard. "I've failed in my duty to you and your household. As for your decision to let Dena decide if Frederic stays or goes, I agree that Dena will be the one who'll be the most shamed when word of her dishonor becomes common gossip, and whether she bears a child or not. I applaud your kindness and generosity in allowing her the choice. But I don't believe the lad is without merit and hope that, given time and a firm hand, he can be a better man."

Gillian slid Bayard a glance. It was unexpected to hear a man, and a nobleman at that, voice such sentiments—as unusual and unexpected as his assurances that he would assume responsibility for his squire's by-blow if Frederic fell short. Many noblemen considered the female servants of a household fair game for their lust, and even that the women should be grateful for their attention. That he did not, despite his reputation, struck her as admirable, although she recalled that he wasn't said to flit from maidservant's bed to maidservant's bed, but from lady's to lady's. Nevertheless, she also believed he'd been honest when he'd said he'd never used lies of love to seduce a woman.

They stopped outside her chamber door. Inside, they could hear Dena weeping.

"My father used women for his amusement far too often," Bayard said, standing close beside her, staring at the closed door as if gazing at a picture. "He seduced them with words of love and the promise of security, only to abandon them when he tired of them, or saw another to take her place. I probably have bastard brothers all over England. I know of at least one, because his mother brought him to our castle when I was a boy. My father called her a cheap, stinking harlot and whipped them both out of the gates. I'll never forget it, or the shame *I* felt, as long as I live."

His attitude and his offer made more sense now. "As long as I'm chatelaine here, Dena won't be mistreated," she assured him.

He nodded and when he looked at her, she saw a relief his eyes that bespoke more than mere gratitude.

Her blood heated until one corner of his lips jerked up in a little grin. "Has anyone ever told you that when you look at someone in that unwavering way, it feels as if you're trying to worm out all their secrets?"

"I'm sorry," she murmured, looking away and flushing with a different kind of heat.

Bayard reached out and cupped her chin to turn her head so that she was looking at him. "Everyone has secrets, my lady. Including you, I suppose."

She couldn't meet his steadfast gaze, didn't want to notice the pressure and warmth of his touch, especially when he seemed to be summoning all her secrets from their hiding places. She feared that if she looked into his dark eyes, she might reveal them. All of them.

They shouldn't be standing so close, either. She shouldn't be noticing the fullness of his lips, the strength of his jaw, the plane of his cheeks. She shouldn't want to turn her face into his hand and kiss his palm. She shouldn't want to kiss him at all.

And much more than that.

She jerked her head away and remembered what she'd heard about him. "If what they say about you is true, you must already support several children."

The light in his eyes dimmed and his lips thinned. "I don't, and if I have a child, I don't know about it."

His expression hardened. "Obviously you've heard what people call me, and why, but I assure you that the number of my liaisons has been exaggerated. I am not the sly seducer rumor paints me. Granted, I've had lovers, but I cared about the women I bedded."

"Although not enough to marry," she countered.

"The same could be said of their feelings for me. We shared some nights of sport, and nothing more. They were as aware of my feelings—or lack of them—as I was of theirs."

He sounded neither pleased, nor proud, nor remorseful. He was matter-of-fact, as if discussing his armor or the weather—as she might sound if she were to tell him about James, carefully keeping the true depth of her feelings from someone she didn't know well.

"I should speak to Dena," she said as she pushed down on the latch and hurried inside, away from him and his dark, troubled eyes, and the sympathy he aroused within her.

DENA SAT ON A STOOL by the window, her shoulders slumped, her hands limp in her lap as if she was too weary to weep anymore.

Gillian's heart swelled with sympathy for her. She understood too well the yearning to give all of oneself to another, the desire that made morals, and rules, and laws seem created only to thwart your happiness. To believe that anything your beloved asked or wanted of you was right, and good, and worth any sacrifice.

Because she did, she'd also experienced the chilling fear that her desire—and the actions it inspired—would be discovered, leading to shame and dishonor if the truth were ever known. That she might, in nine month's time, bear a bastard.

But her courses had come at their regular time, and her shame was still a secret, buried with James.

Unfortunately for Dena, there could be no keeping her seduction a secret. Several of the servants had already seen and heard Dena sobbing in a corner of the hall. She'd been crouched on the floor like an animal in the greatest pain, and more than one of the women had asked her what was wrong.

It had taken all of Gillian's authority as lady of Averette to get the girl to speak, and even then she'd had to strain to hear Dena's strangled explanation. But she *had* heard it, and so had Seltha and Joanna. Such a story would fly through the hall and kitchen, to the stable, and barracks, and armory, and then the village, until everyone in Averette would know of her shame.

Not even the lady of Averette could prevent that now. What she could do, though, was try to ensure that Dena didn't suffer more than she had to.

Dena glanced up when Gillian closed the door. Instead of starting to cry again, as Gillian expected, her eyes flashed with fire and she rose with unexpected vigor. "Oh, my lady, I've been such a *fool!*"

Taken aback by the change in Dena's attitude and her fierce words, not quite knowing what to say because all her comforting words had fled her head, Gillian gestured limply at the stool. "Sit down."

Dena did, only to jump right up again, apparently too agitated to sit. "I've been a ninny, a stupid, silly love-struck ninny." Her angry demeanor crumpled a little. "But when he said he loved me…"

Gillian hurried to put her arm around the girl, wishing she'd paid more attention to what was happening in her household.

Dena shook her off as if she couldn't bear to be touched. "No, my lady, please! Don't pity me! I knew—in my heart, I *knew* that something wasn't right. That he didn't care for me as I did for him. But I—silly numbs-kull!—ignored the warnings of my heart and my con-science and thought that I could make him love me, especially if I…if we…"

Covering her face in hands, she slid down onto the stool. "Oh, my lady, I'm so ashamed!"

Gillian knelt in front of her and gently pried her hands apart to look into her flushed face. "You made a mistake, and while it *was* a mistake, the greater shame belongs to the man who used you, lying to get what he wanted."

Dena sniffled and drew in a ragged breath. "He said I was beautiful, even my hair. Everybody else thinks my hair is ugly, or else it means I'm cursed."

Your hair is like the softest flax.

The words rose up from her memory, sweet and potent and painful. "I understand, Dena. Truly, I do."

Although she didn't doubt that James had sincerely loved her, with all the fervor and wonder of a first and tender passion.

The girl's eyes widened with awe, and hope. "Then you…you won't send me away, my lady?"

"Not if you want to stay, although it won't be easy.

People are going to hear what's happened and cast judgment on you. You may be shunned, or called names, and other men may think you'll come easily to their beds."

"Let them!" the girl declared as she again jumped to her feet, her body trembling with determination. "They'll soon find out I won't! Not again! Never again!"

Gillian rose more slowly. "And if you're with child?"

Dena's gaze faltered, and she ran her hand over her stomach. She raised her eyes, and her lips trembled as tears shivered on her lashes. "If I am, will you make me go?"

"No, not if you don't want to. Are you with child now?"

Dena bit her lip and looked beseechingly at Gillian. "I don't know for certain, my lady, but…perhaps."

Gillian reached out and took Dena's hands in hers. "Then you'll need my protection even more, and you'll have it, Dena."

It was as if all the strength suddenly went out of Dena's legs. She wobbled and nearly fell as Gillian reached out to catch her.

"My lady, oh, my lady, you are so good to me!" she cried as she held tight to Gillian. "I don't know what I'd do if you…"

"Hush now. Hush," Gillian whispered as she led Dena to the bed, afraid any more strain would make the girl ill. "Lie down and rest, Dena."

Dena drew back. "Oh, I couldn't! Not in your own bed, my lady!"

"I command it," Gillian replied only a little sternly.

Moving as gingerly as if the bed were made of delicate threads, Dena did as she was told.

"I knew he wouldn't marry me, my lady," she confessed as Gillian tucked the coverlet around her. "He's nearly a knight and I'm just a weaver's daughter. But many noblemen have mistresses they love and treat as well as they do their wives—even better sometimes. I thought maybe... It may not be honorable, but I would be with him and that would be enough because I loved him so." She choked back another sob and brushed a tear from her flushed cheek. "More fool me, eh, my lady?"

"You trusted him and he played you false," Gillian said as she sat on the side of the bed. "You aren't the first woman to be betrayed by a lover and unfortunately, you surely won't be the last."

"Do you...do you suppose Sir Bayard really meant it when he said he would see that my child and I won't want if Frederic won't—"

"Yes, I believe him." Gillian took the girl's hand in hers and regarded her gravely. "Do you want me to tell Frederic he must leave Averette?"

With her eyes as round as cart wheels and Gillian's coverlet pulled up to her chin, Dena looked even more young and innocent. "Would you make him go for my sake?"

Gillian gave her a little smile of encouragement. "Absolutely."

"And Sir Bayard would agree?"

"He would have no choice in the matter. I command Averette, not him."

Dena's brow furrowed with thought, then she shook her head. "Let him stay. Sir Bayard's a good man and I don't think Frederic's beyond hope. I think he could learn how to be a proper, chivalrous knight from Sir Bayard."

Gillian realized she thought so, too. "You'll

have to see Frederic in the hall or the yard," Gillian reminded her.

"Would I have to serve him?"

"No. You would have my permission to ignore him completely."

Dena managed a tremulous smile that had a hint of satisfaction. "And I will. He can stay."

Gillian got to her feet. "Rest here, Dena. I'll tell Sir Bayard that his squire doesn't have to go. I'll also tell him that Frederic is not to speak to you, or he'll be gone the same day."

Dena's face, which had been so resolute only moments before, dissolved into anguish once more before she buried her head into the pillow. "I'm *never* falling in love again!"

Gillian lightly brushed a lock of auburn hair from the girl's flushed cheek. "You're angry and upset, but you're young. Love may come…"

Again.

The word whispered itself into her mind and heart, although she, too, had been just as certain she could never love again after James had died. She'd stayed certain for years, and when Adelaide had suggested she and her sisters vow never to marry, it had been an easy promise to make.

And now? her heart whispered. *Are you so sure now you can never love again?*

And the answer to that was…

No.

Gillian tried to push aside that realization as she hurried to the hall, where she found Bayard pacing on the dais. He halted and turned to her, query in his dark, penetrating eyes.

"Frederic can stay. Dena hopes you can teach him to be a better man." She softly added, "And so do I."

Bayard flushed, then let his breath out in a long, relieved sigh. "I'll do my best, my lady."

She looked around to ensure that no servants were close by, wanting to spare the girl whatever woe she could until her state became obvious. "Dena may already be with child."

"If so, it will be as I said," he replied just as quietly. "Either Frederic will keep both mother and child clothed, sheltered, and fed, or I will."

Gillian had no doubt about that. Yet she didn't trust herself to say so to his face. Who could say what her own might reveal if she did? "Thank you, my lord. Now if you'll excuse me, I have much to do, and this sad business has taken me from my other duties."

He nodded his agreement, then watched her go.

Today, he'd discovered unexpected gentleness and generosity in Lady Gillian d'Averette. She would have been within her rights to cast Dena out, yet she had treated the younger woman with kindness and sympathy, as if she understood Dena's anguish.

All too well, perhaps?

Was that why she was so cool in her manner to every man with whom she dealt? Had she been betrayed by a man? A lover?

When he'd first arrived at Averette, he would have scoffed at the possibility that Lady Gillian had ever had a lover. Now, though…. Now he could very well believe it.

As Bayard started toward his bedchamber to tell Frederic he could stay, he wondered who might have had the good fortune to have won such a woman's heart, only to cruelly, callously reject her.

THREE NIGHTS LATER, Dunstan, Frederic, and the man called Charles de Fenelon sat sharing the wine Charles had provided. Their faces were illuminated by a fire burning in the small hearth set in the corner of the steward's sumptuous chamber located on the lower level of the family apartments.

The steward might be somewhat austere in his dress but when it came to the comforts of his living quarters, he had more in common with an oriental potentate than an English freeman. There were silken hangings on the bed; highly polished, intricately carved oak furnishings; and a thick, brightly patterned carpet on the floor.

"Are you really forbidden to leave the castle?" Charles asked Frederic, speaking with every appearance of shock and sympathy in response to the youth's complaints.

The steward had been silent since they'd gathered here, seemingly more interested in staring sullenly into his goblet than speaking.

"Not unless I'm with *him*," Frederic sulked, having no need to explain to whom he was referring. "He watches me like a hawk all the time, too. I can't even go to the garden without telling him where I'm going. And I have to sleep in the hall, although who can sleep with all the snoring? It's a low, ungentlemanly form of punishment, if you ask me. I'd rather be whipped."

Frederic took another gulp of wine. "He had me working with the armorer today. The armorer—me, who's to be knighted soon and lord of a vast estate as soon as my father dies."

He thrust his goblet toward the wine merchant. "D'you know what I think?"

Charles accurately guessed he was about to hear it whether he wanted to or not.

"*I* think he's trying to make me leave because the

lady's angry with me and he's *afraid* of her. Mighty warrior—ha!" Frederic scoffed. "My father would cut off Sir Bayard's ears if he knew how I was being treated!"

"So why don't you go home to your father?" Charles asked, pouring him more wine.

"And have Sir Bayard say I ran away? Never!"

"There is that. And it's not as if you did something criminal. Why, I'm sure that girl led you on. They all do, you know, and then later cry rape."

"She never said I raped her," Frederic admitted.

"Because you didn't. And if she'd said you had, you had only to point out that she kept coming back for more." Charles gave the lad a wink. "You must be good."

As Frederic beamed with pride, Dunstan abruptly held out his goblet for more wine.

"You're right," Dunstan muttered, his words slightly slurred. "They do. Lead you on. And then get as frosty as ice when you touch them."

He gestured at them both with his goblet, making the wine slosh over the rim, regardless of the waste or the carpet beneath his feet. "But you're wrong about Bayard. That lout's not afraid of her. He's trying to get her into his bed. Anybody can see that—except *her*."

Dunstan glared at them with enraged and bloodshot eyes. "I thought she was clever, but she's as blind as the rest of them because he acts as if he's another Earl of Pembroke."

"Which he most certainly is not," Charles agreed. "The tales I've heard…"

He shook his head as if too disgusted to continue, but really waiting for them to urge him on, which Frederic eagerly did.

"Well, there's the Duc d'Ormonde's young wife, of course," Charles replied. "He seduced her, although he was treated with every courtesy by her husband. The family's all the same, you know. His father couldn't look at a woman without trying to get under her skirts, they say."

"Lord Armand's a handsome devil, too, is he?" Dunstan demanded, holding out his goblet again.

At this rate, Charles thought, he'd have to start rationing or his wine wouldn't last the week. "Yes, he is— although he dresses like a peasant most of the time."

He remembered too late that Gillian also dressed far below her station. Fortunately, neither Dunstan nor Frederic seemed to notice that particular slip of the tongue.

"Women are all fools when it comes to handsome men," Dunstan mumbled. "Never mind the ones who do all the work and take care of them. Let a fella come along with a pretty face and they're spreading their legs fast enough."

"And so they've spread them for Bayard de Boisbaston," the wine merchant agreed. He waited a moment, then loosed another dart. "I can only hope Lady Gillian is able to resist his easy charm and ready smiles."

He sighed wearily and shook his head, implying that he didn't really believe that was possible.

Frederic leaned forward, a keen excitement gleaming in his eyes. "You think he and she…?"

"I wouldn't be surprised if they have already."

Dunstan threw his goblet to the floor and rose on unsteady feet. "She wouldn't let him! Not her! And they're related by marriage."

Charles picked up the goblet and filled it again. "Naturally I hope Sir Bayard hasn't succeeded," he smoothly replied. "But he'll *try*. It's second nature to a man like that, raised by such a father."

"She *wouldn't*," Dunstan insisted, the forcefulness of

his words undermined by his drunken swaying. "She's too clever. She wouldn't let him take her. Not *her*."

Charles rose and guided the man back to his chair. "Of course, of all women, she'd be the least likely to be fooled by his honeyed words and tender looks. But she is only a woman, after all."

He slid a sideways glance at the squire, who'd been conspicuously silent. "Perhaps someone needs to keep a watch on Sir Bayard, for the lady's sake?" he proposed. "After punishing and humiliating his squire for something far less serious, it would serve Bayard right if his own dishonorable conduct were exposed."

He hesitated for the necessary moment to let his suggestion take root, then continued as Dunstan sat heavily, nearly missing the chair completely. "What, then, will become of the poor, disgraced lady? She'll be humbled and disgraced, as well. She'd have to be grateful to any man who would offer her marriage after that."

As Frederic stared thoughtfully into the flickering flames in the hearth and hope bloomed in the steward's bloodshot eyes, Charles de Fenelon, also known as Lord Richard d'Artage, formerly of the king's court, hid his satisfied smile and poured more wine.

CHAPTER NINE

GILLIAN WALKED BRISKLY along the banks of the pond. Behind her came her escort. Today it was two of Sir Bayard's men, Tom and Robb. Tom didn't seem to mind the duty, but it was clear Robb wished he'd been given almost anything else to do. She didn't relish having two shadows, either, but as long as she might be in danger, she had no choice.

Ignoring the soldiers as best she could, she surveyed the rows of flax stems laid out in the water to rot with a practiced eye. Later, the stems would be beaten and combed into long silken strands, then spun and woven into linen. They'd had a good crop of flax this year and would likely have extra to sell in Chatham.

Or perhaps not. If it came to war, they would need lots of linen for bandaging wounds. And shrouds.

Some serving women were also throwing water from the pond onto stems laid out on grass. It took more time and effort to sprinkle the stems, but the flax that resulted from that labor would be whiter and so would the linen made from it.

"Remember that you're to be given a full length of the best linen as a reward for your hard work, or an amount of silver or grain of equal value," she said to the women, for their task was as backbreaking as cutting hay.

The women returned her smile. "Bless you, my lady," an older serving woman said. "And your sisters, too."

Gillian thanked them, then told Tom and Robb they could wait outside while she went into the long, low shed where the flax was laid out to dry. At one end some of the men were beating the stems, while in the main part of the shed, several women sat on benches arranged in a circle, heckling the beaten stems into long silky strands. Their conversation halted when they saw her, until she picked up one of the wooden combs and joined them.

Hilda, one of the older women and an acknowledged leader of the women, made room for Gillian on the end of one of the benches. "Good day, my lady," she genially began as Gillian picked a stem and started to comb.

"And to you all," she amiably replied. "Has anything exciting happened?"

"You mean other than Sir Bayard scaring the liver out of Felton?" Hilda replied, her tone serious, but her eyes dancing with merriment. "God save me, it's about time somebody did and stopped those two big babies from carrying on the way they do! And over Bertha!"

Gillian kept combing and didn't look up. "I thought perhaps Sir Bayard's presence was too intimidating."

"Lord love you, it was!" another of the women exclaimed, grinning. "I just about fell over in my shoes. Meaning no disrespect, though, my lady, he's not nearly as scary as you in a temper. We thought you were fairly going to flay the poor man alive by the end o' the day."

Clearly, she'd revealed too much of her anger. "I want people to feel sure of getting a fair hearing from me."

"Oh, everybody knows they will," another middle-aged woman named Yllma assured her. "And it don't hurt to have a man with a sword to back you up, especially when those two get going at each other."

Yllma sighed and shook her head as she put her combed flax in the basket beside her and reached for another stem. "I knew that Bertha'd cause no end of trouble. She was a flirty, flighty girl and always chasing the men."

"And letting more than one catch her, too," Hilda added, her lips turned down with disgust.

"Well, what could you expect? She was that desperate to get a husband," Yllma replied.

"*Too* desperate," Hilda said.

Gillian wished they'd talk about something other than marriage.

"Speaking o' marriage," Hilda continued, making Gillian stifle an inward groan, "we wish Lady Adelaide every happiness."

The women all smiled and looked at Gillian expectantly.

"Thank you. I think she's very happy."

"When might she be coming home?" Yllma asked.

"I don't know. She didn't say anything about that in her letter."

The women stopped their labor and several looked at Hilda expectantly. As if in answer to their silent question, Hilda straightened her narrow shoulders and asked, "What's the new lord of Averette like?"

"There is no new lord of Averette," Gillian said, laying her own flax in her lap. She was determined they understand *that* quite clearly. "Regardless of Lady Adelaide's marriage, I'm still chatelaine of Averette. Lady Adelaide will be chatelaine of her husband's castle."

The women let out audible sighs of relief, and Hilda smiled, revealing a few gaps where teeth used to be. "We was sure Lady Adelaide wouldn't marry no cruel or heartless man, my lady, but after your father…"

Her words trailed off as she realized she didn't have

to tell Gillian that her father had been a vicious, cruel, and selfish tyrant.

"Did she say anything about the queen?" one of the younger women, Kat, asked eagerly. Either she was unaware of the sudden tension, or was too curious about Queen Isabel to care.

Gillian suspected it was both, but she was happy to change the subject. "Not in this letter."

"At least the king can marry for love," Kat said with a sigh as she started combing her flax again.

"The king does whatever he wants," Hilda said, and it was clear from her tone that she wished it were otherwise.

It was no secret to Gillian that John was a despised king; she hated him and his capricious, selfish decisions herself. Unfortunately, he was their lawful ruler and to overthrow him would, she was sure, lead to even more trouble for her and her people. They would be torn between warring factions, as if Averette was a bone caught between a pack of wolves.

"He can't be as bad as they say, surely," Kat said hopefully. "I mean, if he won a lady's love, he must have some good qualities."

"He has a crown," one of the other women said with a laugh.

Kat pouted and brushed her flax with hard, swift strokes. "*I* think it was love."

"What do *you* think, my lady?" another of the women asked.

"I'd like to believe it was love that inspired the match," she carefully replied, "and it could be that it did play a part, but there's no denying the match was to John's advantage, too. Isabel had been the promised bride of Hugh the Brown and by marrying her instead, John prevented an alliance that could have meant more trouble for him. As for Isabel's feelings, she's younger than you, Kat, so it may be she wasn't given much choice. However, Adelaide tells me that Isabel enjoys being the queen, as many women would, so perhaps she finds that more than enough compensation if other things are lacking in her marriage."

Not wanting to get embroiled in any more discussions about marriage or the king, and having finished combing the stem she'd taken, Gillian put the flax in the basket by Hilda and got to her feet. "I should go back to the castle."

"My lady!"

She turned to see one of the guards from the gate at the door. Fearing more trouble, her heart leapt to her throat while she fought to maintain an appearance of calm. "Yes?"

"A messenger's come from your sister."

"Which one?" she asked, approaching him. Judging by the perspiration on his face, he'd run from the castle. Dread knotted her stomach.

"Lady Lizette, my lady."

Gillian tried to stifle the concern building inside her, telling herself that if Lizette had sent a messenger, she couldn't be in serious trouble. It was probably just a series of excuses for her failure to have returned home by now.

Nevertheless, she walked quickly back to the castle, with Tom and Robb trotting behind.

Four soldiers from their garrison who'd gone with Lizette as her guards were lounging by the stables while Ned and two stableboys saw to their horses.

Daniel wiped the smile off his face when he saw her marching toward them.

"Where is she?"

"Stamford—at least she was three days ago, my lady," he replied as he reached into the pouch at his side and pulled out a sealed and folded parchment. "She sent you this."

Dunstan came bustling across the yard from the direction of the buttery, his tunic billowing about his ankles. Out of the corner of her eye she spotted Sir Bayard and his squire, swinging their swords at each other near the chapel. She was tempted to call him to join them, but decided he need not be involved. Yet.

"It's word from Lizette," Gillian said as she pried open the seal and began to read.

She wasn't an errant child, Lizette had written, to be called home so abruptly, especially when they had promised her she could travel all she liked. Nevertheless—and although Adelaide's letter had been extremely vague as to why it as so important that she return to Averette—she would obey, albeit it at her own pace.

Gillian noticed Sir Bayard walking toward them and she muttered a curse, earning a shocked look from Dunstan. It was bad enough to have such a letter from her sister; she didn't want to have to reveal Lizette's insolence to Sir Bayard, as well.

"Is it bad news?" Sir Bayard asked as he reached them.

He was wearing only breeches, boots, and a linen shirt that must have been made from the best flax. It was open at the neck, the laces loose and dangling, exposing his muscular chest more than was decent, and he'd tied back his hair from his face with a thin strip of leather. Despite his efforts with his squire, who was hovering nearby, and the warmth of the day, he'd barely broken a sweat.

"Not precisely," she said, prevaricating, although Sir Bayard had to be told about Lizette's letter. "However, there is something we should discuss, so I'd appreciate it if you could join us in the hall."

She caught the annoyed look that crossed Dunstan's face, but that could not be helped. Sir Bayard had to hear the news.

The servants laying new rushes and dusting cobwebs from the corbels took one look at Gillian as she marched toward the dais, and scattered. She threw herself onto the tallest, most ornate of the carved chairs and handed the parchment to Dunstan. "My sister Lizette says that she's not a servant to come when she's called. Nevertheless, she'll graciously acquiesce and come back to Averette—at her own pace."

Dunstan glanced at Sir Bayard before he took the parchment, his expression all but shouting, "Does *he* have to be here?"

Sir Bayard ignored him. "I'm sorry to hear that your sister doesn't appreciate the danger she might be facing. Indeed, she must not or she would come home at once. Perhaps you should write to her yourself, my lady, and try to impress upon her the necessity of returning as quickly as possible."

"I would if I thought it'd do the least bit of good," Gillian said, pushing back her plain scarf that suddenly seemed annoying. "She'll just ignore me. She always does."

Dunstan stepped forward with another suggestion. "Perhaps if you write to Adelaide and suggest *she* send another letter?"

"You know Lizette—she isn't any more likely to obey Adelaide a second time."

Dunstan lapsed into silence and tapped the parchment against his chin.

"If she won't come on her own, someone must go to fetch her," Sir Bayard said.

Gillian gave him a disgruntled look. "You're assuming she could be easily found. She never follows the usual route to any place. She likes to travel off the main roads—to see more of the countryside, she says."

"Surely she won't be alone, and it shouldn't be too difficult to find a large party that includes a young noblewoman.

"Even if it is, someone *must* be sent to bring her home," he concluded in a tone that sounded suspiciously like an order.

"Who do you suggest we send, Sir Bayard?" Gillian asked sweetly, in a way that warned Dunstan, if not the knight, that she was very angry indeed.

"I think Sir Bayard would be the best man for the task," Dunstan declared.

"As much as I'd like to do as you request," Sir Bayard replied evenly, "I must point out a flaw in your plan. You both were loath to believe I had come to help you, or even that I was who I claimed to be. Do you expect Lady Lizette to accept me any easier?"

He was, unfortunately, right. As skeptical as she'd been, Lizette would be worse. Not only that, Sir Bayard didn't know Lizette and how deceptive she could be when it came to avoiding something she didn't want to do.

"Sir Bayard's right," she grudgingly conceded. "If I send an armed knight Lizette's never met before, she probably won't believe he's come to help her. Even if she does, she'll likely dawdle even more.

"I think it must be you, Dunstan. She knows you, and you know the tricks and schemes she's capable of. She'll have a headache, or a backache, or some other complaint that will delay your progress. She'll insist she must make courtesy visits.

"But most of all, she trusts you, Dunstan, and she's always been fond of you. I think she'll do as you ask, as she would not if we sent Sir Bayard."

Dunstan was not at all pleased. "I remind you, my lady, that I'm no swordsman. Sir Bayard is a knight of the realm. He even has the authority of the king, if he wishes to use it. I'm sure he can convince Lizette that she's in danger and compel her to come home. And should your sister be set upon by enemies—"

"She has an armed guard, and you'll have one, too," Gillian said. "Surely that will dissuade any enemies from attacking, unless they bring an army to capture Lizette.

"And they would likely need one," she added under her breath.

Dunstan frowned. "My lady, may I have a word with you in private?"

Gillian heard the edge in his voice, but she was in command here, not him. "Sir Bayard has been sent to help us and since he's related to me by marriage, I think he may be privy to anything you wish to say to me. I know you'd rather attend to your duties here, Dunstan, and of course I wish it could be otherwise, but I truly think you'll have more luck convincing her to return than anyone else, myself included. She likes you, and she respects you, too."

"I don't think it would be wise for me to go away from Averette while Sir Bayard remains here," Dunstan said firmly, regarding her in a way he never had before.

What was she seeing in his face? Suspicion? Anger? Hatred?

She suddenly felt as if he could see all her guilty, shameful secrets. As if he knew the lust she felt, and thought her soiled and unclean. As if he no longer loved her, or even liked her.

Sir Bayard came to stand between them, his hands on his hips as he faced the steward. "Just what are you implying?"

Dunstan took a step back. "I make no accusations, my lord."

"Good, because that would be a mistake."

Dunstan tried to regain his composure. "There has been some talk, my lord, about you, and I fear it has started to include Lady Gillian."

"What *talk?*" Gillian demanded.

"Can you not guess?" Dunstan returned as he glanced at her. "You're a young, unwed lady, and he is a handsome knight known to dally with women."

Gillian put her hand on the back of the chair and gripped it tightly. "Sir Bayard is my relative."

"Which only makes it worse."

If she had sinned, it was only in her heart. Yet if she was to continue to rule here, she must be above reproach, because she was a woman.

So Dunstan must stay. But she still shouldn't send Bayard to bring Lizette home.

"I'll send Iain after my sister," she decided. "He won't be pleased, and neither will she, but he won't fall for any of her schemes, either."

Dunstan smiled, satisfied and smug. "An excellent choice, my lady. For all she aggravates Iain, he loves her like a daughter."

Gillian didn't enjoy seeing Dunstan—or any man—gloat. "While Iain is gone, Sir Bayard will assume command of the garrison."

As Dunstan's frown deepened, the knight's fine lips curved upward. "It would be my honor, my lady."

"Gillian," Dunstan protested, "I don't think—"

"Enough," she said, annoyed that he would question her decision and annoyed with Sir Bayard for telling her what should be done. "I appreciate your concern and advice, Dunstan, but I remind you that you aren't my father, my uncle, my brother, or my husband to tell me what to do. You are my steward and nothing more."

When Dunstan flushed and seemed to shrink a little, she instantly regretted being so harsh.

"Will you tell Iain your decision, my lady, or shall I?" Sir Bayard inquired.

Anxious to get out of the hall and away from the self-confident Sir Bayard, and Dunstan with his wounded eyes, she said, "I will. At once."

WHEN SHE WAS GONE, the door banging shut behind her, Dunstan turned on Bayard.

"She wants to believe the best of you because her sister married your brother," he charged, "but I know the kind of man you are. If you do *anything* to hurt Gillian, I'll see that you regret it."

Bayard's glare had frightened braver men than Dunstan. "You know *nothing* about me, Dunstan. And if you're as clever as Lady Gillian thinks you are, you won't ever make such an accusation about the lady and me again, in my hearing or out of it."

CHAPTER TEN

IF GILLIAN HADN'T already known where to find Iain when she went to tell him about Lizette, all she had to do was follow his shouting.

"Swing harder, man, or I'll rip your arm off and beat you with it!"

"My old mother could do better than that!"

"You *want* to get killed, boy?"

She'd heard this same loud chiding a hundred times before, as had the men. Even so, there was nothing amusing about it if you were the recipient of those harsh denunciations.

At least a person knew where they stood with the veteran soldier. There were no hidden feelings to suddenly flash out, unwelcome, from his eyes. No unexpected passion aroused by a look or touch. Iain was like a better, second father who said what he thought—which was why Lizette disliked him. He never minced words when he thought she'd behaved badly.

When they were growing up, Gillian had often held her tongue and reined in her temper as best she could, for the sake of peace. Sometimes, though, she failed, and that had led to some terrible quarrels with Lizette. Fortunately, Lizette didn't seem to hold a grudge, and she herself was quick to apologize when she saw how their arguing upset their mother and Adelaide. At such times, she felt she was indeed her father's daughter, and she hated the notion that his tempestuous legacy lived on in her.

Iain's presence and his sharp tongue made it easier for her to keep her temper with Lizette. He said all the things she longed to say to her younger sister.

Iain didn't mince words with *her,* either, but unlike Lizette, she would rather hear the blunt truth than prevarications or soothing lies. Iain treated her as an adult, not some poor weak child who needed to be coddled. Neither, she realized, did Bayard.

Upon entering the bailey, Gillian spotted a large group of soldiers stripped to the waist and sweating, swinging wooden swords as they held up their shields and did their best to avoid being the object of Iain's scorn.

Today, the garrison commander wasn't in his chain mail and no wonder, for it was a hot summer's day. Instead, he wore a light leather tunic, dyed linen breeches and boots. The tunic had no sleeves and laced up the center, revealing that although Iain was past his fortieth year, he was still well muscled and likely capable of outlasting many a man on the battlefield.

"Rest!" he called out when he spotted her coming toward him.

The men lowered their weapons and sat on the ground. A few groaned quietly, while two or three examined scratches and purpling bruises.

"Yes, my lady?" Iain asked, beads of sweat trickling down the sides of his lined face.

"We've had word from Lizette."

Iain frowned, making deep furrows in his sun-browned cheeks. "She's not coming?"

"Yes, for a miracle, she is—but in her own good time and by her own odd route, no doubt. She doesn't seem to appreciate that she may be in danger, or that she has no castle or garrison to protect her."

Iain sighed and crossed his powerful arms. "She probably thinks she can hold off an army by herself."

"Probably," Gillian grimly agreed. "So we must send someone to fetch her and I want you to lead the party."

As Iain's thick brows rose, she said, "You're the best soldier in Averette. I could send Dunstan, but if there's danger, and it comes to fighting…"

"Aye, not so good."

"I want my sister home safely," she said, "and I know you're the man to do it. Since Sir Bayard has experience of command, he'll be in charge of the garrison in your absence.

"Lindall's a good soldier," she continued, speaking of his second-in-command who would lead the garrison if Iain were wounded or unable to direct the men in battle and before Iain could protest, "but he's never been besieged.

"Sir Bayard's a trained knight and Adelaide obviously has faith in him or she wouldn't have sent him here. And he does have siege experience, even if it's somewhat limited."

"Limited?" Iain scoffed. "Aye, that's one way to put it."

"Whatever happened in Normandy, Adelaide obviously trusts him. Between Sir Bayard and Lindall, we should be able to cope in your absence. My decision is made, Iain," she finished.

Unlike Dunstan or Bayard, the grizzled veteran knew better than to try to argue with her when she used that tone of voice. "Aye, my lady, I'll bring your sister home."

A gleam came to his eye. "Whether she comes peacefully or no."

A FEW DAYS LATER, Gillian tripped over an uneven cobblestone in the yard and nearly dropped her basket full of bread.

"Careful, my lady!" Dena warned with a giggle.

Gillian smiled, taking no offense at Dena's laughter. Unfortunately, she was often preoccupied these days, wondering if there really was a conspiracy afoot and how it might endanger Averette; worrying about Lizette, unsure where she was and if Iain had found her; concerned about the harvest, and the myriad tasks, and people involved; keeping track of the household needs and expenses; and trying not to be distracted by the now very distracting presence of Sir Bayard de Boisbaston.

Not that she saw or spoke to him any more frequently than she had before. He appeared at meals and ate with a hearty appetite. He answered her questions succinctly, without exaggerated praise or complaint. When she asked him his opinion about the fortifications, he replied in a way that proved he was knowledgeable about such matters. He even reminded her of Iain sometimes.

The one thing he never spoke about was the king or his policies, or the recent campaign in France, although whether that was because such talk disturbed him, he had no interest in it, or he thought it safer not to discuss, she couldn't tell.

Today, since ensuring the safety of Averette was still her responsibility, she'd decided to see for herself how Sir Bayard was handling his command and the soldiers of the garrison. As far as she could tell, Sir Bayard's men and her own were amiable to each other, and Sir Bayard had won the respect of her men. Yet she had only ever seen them in the hall, when the day was over. Helping to take the noon meal to the soldiers seemed a good excuse to see them during the day, when she wasn't expected.

"There they are!" Dena cried, pointing at the men training in the bailey as if she'd honestly expected them to be somewhere else.

Gillian recognized Bayard immediately, although his back was to her and he was half naked as he strode through the equally half-naked ranks of his men fighting in pairs.

Unlike Iain, he wasn't shouting. If he spoke, it was only loud enough for those nearest him to hear and while he carried a long, slender wooden stick, he used it to guide a stroke or an arm as his men fought, not to strike in punishment.

Of course, he wasn't Iain, so naturally he would command differently, the same way she gave orders in a manner different from Adelaide, or Lizette, who merely made suggestions.

And she would not stare at his remarkably fit body. Or his broad shoulders and narrow waist. Or note the several small scars that marked him as a trained warrior, not a pretty courtier who only spoke of battle and paid a scutage rather than fight, so he could stay safe at home.

Frederic was there, too. She slid a glance at Dena, but either she hadn't seen him or she was purposefully avoiding looking in the young man's direction.

Bayard soon noticed Gillian at the head of the small parade of servants bearing food and drink.

"Rest, men! You've earned it," he called out before he hurried toward a pile of clothes and pulled on his shirt.

Meanwhile, the women who'd brought the baskets of food and jugs of ale began to distribute the refreshment to the grateful men, who talked among themselves and tried to entice the maidservants to provide a second loaf or more ale.

"Have you had news from Iain or your sister?" Bayard asked when he joined her.

"No, not yet."

"It's only been a few days," he replied with a shrug. "And it rained for two. That might have slowed them down."

Even though she didn't need his comfort, his words were unexpectedly welcome. "I thought I should find out if you're having any trouble with the men."

He looked genuinely surprised. "No," he said as he took her basket, keeping one of the small brown loaves for himself before handing it off to a nearby soldier. "Here, Ralph, give these out."

Bayard raised his voice and called to the rest of the men with apparent annoyance, "Not too much ale, you louts, or it'll be the buckets! We've more to do today."

"Have they been difficult?"

"Not at all," he said, turning back to her with the hint of a smile. "But I don't coddle soldiers. Makes them soft."

"What did you mean about the buckets?"

Bayard nodded at the far end of the field. A well-muscled man with fair hair stood there, his legs slightly more than shoulder-width apart, his arms outstretched, holding two buckets. Even from this distance she could see that the effort was making his arms tremble and that his face was as red as if he'd marched for miles in the noonday heat.

"You can put those down now, Elmer," Bayard shouted to him. "You won't be too much the worse for ale again, will you, my man?"

"No, my lord!" the man answered as he lurched forward, almost dropping the buckets. Water sloshed over their sides, but they didn't fall over. Rubbing his arms, Elmer left them there and went to join the other men.

"He got drunk last night, then was too ill to practice this morning," Bayard explained as he finished his loaf of bread. "He won't do that again. When you're holding two buckets full of water like that, even the shortest time can seem an eternity."

"You sound as if you know that for a fact."

"I was punished that way many times, and worse," he replied without rancor, brushing crumbs off his shirt. "Raymond de Boisbaston wanted his sons to be the hardiest, best knights in England. He was a firm believer in a heavy hand to achieve that end."

"At least he paid attention to you," she blurted, then wished she'd been more circumspect. Even if her father had acted as if she didn't exist most of the time, Bayard didn't need to know that.

"Lord Raymond paid attention to Simon, his eldest, and me," Bayard said, "but the only time he acknowledged Armand was to criticize or punish him."

Another clue, perhaps, as to why Bayard would want to help his half brother. "I'm sorry."

"My father made us tough and strong, just as he wanted. So I learned that holding buckets is painful, but not enough to do serious damage."

"Iain would have had that man in the stocks," she noted.

"Too humiliating," Bayard replied without hesitation. "I'd save that for something more serious, like thieving. Take away a man's dignity for a minor infraction, and you've lost his respect, and likely that of others, as well."

"Iain wouldn't consider that sort of behavior a *minor*

infraction and he most certainly has the respect of his men. They obey him without question."

"As they do me," Bayard said, turning on his heel. "Men! In lines!"

Although he didn't exactly shout, his deep, booming voice carried easily to the far wall.

The soldiers immediately abandoned their food and drink. They grabbed their wooden swords, jumped to their feet, and formed four even rows, arms and swords at their sides, staring straight ahead, as disciplined as they had ever been under Iain's command.

It was, she had to admit, "Very impressive."

He shrugged, then gave the order for the men to rest again.

"You genuinely care about them, don't you?" she asked, realizing that was true.

"As you care about your people," he answered. "You don't sit on the dais issuing your orders or have Dunstan pass them along to the servants. You talk to your servants, and sometimes do a task yourself, just as you brought the basket of bread today. And I was sure you were going to get stung the other day when the bees swarmed."

She blushed again, like the most silly, moonstruck girl. "Bees are too full of honey to sting when they swarm. You ought to know that."

"I do, but I was worried about you nonetheless."

He meant that and because he did, she felt even more foolish, and girlish, and giddy.

There was no reason to stay here and feel giddy or girlish. After all, she was chatelaine of a castle and there was much to do at this time of year.

Calling for Dena and the others to gather up the baskets and follow, she bade Bayard farewell and started back to the inner bailey.

"Until later, my lady," Bayard murmured as he watched her slender, graceful figure walking back to the castle she presided over with more skill and efficiency than many a man he could name.

Although she was most certainly a woman.

RICHARD D'ARTAGE, ONCE A favorite of the queen and a lord in the King John's court, more recently pretending to be wine merchant Charles de Fenelon, drew his horse to a halt at the wooden drawbridge of Lord Wimarc's castle and called out the password. The portcullis began to rise, and the gate beyond swung open. Urging his mount to a trot, he rode into the yard of a fortress that wasn't very large, yet would be difficult to take because it was manned with the most fierce, skilled mercenaries in all of Europe.

Richard leapt from the saddle as a skinny, middle-aged groom hastened from the stable to take hold of his reins.

"Is Lord Wimarc in the hall?" he demanded of the dim-witted dolt.

The oaf shook his head and glanced up at the window that Richard knew from previous visits was the lord's bedchamber.

Scowling, Richard strode across the courtyard. Since he was known to be a close friend of Lord Wimarc, nobody interfered with his progress, even when he entered the stairwell leading to Wimarc's private chamber.

Francis de Farnby had died for their cause, while he himself had been accused of treason and barely escaped with his life. Lately, he'd been forced to play the part of a common merchant, while Wimarc stayed in his castle enjoying his women and weaving his schemes like a spider in a thick, but very safe, web—because he was richer than Croesus and more sly than a coven of foxes.

When Richard reached the luxuriously appointed chamber, he didn't bother to knock. He opened the door and marched into the room.

A woman shrieked. The naked man who'd been atop her in the curtained bed rolled off, simultaneously pulling a dagger from beneath the pillows and preparing to defend himself.

"It's Richard," the erstwhile wine merchant declared.

The fierce expression on Wimarc's features relaxed. He straightened and assumed his usual courtly manner, although he was naked except for the rings on his fingers.

"It's considered polite to knock before entering a gentleman's bedchamber, Richard," Wimarc remarked as he tossed the dagger on the table and reached for the scarlet silken bedrobe flung over a nearby chair.

"I've come on important business."

"So I should hope," Wimarc replied as he drew his robe over his slender, leanly muscled body. Glancing at the girl still cowering in the bed, who was probably a singer or dancing girl, he barked, "Leave us."

She scrambled from the bed and as she did, Wimarc took a plain silver ring from his finger and tossed it at her.

With a delighted cry, the girl deftly caught the bauble before gathering up her motley collection of clothing. Then she dashed out of the chamber, as slender and lithe as a deer.

Richard felt a pang of envy, but only for a moment.

He had more important things to consider than the needs of his body.

"It's about Lady Gillian," he said as Wimarc smoothed his hair, then his robe, before sitting on an ebony chair of ancient and delicate design.

Wimarc gestured for Richard to take another chair, less finely wrought. "Is she dead?"

"Not yet. I thought I'd have a chance at the hall moot, but there's been a complication."

"What kind of complication?"

"Armand's sent his half brother to Averette with a warning, and apparently the man intends to stay. There were nearly as many soldiers as villagers in the yard that day."

Richard could read nothing in Wimarc's face as the man twisted a ruby ring around his slender index finger. "So it won't be easy. Or are you here to tell me you can't do it?"

Admit he'd failed and allow the de Boisbastons and that whore Adelaide escape unscathed? *Never.* "I came to get more men. Lady Gillian no longer ventures out of the castle unescorted, and it'll take more than a single man to bring Bayard de Boisbaston down."

Wimarc settled himself more comfortably on his chair. "I see. And who is to pay for these men?"

Richard struggled to contain his anger. Wimarc had more money than he, Francis, and the others put together. Wimarc had come up with the plan to rid John of the men most capable of keeping him under control. Once John was given free rein, his own nature would soon ensure that the rest of the country turned against him. "I had assumed, my lord, that you already had such men in your employ.

"And there is more," he continued. "Taking Averette

is not going to be as easy as you seem to think. The garrison is extremely well trained and Lady Gillian's people are very loyal."

"Perhaps I should consider sending another, more experienced—"

"With enough men I can do what needs to be done."

"And heaven forbid I should rob you of your vengeance," Wimarc replied with a smirk as he rose and sauntered over to the bedside table.

On it stood a silver carafe studded with jewels, two silver goblets, and the remains of bread and sweetmeats. A narrow beam of sunlight shone through the closed shutters, falling across the expensive, rare and brightly colored carpet.

Wimarc poured some rich red wine into one of the goblets. The silver vessel glittered in the sunlight as he handed it to Richard.

"Naturally I have every confidence in you," Wimarc said when he returned to his chair. "That's why I chose you for such an important task." He steepled his fingers. "How many men do you want?"

"Twenty."

Wimarc raised a questioning brow. "So many would be a little conspicuous, don't you think?"

"If they went into the village, yes. They can make camp some distance away until a suitable opportunity arises to do the deed that should bring Adelaide and Armand to Averette, as we wish."

"If you kill the de Boisbastons and take command of Averette, the lovely Lady Adelaide and her sisters will be completely in your power until—and if—the king bestirs himself," Wimarc noted. "How delightful for you."

"I don't care about them."

"Liar, at least as far as the beautiful Adelaide is concerned," Wimarc said, smiling, and his eyes glittering with the certainty that he knew his minion well. "I don't care what you do with her. Rape her, kill her, do both or neither, as long as you get rid of the de Boisbastons. And when we have our new king, the de Boisbaston's estates, as well as Averette, will be yours."

CHAPTER ELEVEN

"NO, A LITTLE more to the left," Gillian instructed the servants who were hanging the tapestry that had arrived that morning from the convent of the Sacred Heart.

It had only been completed yesterday, although Adelaide and Lizette had started it after their mother had died eight years ago. They'd kept a secret from their father and gotten the money for the materials from Dunstan's kind-hearted father. Lizette had worked on it for a week, Adelaide every day until she left, and Gillian not at all, because she hated sewing. Three nuns from the nearby convent had finished it, for which their convent would receive ten sheep, three cows, and five hens as Gillian's thanks.

It depicted an orchard and four ladies who were supposed to be Adelaide, Lizette, Gillian, and their mother, and it was as lovely as Adelaide had said it would be, especially the portrait of their mother.

She wished Adelaide were here to see it once it was in place behind the dais. Hopefully, this trouble with the conspiracy would soon be over, and she would be able to come home.

With her husband.

Dunstan came sweeping into the hall, and one glance was enough to tell Gillian he was peeved. He'd been peeved since Sir Bayard de Boisbaston had arrived, and she was starting to get impatient with his manner.

There was, after all, no reason for him to be so upset. Sir Bayard fulfilled his duties as garrison commander, and that was all.

She turned back to the servants. "Now a little more to the right. That's it. Excellent!" she said when it was straight. "Now you can go back to your regular duties."

The men gathered up their tools and departed from the hall, leaving Dunstan, Gillian, and a few female servants who were cleaning the various furnishings with sand, water, and wax.

"My lady, have you heard what Sir Bayard has your soldiers doing today?" Dunstan demanded.

Gillian said a silent prayer for patience and guidance before she faced her irate steward. "No."

Bayard never told her what he planned to do, and she never asked. She never spoke to him at all if she could help it. He made her feel too…uncomfortable.

"He has apparently arranged some sort of competition between the farmers and your men. To *cut hay!* And *he's* leading the soldiers!"

She was sorry Dunstan had fallen for what had to be a joke, but surely he should have realized that couldn't possibly be true. "Somebody's jesting, Dunstan. No true knight would ever do a peasant's work."

"No, no *true* knight would," Dunstan agreed, looking grimly satisfied. "I've told you some of the things I've heard about Sir Bayard de Boisbaston, but I've also learned that many people believe he's not really Raymond de Boisbaston's son at all."

Gillian regarded him skeptically. "Whose son do they think he is?"

"It's said that his mother lost her own child at birth and bought another baby from a band of traveling 'Gyptians. It's another reason they call Bayard the 'Gyptian lover."

She frowned, annoyed that Dunstan was still so antagonistic toward their guest. Bayard had proven to be helpful, and honorable, and a far cry from the lascivious scoundrel the wine merchant had described. "Whatever gossip and rumors attend Sir Bayard, I believe him to be an honorable man. And I suppose if he wishes to cut hay…"

She paused and shook her head. "No, that can't be true. It must be somebody's idea of a jest, to tell you such a thing."

Dunstan got a stubborn look in his eyes that she knew well. Usually he would defer to her without protest, but this was not going to be one of those times. "I passed him on my way from the village and he was carrying a scythe. So were several of his men, including that big oaf, Robb."

Dunstan didn't add that the arrogant Bayard—who surreptitiously watched Gillian when they were at table, who made her smile when he spoke of the men and their drills, who was too damnably attractive by far—had given him an insolent smile and bid him good day as he strolled by. Or that he'd been followed by a bevy of young women all too eager to admire the handsome nobleman, including that red-headed witch Dena. She should have been sent away after her sin was discovered. What kind of example was that for a noble household? Sometimes Gillian was too compassionate by far.

"It's true, my lady," Seltha offered as she paused in her waxing of a chair that had been moved to the side of the dais while the tapestry was being hung. "The men were talking about it when they broke the fast this morning.

He's offered a prize, too—a cask of ale to the group that does the best job."

"And who is to decide that?" Dunstan demanded.

"Hale, o' course."

"Hale agreed to this?" Gillian asked, still not quite willing to believe it.

"He couldn't have," Dunstan protested. "Why, soldiers will ruin the harvest. They have no idea how to cut grain!"

"They aren't all going to cut," Seltha said. "Just them as knows how."

And that included Sir Bayard de Boisbaston? Gillian thought incredulously. When and how would he have learned to cut hay?

"I believe I should see for myself if there really is a competition or if you've been deceived," she said to Dunstan.

"I'll come, too," he replied, his expression grimly skeptical. "I'd like to see a knight cutting hay."

As THEY NEARED THE FIELD, it quickly became apparent that something unusual was indeed afoot. Cutting hay wasn't generally watched by cheering crowds of villagers, nor merchants who must have abandoned their stalls for the afternoon.

Gillian could easily discern the women in their skirts and scarves, the farmers in their smocks, and their sons in their rough homespun. Other men sat at the far end with their whetstones, sharpening scythes. Children scampered about, their older sisters watching them, while nursing mothers sat in the shade of a chestnut tree suckling their infants. Hale stood near the men with the whetstones, overseeing the cutting. Little Teddy was beside him, jumping up and down and clapping with excitement.

His father looked nearly as excited, although his gaze was focused on the men working.

More surprisingly, several soldiers were also gathered there in excited knots, clearly making wagers as they watched the activity in the field.

Where ten men were moving with slow deliberation, swinging their scythes to cut the grain, followed by women binding the cut hay into sheaves.

Five of the men were villagers, including Old Davy's grandson. Young Davy was easy to recognize from behind, for he was an exceptionally skinny young man. Even so, he possessed great stamina and would still be mowing when many a larger, older man was panting for breath and calling for water. To either side of him were four more farmers from the estate, men who she knew were notable experts with a scythe.

In the other half of the field were four soldiers who'd arrived with Sir Bayard, including Robb. In the center of them, swinging a scythe with ease and practiced skill, half-naked, broad-shouldered, and with dark hair nearly to his shoulders, was Sir Bayard de Boisbaston, working as if he'd been born and raised a peasant.

"I wouldn't have believed it," she murmured as she watched the line of men moving inexorably forward.

"Perhaps he's not a true nobleman's son after all," Dunstan suggested, obviously delighted at the possibility that Bayard de Boisbaston might be a vagabond's child and not the son of a nobleman.

She wanted to tell him envy and jealousy didn't endear him to her, but she held her tongue. After all, one day Bayard de Boisbaston would leave and Dunstan would remain, hopefully a loyal and faithful friend and steward even if she could never love him the way he wanted.

Dunstan swore under his breath. Bayard and his men were in the lead and gaining slowly. But in the next moment, with a great effort, Young Davy's men surged ahead. The two groups were neck in neck, then the soldiers gained a little. Then the farmers. Gillian clasped her hands and moved forward, trying to see better. Young Davy was mowing with great speed and agility, his head bent, seeing only the remaining grain before him.

Bayard had caught up to him and was gaining, until he looked over to see where Davy was.

"Don't do that, you fool!" Gillian whispered.

In that brief lapse of concentration, Davy moved ahead another foot to finish with a flourish, followed by his men, their triumph greeted with a huge, happy roar from the farmers and villagers.

A collective groan went up from the soldiers as their sweating and panting comrades finished, then collapsed on the ground.

"A valiant effort!" Hale called out, beaming, as Gillian and Dunstan came closer. "Wonderful! And well done, too. Ale for all!"

"Thank God. I'm parched," Bayard said, straightening and arching his back, his scythe still in his hand. "That's damn hard work."

"Threshing's worse!" one of the peasants shouted with a laugh.

"No, stacking!" cried another.

"Oh, you men!" a woman exclaimed from beneath the chestnut tree where she nursed her child. "Try having a baby! Now *that's p*ainful!"

The whole gathering burst out laughing, including Bayard.

Gillian had never heard him laugh like that before. It was a wonderful laugh, deep, and rich, and full of good humor. A laugh to warm your heart, to make you simply glad to be alive. To want to be part of such a man's life.

Well, in a way she always would be, she realized, since he was Adelaide's brother-in-law. Any other, more intimate way, would therefore be impossible. Church law would forbid such a union—if she wanted it, which she didn't. She didn't want to marry anyone and leave Averette.

"Ah, here is my lady!" Hale cried, and the people all turned toward her, happy and smiling.

Including Bayard.

Blushing at the sudden attention, she nevertheless straightened her shoulders and started across the field, skirting the sheaves and kicking up little bits of chaff.

"As you can see, my lady," Hale said, "the last field was finished sooner than expected."

"I'm most impressed," she said, "although I appreciate these were exceptional circumstances. I won't expect every field to be cut with such speed in future."

"Good!" Young Davy groaned, making the crowd laugh again, while Gillian smiled.

"Please, refresh yourselves now and at the feast later," she said. "You've all worked hard, and I thank you."

A cheer went up from the crowd while Gillian smiled and managed not to look at Bayard de Boisbaston.

THE PEOPLE OF AVERETTE really did love their lady, Bayard reflected as he watched her.

He could understand why. She might be arrogant and aloof to him—and she was—but she wasn't to anybody else. She treated even the lowliest servant with kindness and often seemed to be doing work many another lady would assign to an underling.

And she was often smiling, except when she was near him.

As for her dealings with him, they'd managed to maintain a truce, albeit a seemingly delicate one, and since he was determined to fulfill his promise to Armand, he was resolved not to be the one to break it.

Fortunately, she was apparently too busy running the castle and estate to quarrel with him, flitting about like a very busy bee, which made it was much easier to keep the peace between them.

There was a brief tug on his breeches and he looked down to see Teddy holding up his shirt.

"My papa says you're good at mowing," he announced with pride. "He says I'm good, too."

"I don't doubt it," Bayard replied, pleased that the little fellow didn't bear him any ill will.

"I'll take you to your papa, shall I?" he asked after he'd put on his shirt.

When the boy eagerly nodded his assent, Bayard reached down and, in one swift, easy motion, swung him up on his shoulders.

The boy laughed with unbridled glee as they crossed the field, skirting the standing sheaves leaning against each other.

"Look at me, Papa!" he crowed with delight. "Look at me!"

Hale and several other people gathered around the field saw them and smiled. Bayard tried not to look for Gillian, but felt a surge of pleasure when he caught a glimpse of her watching them with a smile on her face. Unfortunately, the steward stood at her elbow, glaring.

He'd had rivals and enemies before, and in the past

he wouldn't have considered a man like Dunstan, who was gloom in a tunic, to be any competition at all. The man wasn't particularly attractive or charming. What he did have, though, was the lady's obvious good will and affection, which could be a problem—if he were competing, of course.

In this instance, he was not. Could not, even if he wanted to, and even though his recent dreams had been full of arousing images of Gillian in his arms, returning his embraces with unbridled passion. For one thing, Armand trusted him to act with honor and dignity while he was at Averette; for another, he was related to her, if not by near degree.

Hale smiled as they reached him. "Careful not to hurt the man, my son," he warned. "After all, he's a knight, one of the king's own men."

Bayard was not pleased to be reminded that he'd sworn his oath to John before he knew the true nature of the man. Nevertheless, he genially said, "Today, I'm merely a mower of hay, and at the moment, a mighty destrier."

With that, he neighed and pawed at the ground with his foot before lowering his head and making a charge at the nearest upright sheaf, causing the swaying Teddy to shriek with laughter.

He made a few more passes before lifting the boy down, pleading exhaustion. "Even a mighty destrier requires food, drink, and rest," he said, tousling the little boy's hair.

With a look of regret, Teddy nodded and went back to his father, while Bayard walked toward the trestle tables bearing food and ale.

He rarely contemplated having children, consigning the idea to the foggy future, along with marriage and other necessary duties, but today, here, surrounded by the happy, celebrating people of Averette and with the memory of little Teddy's gleeful laughter in his ears, he thought it would be a wonderful thing to have a son of his own, provided he could find a suitable wife.

As to what sort of woman might be suitable… His notions about that had, he realized, undergone a change.

But marriage still lay in the unforeseeable future, so he put such thoughts from his mind when he reached the table. The aroma of fresh bread made his mouth water. There were thick rounds of cheese, and jugs of rich ale waiting, too, with mugs beside them.

Armand had told him that when he'd been imprisoned, he'd craved bread more than any other food, and as Bayard bit into his loaf, he could understand why. When a man was truly hungry, was there anything better?

Well, perhaps cool ale if he was thirsty, Bayard reflected as he downed a mug in a single gulp.

He was wiping his lips with the back of his hand when Gillian appeared before him.

To his chagrin, he felt himself blush as if he were a lad again, for he was sweaty, dressed like a peasant, and probably smelled.

"I was surprised to see you cutting hay, my lord," she said.

He couldn't tell if she approved or not, but he had no regrets. "Obviously I'm skilled in more than fighting, my lady."

"Obviously," she replied. "Where did you learn how to cut hay with such skill? Usually it takes years to become so proficient."

Had she heard the rumors about his birth, rumors that had been circulating well before his father's death?

"The late Lord Raymond de Boisbaston had some unusual notions about training," he truthfully replied.

"He believed working in the fields strengthened his sons' bodies and built stamina. It also meant he had extra hands at his disposal, ones that didn't require payment."

She raised a light brown brow. "Your father considered mowing hay a sort of martial exercise?"

"Among other tasks. I've picked apples and crushed them for cider, worked in the brew house, helped the carter fix wheels and axles, and the cooper make barrels, shod horses, plowed and sown seeds. Whatever needed to be done, we did.

"For my own part, I thought a little competition would relieve some of the tension among the men."

"Are they anxious?"

"They'd be fools not to be. Who can say when the king will start another war? Or when we might be attacked? If either happens, they will bear the brunt of it. Training can prepare them to fight, but the waiting is the worst. Sometimes a little entertainment is more helpful than another sword drill."

"I see."

He thought she really did. "However," he admitted with a little smile, "it's been some time since I've done such labor. Likely every bone in my body will ache tomorrow."

Out of the corner of his eye, he caught sight of the steward, who was lingering nearby like a bad smell.

"Dunstan should take a turn in the field," he suggested. "It'd put some muscle on those arms and shoulders of his."

He realized at once he should have kept quiet, for her expression soured as if he'd insulted *her*.

"While you may have some cause to be vain of your physique, my lord," she said primly, "I remind you that vanity is one of the seven deadly sins. And although you may see no harm in behaving like one of the tenants, you are still my guest here. What will other nobles say if they hear of this? They might believe I made you do it."

He regretted what he'd said, but he didn't appreciate being chastised like a child, especially in public. "Then I would have to tell them there is very little you could *make* me do, my lady. As for my vanity, I'm well aware I have much to be humble about. Now if you'll excuse me," he snapped, not wanting to hear if she excused him or not before he joined his squire.

Frederic was leaning against a tree, looking as sullen and stubborn as a lad of fifteen could. Bayard knew why: Frederic had been appalled at his plan for the competition, claiming it was beneath a knight to cut hay or do anything a peasant might.

The lad still had much to learn.

Approaching his disgruntled squire, Bayard gestured at the men and women taking their ease, laughing, talking, eating and drinking. "Well, Frederic? Do you think they don't respect me now?"

Frederic kicked at a lump of dirt with the toe of his fine leather boot. "I still think it's not right."

Bayard struggled to be patient. How the devil had Armand managed it all these years? He'd been more insolent in his youth than Frederic.

"A knight does whatever is required of him," Bayard explained again. "And it's never amiss to spend time with the men and women who provide the food you eat, the clothes you wear, and the arms you bear. Have you not noticed that although Lady Gillian dresses simply and plainly and does several tasks that by rights she could assign to others, she is obeyed without question and even spoken of with affection?"

"So you think I should cut hay?"

"I think you should do whatever you're ordered to do. As it happens, the haying is finished. But if I ask you to unload a wagon or help gather the sheaves, I expect you to do it without complaint or question."

"Yes, my lord," the lad muttered.

"Now go get something to eat."

Bayard sighed as Frederic nodded and walked away. He still had hopes for the boy, but it wasn't proving as easy to inspire him as he'd thought it'd be.

He heard Lady Gillian laugh, then spotted her among the women. She was holding a babe in her arms and tickling the mite under its chin.

How much she belonged here, in this place and among these people.

Where did *he* belong? At the side of the king he loathed? At the estates that had been his mother's dower and bequeathed to him on her death, estates she would do anything to prevent Armand or their father inheriting?

Was he truly his father's son, or were those rumors of a changeling true?

He would never know.

What he did know was that Armand had asked him to come here, and so he would stay, even if that meant fighting a desire he wished had never blossomed, for a woman who stirred his passion, dressed like a peasant, and governed like a benevolent queen.

CHAPTER TWELVE

THAT NIGHT, GILLIAN WATCHED as the men and women of the village danced by the light of a bonfire in the center of the green. The trestle tables had been moved near the smithy and now bore bread, roasted beef, mutton stew, sweetmeats, and honey cakes from the castle kitchen, as well as more kegs of ale.

While the dancers made merry, boisterous children ran about, weaving their way among those eating, drinking, talking, and laughing. Little Teddy and some of his friends, tired out from their sport and the excitement of the day, lay sleeping on blankets near the women who sat with babies on their knees or in their arms. Old Davy was with other elders, beating time to the music of the harp and drum on his knee, and reminiscing about harvests past. In the shadows, couples whispered and kissed, and a few slipped away into the darkness.

The smith danced with particular relish. He held the hand of Peg from the Stag's Head and swung her with such abandon, it was a wonder they didn't collide with the other dancers. Keeping a wary eye on them were the miller and his wife. It seemed fairly obvious that Geoffrey and the statuesque Bertha had made up after another quarrel, the truce no doubt encouraged by the free food and drink.

Normally, Gillian would be dancing, too, for she enjoyed it, but not tonight. Tonight, she preferred to watch with quiet contentment, while incidentally avoiding Dunstan, who'd been drinking too much wine.

Her gaze scanned the crowd and sure enough, there was the wine merchant, back from London. Perhaps it had been a mistake to encourage Charles de Fenelon to return to Averette, although if Dunstan wanted to get drunk, he didn't need Charles de Fenelon's wine to do it. There was plenty enough in the castle buttery and Dunstan had the keys, the same as she.

Sir Bayard de Boisbaston was there, sitting among the men of the garrison, talking to them about battles and tournaments, strategy, and arms. They listened with rapt attention, pausing only to take a drink of ale or ask a question.

His squire stood nearby, obviously not enjoying the talk nearly so much. His arms were crossed and he had a disgruntled expression on his face, as if he'd heard all this before.

Perhaps he had, and perhaps it had not been wise to let Frederic stay, regardless of what Dena thought. Maybe it would have been better to send him home.

She looked around, wondering where Dena had got to, then spied her by the tables smiling shyly as she talked to Robb. Gillian hoped that she was feeling better, and not just physically.

At the same time, though, she felt a little ache of sorrow and self-pity that she immediately condemned. After all, she had more to be happy about than many these days. Here at Averette, all was well—at least for now—and perhaps that was all one could hope for in such times.

"Ah, here you are, my lady!" Dunstan cried, stumbling a little as he came toward her although the ground was even. He'd been drinking a *lot* of wine, to judge by the scent of his breath.

She wasn't pleased, but even a steward should be allowed an occasional lapse of dignity, she supposed. "Good evening, Dunstan. A fine night, is it not?"

"It is," he agreed. "Very fine. Very, very fine."

He lunged forward, grabbed her hand and pulled her out of her secluded corner. "Come, Gillian, let's join the dancers!"

Far from pleased by his action, his tone and his familiar address here in public, Gillian tugged her hand free. "I'm a little tired tonight."

He frowned, looking as petulant as a child although he was older than she and of an age with Sir Bayard. "Not even one dance with an old friend?"

He *was* a friend. And had she not danced with him several times before? Besides, people were looking at them now. What would they think if she refused Dunstan?

And she'd been unusually grim these past few days waiting for a reply from Adelaide while fearing some sort of attack. Her people might be troubled if she seemed too anxious to celebrate. "Very well, I'll dance."

His smile reminded her why they were friends. He was a good man, and although she couldn't love him, she liked him a great deal. Her days at Averette would also be much more difficult without his help and calculating skills.

So as she walked to the green beside Dunstan, she made up her mind to treat him as she always had, and to enjoy herself. The crops were good, the land was at peace—albeit a precarious one—and she was young and healthy.

The people welcomed her appearance in the circle and

clapped in accompaniment as she stamped, and twirled, and joined hands with the somewhat wobbly Dunstan.

Soon the music took hold of her, and it seemed her feet had a vitality of their own. She forgot her cares and responsibilities, her worries and doubts. She became simply Gillian, not the chatelaine of an estate or the possible prey of an unknown, unseen enemy. Just a woman on a night of celebration, dancing with her friend.

By the time the dance was finished, she was winded but happy, feeling more carefree than she had in days. Dunstan bent over, his hands on his knees as he drew in great, ragged breaths. "Holy Mary, I'm done!"

Fearing he might collapse from both too much wine and too much enthusiastic dancing, she put her arm around him and led him to the nearest bench, where he sat heavily. Then, in full view of everyone around the green, he tugged her onto his lap.

"Dunstan!" she cried, leaping up at once, all her pleasure ruined by this unexpected and unseemly action. "You forget yourself!"

"Gillian, forgive me," he said, rising unsteadily, looking stricken. "I never... I shouldn't have... It's the wine!"

His face twisted, then he clapped a hand over his mouth and shoved his way though the crowd toward the river.

Embarrassed and dismayed, Gillian hardly knew where to look or what to do, until Bayard's voice came from behind her. "Poor fellow can't hold his wine."

She swivelled on her heel and encountered eyes gleaming in the firelight with what was suspiciously like amusement. Bayard looked like the lord of misrule himself—if the lord of misrule was also an incredibly attractive young man.

"Dunstan rarely drinks to excess," she said in her steward's defense.

"Neither do I," the knight replied. "Dulls the senses."

She didn't want to think about Bayard's senses, or anything else about him. She started to back away as the drummer began a swift and throbbing beat, not unlike the blood pulsing in her ears.

"Will you dance with me, my lady?"

He seemed to ask the question expecting her to refuse. Was it because he didn't think she would accept? Because he didn't think she'd want to dance with him? Because she feared gossip and censure?

Because she was *afraid?*

If so, he had much to learn about Lady Gillian d'Averette.

She gave him a bold smile and held out her hand. "With pleasure, my lord."

His lips jerked up in the smallest of smiles, but she felt his approval and was glad.

She immediately rued being so pleased by any man's approval, except by then he'd grasped her hand in his strong, calloused one and led her into the center of the circle. He bowed to her as if they were in the king's hall in Westminster and she the most lovely of ladies.

That inspired a very strange sensation.

And then they danced. It took only a few steps to realize that Bayard danced very well, with a lithe, yet masculine grace and a confidence that told her he danced often. Watching him, she could believe the stories of a 'Gyptian heritage might be true.

Determined not to be outdone, she danced as she never had before. She twirled and spun, clapped, and leapt to and fro as the dance, and her own desire, demanded. The way Lizette would dance.

Until the harp and drum ceased and she was panting and breathless, hot and disheveled. Bayard applauded, and so did all the other people gathered there.

She immediately wondered if it had been a mistake to give herself free rein. Maybe she should have danced with more dignity and decorum.

"Would you care for something to drink, my lady?" Bayard asked.

She was thirsty and wanted to leave the green so, lifting her chin as regally as if this were the hall and she attired in her best gown, she walked away beside Bayard, likewise doing her best to ignore the surreptitious glances the villagers and farmers exchanged.

This may indeed have been a mistake, and yet…she didn't feel very sorry. Instead, she found herself remembering the thrill of dancing, touching Bayard's hand, seeing him move with such skill and power, watching him come so close, his body so near…

Handing her an ale, Bayard's fingers brushed over hers and a desire she hadn't felt since James had died bloomed within her, warm and strong and urgent.

"You dance very well, my lady," Bayard said as they walked to an empty bench a short distance away from the tables, shrouded in the shadow of the smithy.

Too shadowed, perhaps, but she didn't want to feel the prying eyes of the villagers upon them as they talked. "So do you," she replied, sipping her ale, "as if…"

She hesitated when she realized he might not appreciate any comparisons to vagabonds who were said to be descended from people who'd refused to help Joseph and Mary on their flight from Egypt, or perhaps from Noah after the flood.

"As if I had 'Gyptian blood?" he said, the downturn of his lips revealing his displeasure.

It seemed she was too late, or perhaps he'd had such similarities noted before. "I didn't mean to insult you. It's just that I've rarely seen a man dance so well."

"Then I accept your compliment and ask your forgiveness for taking offense where none was intended."

It was even easier to see how so many women would want to be intimate with him when he spoke in that low, deep voice, and regarded her with those dark, intense eyes. "Please sit," she said. "You must be tired."

"Yes, I am," he agreed as he sat beside her. "Tired of the speculation that I'm not my mother's child, but a 'Gyptian's son bought or stolen to replace her own dead babe."

"I know how upsetting rumors can be," she said, because she did. "People are forever claiming my sisters and I are going to be married, or ought to married. They have several opinions about who we ought to marry, too. Or because we haven't, they say we must be unnatural, or ill-formed, or fools."

"Frustrating, isn't it?" he said, clasping his hands and leaning forward, his forearms on his thighs. "Unfortunately, while you can be sure you're not unnatural, or ill-formed, or a fool, I can't be sure I'm *not* some 'Gyptian's changeling child. My mother had difficulty giving birth to her one and only child, and never bore another.

"It was also no secret she hated my father, nor that on her death, her dower property was to go to the children of her body, not her husband or her stepsons, for Lord Raymond had two older sons before me—Simon, who died preparing to go on Crusade, and Armand, whom she loathed.

"Even *I* can believe that if her own child had died during birth and she'd been told she'd been too damaged to bear another, she would buy or steal a babe to prevent her husband or her stepsons from having any claim to her dower property."

He slid Gillian a wary glance. "She sounds monstrous, doesn't she? Who knows what she would have been like if she hadn't been forced into marriage by her family, on pain of banishment to a convent? Unfortunately, she was, and that made her bitter and resentful. My father tried to demean her every chance he got, and she would never back down. Armand and I grew up in a battlefield, or so it often seemed. Instead of being enemies, though, we became allies, trying to find a little peace."

No wonder he cared so much for his half brother, and would do whatever he asked. "Our home wasn't a happy one, either," she admitted, cupping her mug in her hands. "But unlike yours, my mother never stood up to my father, who was desperate for sons. She was too timid, too weak. So was I."

"I find that hard to believe."

She gave him a rueful smile. "Oh, I was. I used to run away to the village and stay with Old Davy and his wife rather than listen to him rage at her."

She felt the heat of shame color her face. "I left it to Adelaide to deal with him. *She* was the brave one. I'll never forget the day she stood up to my father when he hit my mother. She called him a coward to strike a woman.

"The look he gave her then! It wasn't hate. We were used to that. Or disgust. We were used to that, too. It was a sort of respect. I learned that day that strength didn't depend on muscle, bone, sinew, or size. Adelaide's the strongest person I know, and if I could be half as brave, and strong, and good as she is, I'd be content."

"You are," he said softly, "and I'm not sure she could run Averette half as well as you."

It was the greatest, most thrilling compliment she'd ever received, and for a moment, she was too overwhelmed to reply.

He rose and stood before her, his scar more visible in the flickering light of the bonfire. "I suppose you've heard me called another name—another reference to my supposed 'Gyptian heritage?"

"Yes," she whispered.

"I'm no monk, but I want to assure you, Gillian, that even at my worst, I didn't go around the countryside seducing every woman who came across my path like my late, unlamented father. Armand and I saw all too clearly the pain and ruin such a man leaves behind him to ever follow in those selfish footsteps."

Gillian got to her feet and regarded him intently, wanting to see the truth in his eyes if she could. "Then you weren't dallying with your captor's wife while you were waiting to be ransomed in France and your brother languished in captivity elsewhere?"

"No! The duke's wife was young and lonely and she found me attractive, but there was nothing more between us." He ran an agitated hand through his dark hair. "I could have been her lover if I had wanted to, I suppose, but I did *not*. I was the duke's guest as much as his prisoner.

"As for the surrender of the castle I was charged to hold, I received a message, apparently from the king, telling me to surrender. That it wasn't worth the loss of men to hold it.

"At the time, I didn't question from whence that order came. I recognized what looked like the king's seal and it was signed in what looked like his hand, but when I returned to court, he refused to acknowledge sending such an order—which sadly doesn't mean he didn't. He may have been trying to cover a mistake, to excuse yet another disaster. Those of my men who managed to get away were sent immediately to join the forces with the king for his personal protection, I don't doubt."

"Yet you support him."

"Because I swore an oath, my lady, and honor demands that I keep it. To my regret, I swore it before I knew the kind of man John was—before I fully understood the depths to which he'd sink."

Bayard shook his head. "I was young and eager to be knighted. God help me, I probably would have sworn to be loyal to Satan himself if a knighthood was the price."

He took hold of her shoulders and spoke with fervent conviction. "But I want you to believe that I'm not a lecher, that I was following orders when I surrendered, that I truly didn't know Armand was suffering, although—God and Armand forgive me!—I should have realized that after John let the men of Corfe starve to death, his enemies would be less than chivalrous. I should not have assumed they would all be like the duke."

She laid her hand lightly on Bayard's arm to calm him and offer what silent comfort she could. Yet as she did, she became achingly aware of the feel of his flesh and muscle beneath her fingertips. Of his proximity and the masculine scent of leather and wool attending him. Of his lips so close to hers.

But he was Adelaide's brother-in-law, sent to protect her. Not to woo her. Never to court or kiss. Never to wed. Or love.

He drew her to him. She should stop him…protest… refuse…run….

She couldn't. Didn't want to. She needed….

The moment their lips met, the walls she'd erected

around her heart broke into a thousand pieces, destroyed by his touch. Desire, so long held in check, burst free from its restraints and the longing she had tried to deny leapt into life.

She wanted to be in Bayard's arms, to feel and experience passion once again, and to be desired in return.

So she kissed him fervently and with an almost desperate longing, as if she were a wanton with no more thought for the future than warming a man's bed.

This man's bed.

She shoved one hand into the thick mass of his hair and with the other held him tight. His muscles moved and bunched as he embraced her, holding her as if he'd never let her go.

Desire, yearning, increased tenfold as he caressed her. Panting, wanting, not thinking, she kissed him as if she would devour him.

She had loved and been loved before, by a young man just past the threshold of adulthood. With all the hunger for love engendered by her neglected childhood, she'd gladly accepted and returned that love, willingly giving her body. And her heart.

What she felt now, in this mature man's arms, in his powerful embrace, overwhelmed her even more. She knew where this lust could lead, and she didn't care. She had no apprehension about who or what he was, or what he'd done. All that mattered was kissing him and returning his passion.

Until someone grabbed her hard by the shoulder and yanked her from his arms.

CHAPTER THIRTEEN

"You disgusting, sinning *whore!*" Dunstan shouted as he shoved her away.

As she stumbled back, Bayard stepped forward, looking even larger and more powerful, his voice stern and commanding. "Lay a hand on her again and I'll kill you."

Oh, God help her! What had they done?

She stepped between the men, determined to stop them before someone was hurt. "Dunstan, please—"

"I know what I saw!" he charged. His whole body quaked with rage as he jabbed a finger at her. "You weren't resisting. You were letting him kiss you. You were kissing him back."

His hate and anger changed into anguish. "Dear God, you *wanted* him to kiss you!"

"It was a mistake," she said, moving toward him. Bayard tried to hold her back, but she shook him off.

"Mistake?" Dunstan jeered as he drew a dagger from his belt. "How many things have I done for you, you ungrateful harlot? How patient have I been, believing that if I served you well and treated you with the respect you crave so much, one day, you would see my merit and my worth? I thought I could win your love, despite my humble birth. What a fool! What a stupid fool to think you were worth such effort!"

"Put up your dagger," Bayard commanded, aware of

Gillian, but not taking his eyes off the enraged man. Dunstan was no knight, but he was impassioned and therefore the most dangerous kind of opponent, for he would fight with only one objective: to kill the man he thought his enemy.

"Yes, Dunstan, put up your dagger," Gillian pleaded as she stepped forward. "There is no need for violence here."

Again Bayard took hold of her to keep her out of Dunstan's reach.

"Take your bloody hands off her!" Dunstan cried, lunging.

Determined and overwrought he might be, but Bayard was a trained knight. He easily avoided the blow, grabbed the man's wrist and twisted, forcing the knife from Dunstan's hand.

Bayard swiftly bent down and grabbed it.

"Leave, Dunstan," he ordered. "Go back to the castle."

"Do you think I'm afraid of you, you lustful sinner?" the steward cried, nearly hysterical. "You march in here like the king, taking what you want, and I'm supposed to let you?"

"Dunstan," Gillian said, "I'm so sorry you—"

"Sorry?" he scoffed. "You're not sorry! I've known you all your life, and I know you too well to be tricked by what you say. I saw the truth in your embrace. You want him as you've never wanted me."

"Dunstan, I may not be able to return your love," she said gently, "but I do care about you, as I would a brother."

"Brother?" he exclaimed with disdain, his face red as holly berries. "This man is your brother more than I!"

She had no words to reply to that, because he was right—or at least the church would say so.

"Dunstan, go to the castle," Bayard ordered again, this time taking a step closer to the steward.

"Yes, Dunstan, please go back. We can discuss this later," Gillian said, "when you've had time to—"

"What? *Calm down?*" Shaking his head, Dunstan began to back away. "Do you think I'm that much of a fool that I'll believe your lying explanations, your pathetic excuses? You disgust me, the pair of you. To think of the years I've wasted, hoping…"

He shook his finger at her. "I'm going to write to Adelaide. She should learn the sort of scoundrel her brother-in-law is and that her sister's no better than a whore."

He turned and stumbled toward the castle.

"Dunstan, wait!" Gillian called out, starting after him until Bayard pulled her back.

"Leave him. He's too upset now. He won't care who hears the charges that he makes, or whether they're true or not."

She shook off the hand that moments ago had aroused her so. "What are we going to do?"

"Write your own letter and explain to your sister what happened."

"And what is that?" she demanded, her gaze searching his inscrutable face. "What *is* happening between us, my lord?"

Although his eyes held hers, she couldn't even guess what he was thinking. "What other truth can there be but that we, being fallible and thrown much together of late, became too friendly? Our affection drifted into a wrong course until we did something regrettable, and Dunstan saw us. Tell her that she has no cause to worry, for we'll make no such errors again."

He sounded so calm, so cool, as if that kiss had meant little more to him that tripping over a stick. But what more *could* it mean, given her vow and her desire to remain here in Averette where she belonged, as well as the marriage of their siblings. "What about Dunstan? What will we say to him?"

"You are the lady of Averette. He's your steward. You owe him no explanation for your conduct, and neither do I."

"Except that he's also my friend."

"Your friend just called you vile names, drew a dagger, and threatened you. Even if you wish to excuse him, you should relieve him of his duties at the least. You can no longer trust him as you have."

However right Bayard might be, and even if she agreed she could no longer have complete faith in Dunstan, she didn't want him telling her what to do. "I'll consider it."

"The man's pride has been dealt a serious blow. He's not likely to forgive that, or you, or me, any time soon. If he stays, he'll likely create conflict and strife."

"He was my *friend!*" she cried, unable to restrain her dismay and frustration any longer. "I trusted him. I relied on him. I simply cannot order him to go—not when *we* did wrong!"

Glaring at her, Bayard threw up his hands. "Then do what you will, if you're prepared to bear the consequences. God knows why I even offered an opinion!"

"Perhaps, my lord, you should go, as well. Dunstan will tell people what happened here."

Bayard's expression grew as grim as a death's head. "I've told you, my lady, I'm staying here until Armand or Adelaide give me leave to go. That is what Armand asked of me, and so I will. But I assure you, my lady, on my word of honor as a knight, I'll never kiss you again."

Then he turned on his heel and left her.

GILLIAN WAITED IN THE SHADOWS, trying to catch her breath and calm her racing heart.

God help her, she'd been a fool—a weak-willed, moon-struck fool, giving in to her lustful impulses when she had so much to lose: Dunstan's friendship and counsel, the respect of her people, her respect for herself....

For what? A kiss, an embrace? To feel like a desirable, attractive woman? To feel loved and beloved?

She had thought herself so strong, so resolute, not needing any man's help or succor or good opinion. She had wanted only their respect.

Until she met a man who gave her that, and so much more.

At what cost?

If she lost the affection and respect of her people, if she lost Averette, she had nothing. She *was* nothing.

No feeling, no love, no desire, no man, was worth that.

Not even Bayard de Boisbaston.

DIZZY, NAUSEOUS, HIS MIND still reeling from what he'd seen, Dunstan stumbled into his chamber. Closing the door, he leaned back against it, drawing in great gasping breaths.

All he could see, all he could think about, was Gillian in Bayard de Boisbaston's arms, kissing him passionately. Willingly. Her whole body pressed against his, as if they'd been lovers for days, maybe from the first day he'd arrived.

Surely not. Not Gillian. He would have realized… known…seen…

Yet she'd treated *him* like a leper for simply pulling her onto his lap.

All his hopes, all his dreams, were in ashes around him. All the plans he'd made for all these weeks, and months, and years—that he would one day prove himself worthy of her love. That she would look at him one day and he would see desire for him in her eyes, a passion that mirrored his own. And they would have enough money saved over the years from her frugality and his careful management that they could offer the king a sum that would ensure his agreement to their marriage.

Then he would take Gillian for his wife, and to his bed.

Instead, what had his patience, his careful calculation, his waiting, yielded? He'd been overlooked and passed over for a knight with a handsome face and powerful body and a reputation as a scoundrel and a coward.

She had rejected him for Bayard de Boisbaston.

He should denounce Gillian. In the hall, in front of everyone. And in the village, too. Let Dena, who admired her so, and the other servants in the hall and castle, the people in the village, know the sort of lustful whore their mistress was, and the kind of scoundrel Sir Bayard de Boisbaston, the 'Gyptian lover, was.

He *should* denounce them. He had every right to. And he should write to Adelaide, just as he'd threatened.

Except…what would happen to Gillian if her sin and shame became known? What would Adelaide do? And the people of Averette? They might force her to leave, to go to some convent somewhere, to hide her shame.

That would destroy her. She loved Averette too much…as much as he loved her.

A sob choked him. Then another, as he slowly slid to the floor. He couldn't do such a thing to her. He loved her. In spite of what he'd seen and what she'd done, he loved her still.

He'd loved her from the time they were children playing childish games, and she would take his part when Lizette teased him. He'd loved her when James d'Ardenay came to visit, and when he'd feared he'd lost her.

He loved her even if Bayard de Boisbaston had seduced her, even if she could never be his.

MUCH LATER THAT NIGHT, unable to sleep, Bayard paced in his chamber like a beast on a leash. He never should have touched Gillian. God help him, he never should have kissed her.

Not only had he put Gillian's reputation at risk, he'd seen the guilt in her eyes. The shame. The remorse and dismay, as if they'd committed a terrible crime.

Once again, he went to the window and looked at the clouds scudding across the moon like spirits. Had Dunstan gone to his chamber to write a scathing letter to Adelaide denouncing her sister and painting him as a lascivious scoundrel, one even worse than his father? Or was the steward drinking himself into a stupor?

What would Adelaide think if she received such a letter? God help him, what would Armand?

How many days would it be before Armand summoned him and demanded an explanation, or denounced him, too?

He should speak to Dunstan alone, man to man, while there was still time and before he told everyone what he'd seen, if it wasn't already too late. He would try to explain that it was a mistake, an urge he should have controlled. *His* shame, *his* sin, *his* fault. He would take sole responsibility for what they'd done and spare Gillian if he could.

If Dunstan truly loved Gillian, if he retained any tender feeling towards her at all, and even if he didn't truly believe Bayard's explanation, he should be willing to spare her humiliation and shame, and not ruin her reputation and position in the world. He shouldn't want to turn the people she cherished against her.

And if Dunstan would not forgive her and keep silent?

He would find a way to convince him.

Grabbing his tunic, Bayard tugged it on over his shirt and breeches. He pulled on his boots, then opened the door to his chamber. The steward's quarters were on the bottom floor of the family apartments, and were entered directly from the yard.

Bayard waited until a thicker cloud covered the moon, then slipped into the steward's doorway. He knocked softly and pressed his ear to the door, listening for an answer.

Nothing.

Maybe the steward hadn't heard him. Maybe he was too busy composing his letter. Or maybe he had gotten drunk and passed out.

Not willing to return to his chamber until he knew the answer, Bayard cautiously opened the chamber door and slipped inside. At nearly the same moment, a shaft of moonlight shone in through the chamber's open window.

Bayard stood motionless with amazement. This chamber was as luxuriously furnished as any he'd ever seen. It was also in complete disarray. Clothes, papers, scrolls, small boxes, and boots lay scattered about, apparently tossed anywhere and everywhere. A shattered pitcher was on the floor near the washstand beside an overturned, broken chest.

Striking a flint on the bedside table to light a candle, Bayard slowly surveyed the room. Thank God there was no body there, no blood, no dead face staring up at him.

Perhaps someone had broken into the chamber with robbery in mind while Dunstan was at the celebration on the green. If so, where was the steward now?

Bayard surveyed the disorder again, noting what appeared to be missing, and what was not. Clothes had been taken, he was fairly certain, and perhaps jewels from the small cask discarded in the corner. But if thievery had been the goal, why leave the silver candleholder that he held in his hand, the thick, studded leather belts and boots, the finely wrought bronze basin and ewer?

It was more like someone had packed in a great hurry.

Bayard blew out the candle and returned the holder to the table. He left the chamber as silently and cautiously as he'd entered, then walked across the yard to the gate.

The guards on duty, Bran and Alfric, stiffened, clearly taken aback by Bayard's arrival in the middle of the night.

"Just making sure you're not asleep on watch," Bayard lied. "Has Dunstan come back yet?"

Grinning, Bran shook his head, his face illuminated by the torch flickering in a sconce on the wall. "Not yet. He seemed right anxious when he rode out. I think maybe he was afraid Peg wouldn't wait for 'em and take another."

"Peg?"

Frowning, Alfric nudged his companion in the side. Bran shoved him back. "What? So he goes to town and has some fun. Nothing wrong with that."

"No, there isn't," Bayard agreed, wondering how long Dunstan had been visiting this Peg, if Gillian knew about it, or if that was really where he'd gone. "When does he usually return?"

"Lauds, sometimes a little later, never after prime."

"I think it'll be after prime this time, my lord," Alfric said, apparently willing to give information now that he knew Bayard wasn't angry. "He had a bundle with him. Looked like extra clothes, as if he might be stayin' awhile."

Bran snorted a laugh. "Maybe a couple o' days, judging by the size of it."

Or perhaps never to return, Bayard thought. If Dunstan had gone without a word to anyone of their misdeed, he could only be grateful. "When he comes back, tell him I'd like to speak with him. It's important."

"Aye, my lord, we will," Alfric cheerfully replied.

HAVING SUCCESSFULLY PASSED the sentries by giving them the password, Richard strode through the trees toward the flickering fire of the mercenaries' camp on the southern border of Averette.

"Where's Ullric?" he demanded when he reached the open area where the mercenaries had gathered. He ignored the three big louts who clambered to their feet and drew their swords.

The Saxon leader of Wimarc's men rose. "It's Richard," he said to his wary men, who sheathed their swords and sat down again.

Holding a wineskin, Ullric belched and gave the nobleman an impertinent, questioning look.

Richard curled his lip with disgust. He could smell the Saxon from here. "When are you going to attack?"

Ullric took a gulp of wine—part of his payment, no doubt—before he answered. "When I'm ready."

His hand on his sword, aware of the dagger in each boot and the other in his belt, Richard took a step closer. "You were paid to kill them, not sit around a fire getting drunk."

"Not enough to get killed doing it," Ullric said as he tossed the wineskin to one of his equally filthy, bearded companions.

Not all of them were Saxons or Angles, or from German tribes. There were a few Spaniards who used the curved swords of the Moors, as well a couple of Irishmen and three men from Wales with their longbows. They chuckled and nodded appreciatively when Ullric added, "Money's no good if you're dead."

"It was my understanding you were the best money could buy. If that's not true, I suggest you return the fee to Wimarc."

Ullric laughed again. "He can come and get it."

"Do you think he won't?"

Dread dawned in Ullric's beady little eyes. He knew, as Richard did, that Wimarc was not a man you wanted for an enemy. The best thing you could hope for then was a swift death.

"He won't come himself, of course," Richard said, stabbing a little harder with his verbal weapons, the ones he wielded so well. "He'll send his personal guard. I hear they can take a week to kill a man."

"She's too well guarded," Ullric defensively replied. "And you should have told me Bayard de Boisbaston was here."

"You know him?"

"We hear things. His father trained his sons hard

and they're ruthless in battle. Fierce when fighting, they say."

"Bayard's just one man and there are fifteen of you," Richard returned, wishing he'd insisted Wimarc give him twenty men. He never should have settled for fifteen.

"And we'll do the job—when *I* say the time's right, not you."

The sound of voices and rustling leaves interrupted them. All the men got to their feet as two of the lookouts arrived, dragging a third man between them. He was beaten and bloody, with his hands bound.

Richard grabbed a burning branch from the fire and held it aloft as the two mercenaries threw their prisoner on the ground, then Richard turned him over with his foot.

Whimpering with pain, his left cheek bruising, his lip cut and bleeding, and his right eye swollen shut, Dunstan looked up at Richard. "Charles! Help me!" he gasped.

Richard smiled and said, "Well, well, well, Ullric. I believe your men have found some bait."

CHAPTER FOURTEEN

THE NEXT MORNING Gillian stood beside Bayard in the chapel as the priest said mass.

The small building was made of stone, with pillars down the sides and an altar likewise of gray stone. Her mother had made an altar cloth for part of her dower, and it was still the only decoration, besides the necessary candles and the statue of the Virgin.

She was paying little heed to her surroundings, or to Father Matthew, because for the first time since her father had died, she'd been afraid to leave her bedchamber this morning. She'd dreaded seeing any change in her people's behavior toward her after Dunstan had revealed what he'd seen. Although Dena had behaved normally when she'd brought her water to wash, Gillian had wondered if she simply hadn't yet heard the gossip.

But then the servants and soldiers in the hall had greeted her as they normally would. She was relieved but confused until she reached the chapel and an explanation had presented itself.

Dunstan wasn't there. It was possible he hadn't yet told anyone what he'd seen.

Perhaps he'd gotten a wineskin and drunk himself into a stupor.

Or maybe he'd spent the night in the village and had yet to return.

Wherever he was, word of her shameful conduct obviously hadn't yet reached the castle and her household. It would soon enough, though, and then everyone would know. He could even now be regaling the villagers with what he'd seen last night, and he could return at any moment to denounce her.

She glanced at Bayard, his head reverently bowed. Looking at him, she could believe he was full of guilt and remorse, except that he'd always appeared devout at mass. She'd noted it the first morning he'd been there. Then she'd wondered if his dedication was sincere or merely intended to impress her.

If he wanted to impress her, he had, especially since he never said or did anything to draw attention to his devotion. But how, if he was a God-fearing man, could he have kissed her?

Perhaps because, like her, his desire had overpowered his reason.

And now she might lose the respect she'd worked so hard to deserve, and perhaps her people's affection, too.

The mass concluded, she went to the door, expecting Bayard to stay behind, as he often did. Instead, he followed her into the yard, causing several of the servants to cast curious looks their way.

"You shouldn't have followed me," she quietly chided.

"I have to speak to you," he answered, urgency in his voice and grave concern in his dark eyes. "Dunstan's gone."

She halted abruptly. "Gone?"

"Bran and Alfric were on guard at the gate last night and they told me he left the castle carrying a large bundle. Apparently he sometimes visits Peg, a woman at the Stag's Head."

Gillian thought she knew Dunstan well, but obviously he had secrets, too.

"I gather he usually returns before lauds," Bayard continued. "I asked the guards to send him to me when he returns. He hasn't. Either he's lingering longer with this Peg than he habitually does, or else—as I suspect from the disarray I found in his chamber—he's left Averette.

"I went back again this morning. It looks as if most of his clothing and a few other items are missing, but nothing of value. I think that he's taken his clothes and gone."

Undeniable relief warred with dread. "Why would he leave?"

Bayard's expression softened. "Perhaps because he still cares for you. He left without telling anyone anything, it seems."

So their secret, their shame, was safe. Perhaps. For now.

"Bayard," she began, once again thinking he, too, should leave Averette, but before she could continue, a hoarse voice shouted, "My lady!"

Panting, Hale stood at the gate, one hand splayed against the open wicket, the other holding his side, and his face dripped with sweat.

With a cry of dismay, she gathered up her skirts and ran toward him. Bayard outstripped her and reached the gate first, but it was Gillian whom Hale addressed. "It's Dunstan, my lady," he gasped. "He's dead!"

"Dead?" she repeated incredulously. Dunstan couldn't be dead. He'd been here last night, alive and well. Alive when he rode out the gate, Bayard had said.

"Where? When?" Bayard demanded.

"I don't know, my lord," Hale answered, his breathing slightly less ragged. "I found him tied to a tree. In a meadow. He'd been beaten, my lady, and cut, and they took his—"

Hale swallowed hard and shook his head, averting his eyes. "What they did isn't fit for your ears, my lady."

The guards and soldiers at the gate and on the walk who'd overheard looked as sick as Gillian felt. Seltha, on her way to the well, started to cry.

Dunstan had fled Averette and become the prey of evil men.

He'd left because of what he'd seen. Because of what *she'd* done and felt.

Because of *them*.

He was dead. Gone. Murdered and mutilated.

"Did you touch him?" Bayard demanded.

"No, my lord."

"Good."

Feeling ill and dizzy, Gillian laid a hand on Hale's arm. "Teddy wasn't with you, was he?"

"No, my lady, thank God. He stayed the night with my sister."

"You saw no sign of the people who did this?" Bayard asked.

Again Hale shook his head. "No, my lord, not a sign, but I didn't take too close a look."

Gillian couldn't blame him.

"I fear, my lady," Bayard said, "that this isn't the work of simple thieves or outlaws. Such men would have left Dunstan where they found him, or tried to hide his body. They wouldn't have mutilated him and put him on display."

Poor Dunstan. Her poor friend. Murdered, and savaged, and treated like carrion.

She would have justice done. She would see that Dunstan was avenged.

"Whoever it was," she said, her voice hard and cold as iron, "I want them found. *At once.*"

Bayard's face mirrored her own anger and resolve to find the killers as he bowed his head in acquiescence. "I promise you, my lady, that I'm going to catch whoever did this, and God help them when I do."

"I want them brought back *here* for justice, Bayard," she said. "The king's justice for traitors. A quick death is too good for them."

"Have all the men called out," Bayard said to Lindall, who had come toward them from the armory. "I want four extra patrols mounted and out the gates by the time the chapel bell tolls terce—one to go north, one east and the other west to circle round and meet the one already on the border of the estate, and another with me and Robb. Get a wagon for the body. Lindall, you'll be in charge of the gates. No one goes in or out unless you know them. Frederic!"

"Here, my lord!" his squire answered from the hall steps. He, and many others who had been inside breaking the fast, had heard the growing commotion in the yard and come to see what was happening.

"You'll ride with me," Bayard said, "after you help me into my mail." He went to pass Gillian, then checked his step. "You should be safe here, my lady."

No, she wouldn't. "I'm going with you."

"I think you should stay here, my lady," Hale ventured. "Dunstan's no sight for a lady's eyes."

"Dunstan was my steward, and my friend, and I loved him as a brother," Gillian replied in a tone that would brook no dissent. "Regardless of what those animals did to him, *I* will bring him home."

Fearing for her safety, mindful of what he'd been charged to do, sickened by what had happened to

Dunstan, Bayard was about to protest, until he saw the look in Gillian's eyes. "As you wish, my lady."

IT WASN'T MANY MILES TO the place where the men who'd murdered Dunstan had left his body, yet it seemed hundreds as Gillian sat beside Ned on the seat of a wagon, rocking with its motion.

Bayard rode at the head of the cortege, with Frederic at his side. Half of the patrol came behind him, the other half after the wagon.

Although her throat felt as if a leather strap had been thrown around it and pulled tight enough to strangle her, Gillian wasn't crying. She couldn't. It was as if what had happened was too terrible for tears, too awful for her mind to fully accept, too impossible for her to mourn.

It seemed like the whole world had changed since last night. Dunstan was dead, and the safety and security she'd tried so hard to create since her father's death had been shattered. Not just for her, but for everyone in Averette.

Now, every sound, every whisper of the breeze through the oak and chestnut, alder and rowan leaves, made her shiver and fear that terrible men lurked nearby, waiting to attack regardless of the presence of Bayard and his men.

At last they reached the edge of the far meadow, where sheep and cows grazed in the spring. In the middle of it stood a single oak. As Bayard called out for the cortege to halt, several crows rose cawing from the tree and something tied to the trunk.

God help her, it was Dunstan.

If she hadn't kissed Bayard and Dunstan hadn't seen them, he wouldn't have left the castle. He would still be in Averette, alive.

Bayard nudged his horse back to her. "I think it would be best if you stayed here, my lady. Frederic, Robb, and I will take Dunstan down."

She was the lady of Averette and she had to be strong. "Dunstan was my friend and a friend's hands should help him."

Bayard's dark eyes softened with sorrow and pity. "He's dead, my lady, and only prayers can help him now. It would be better if the ground around him is left as undisturbed as possible until Robb and I can examine it."

He lowered his voice and spoke with gentle sympathy. "I think he would rather you remember him as he was, my lady, than as he is now. I assure you that we'll treat him with all the respect and dignity he deserves."

If fewer people around Dunstan now ensured they caught the guilty men sooner… "Very well."

Bayard dismounted and held out his gloved hand.

"Be gentle with him," she said as she put her hand in his, and his strong fingers closed around hers to help her to the ground.

"I will," Bayard vowed as he let go, his hand slipping from hers before he remounted.

He issued a few brief orders and with Frederic, Robb, Ned, and the wagon, left her and the rest of his men behind.

BAYARD HAD BEEN IN BATTLE, and any man who'd been in battle had seen gruesome remains of what had once been men.

But Dunstan's mutilated body was like nothing Bayard had ever seen, and as they took down the bloody corpse, he fervently prayed he never saw anything like it again. Not only had Dunstan been savagely beaten, there were signs of torture on his body, and not of the sort to extract information.

What had been done to Dunstan had been done for pleasure, the pleasure some men got from inflicting pain.

Thank God he'd asked Gillian to stay behind, and thank God she'd agreed. The sight of this body would sicken her, just as it sickened Frederic, who was still losing what remained of his morning meal behind the tree.

Bayard regretted bringing the youth this close. He'd thought Frederic ought to be made aware of the evil nature of some men, but if he'd known how brutal they'd been, he would have spared the lad. This was a sight to trouble sleep for years.

Including his.

Ned had paled, but he was older and he managed to do as Bayard asked, so that now Dunstan's remains lay on the bed of the wagon covered with a blanket. Robb, meanwhile, continued to study the muddy ground around the tree.

"Tell Alfric twenty men are to go back to the castle to guard the lady," he said to the groom. "And don't let Lady Gillian look beneath the blanket. That's an order."

"Aye, my lord. What about you and him?" the groom asked, nodding at Frederic, who staggered to his feet and leaned against the trunk of the massive oak.

"Frederic, you can go back to the castle with Lady Gillian and the others. The rest of the men should stay where they are until I've finished looking around here."

"I'd rather stay here with you, my lord," the youth replied.

Bayard studied Frederic's face. He was still green

around the gills but looked better since Dunstan had been covered. "Very well. Ned, take the body."

"Aye, my lord. A nasty business this. I hope you catch the bastards," the groom replied as he picked up the reins.

"I will," Bayard replied. "With God's help, I will."

FROM THE COVER OF THE nearby wood, Ullric muttered an earthy Saxon curse. "That many men makes it too dangerous," he said to the now-clean-shaven Richard.

"You have to attack. When will you have a better chance?"

Ullric curled his thick upper lip. "We're to risk our lives on your say-so while you stay here like a little girl?"

"*You* were hired to kill him."

"So *I* decide when to attack. I told you, I don't take stupid risks."

Richard regarded the Saxon with scorn. "What are you going to do, wait for an invitation?"

"I'll wait till he's out with a smaller patrol. I didn't expect him to bring so many to get a body."

Richard studied the group of soldiers arrayed at the edge of the meadow. He hadn't expected Bayard to bring so many, either.

Bayard's party began to split in two, one obviously going with Lady Gillian and the wagon, the other to stay with Bayard—twenty with the lady and at least that many with Bayard.

"He's no fool, either," Ullric growled, stroking his cheek with the butt of his ax's shaft. "I might have to split my own men up. Fire a few farmhouses to make him cut his force into small patrols, then wait for him to come out with one of them."

Richard swore again. "I wasn't planning to spend the rest of my life trying to kill Bayard de Boisbaston."

"Then go. Leave him, and the woman, to us."

As much as Richard chafed at the notion of taking more time to kill Bayard and Gillian, he wanted to stay here until Armand and his beautiful wife came so that he could exact his own particular vengeance on them. He especially wasn't about to leave Adelaide for Ullric.

Richard got to his feet. "Just kill him, and soon. I don't want to waste any more time here than I must."

CHAPTER FIFTEEN

For Gillian, the rest of that terrible day passed in a nightmare haze of sorrow, despair, guilt, and remorse.

She didn't look at Dunstan's body before she relinquished it to Father Matthew. Weak it may be, and cowardly, but this once she would be weak and cowardly. As Bayard had suggested, she wanted to remember Dunstan as he'd been—in the prime of his life, a friend, a companion, and a brother.

Until his affection for her had changed, and Bayard de Boisbaston had come.

After returning with Dunstan's body, and despite her own sorrow, she had to act as if she was calm, and confident, and that all would be well. She gave her orders for the clearing of Dunstan's chamber and the packing of his possessions that remained in his chamber, deciding his property should go to the church since Dunstan had no family living. She spoke to Father Matthew about the funeral mass, and vigil, and the prayers to be said for Dunstan's soul. She wrote to Adelaide and dispatched a messenger with a ten-man escort. She presided over a subdued evening meal, although she hardly ate anything. She wasn't hungry.

Afterward, she went to the chapel to pray for Dunstan's soul, for justice for her murdered friend, and for mercy, and forgiveness for own sins, and Bayard's, too, kneeling before the bier that bore Dunstan's shrouded body.

Of all the things she regretted, the greatest was that she hadn't spoken to Dunstan sooner about his feelings, and hers. Perhaps if she had put an end to his hopes when she first noticed the alteration in his manner toward her, perhaps if she had explained the vow she'd made with her sisters, she could have prevented his jealous rage and the sudden departure that had put him in harm's way.

But she shouldn't have kissed Bayard, either. She shouldn't have surrendered to her desire, especially not for him. She knew any respectable, honorable union between them was forbidden, no matter how she felt, and even if she loved him as she'd never hoped to love again, with a love deeper and stronger than the infatuation she'd felt for James. She had loved James as a girl, full of girlish hopes and dreams.

What she felt for Bayard was the love of a woman's heart, a woman who saw that he was handsome, but also so much more than that. He was loyal, compassionate, generous, and good, honest, and vulnerable. They could be together, if they could marry and she could give him a home, she might know a happiness and contentment few women were ever fortunate enough to experience.

The door to the chapel opened and closed. It was Father Matthew, perhaps, or someone else come to pay their respects to the well-regarded Dunstan.

"Lady Gillian?"

Bayard.

She closed her eyes and prayed for strength as she rose slowly, her knees aching from kneeling on the cold stone floor. He'd removed his armor and washed. Now he wore his tunic, shirt, breeches, and boots. Attired thus, he no longer seemed the stern commander. He looked like a friend. Or a lover.

"Did you find the murderers?" she asked.

He shook his head. "No. There was no sign of the blackguards. I *can* tell you that Dunstan wasn't killed near that tree, though. There wasn't enough blood. Tomorrow, we'll try to find the place where they did the deed."

"What does it matter where it was done?" she asked, trying to make her mind work in spite of her grief, and fatigue, and the other emotions roiling within her.

"There may be things left behind that will tell us who the men were, or where they were from, and perhaps a sign as to where they've gone."

His brow furrowed with concern. "Will you not retire and try to get some rest, my lady? It'll distress the people, who are upset enough, if their lady falls ill."

"The least I can do for Dunstan now is keep vigil. Leave me alone with my dead."

Her dead. Dead because of them and what they'd done, the desire she couldn't subdue. Dead, never to hear her say how sorry she was for hurting him. For not being honest with him.

"Gillian."

Her name. A word. Soft in the stillness.

Quietly spoken, passing Bayard's lips that had kissed her so passionately.

"Gillian," he whispered again, his whole body tense as if he was holding himself in check, his hands still at his sides.

As if he wanted to take her in his arms, but didn't dare, as she longed to hold him, but couldn't. He was her relative, sent to protect her, not a lover come to woo and win her.

Or he would already have succeeded.

"My brave Gillian!"

She covered her face with her hands. "Bayard, please go."

And then the tears came, so hard and so fast that her sobs wracked her body and choked her very breath.

His arms encircled her, holding her close. His voice was a ragged, broken whisper of remorse and longing, regret and comfort, as his hand stroked her hair.

The hair that James had called soft as flax. James, whose love had, she thought, prevented her from loving Dunstan, or any other man. Until now.

She should order Bayard to leave and she did try, but the words would not come. She couldn't bear to let him go. She would drown in the raging currents of her grief and guilt without his support.

He was so sorry, he whispered. So very sorry. He hadn't meant for anything like this to happen. He'd been sent here to help and that's all he wanted to do, not cause a good man's death. He wished with all his heart she could forgive him for being weak. For giving in to his desire. For wanting her. For wanting her still.

God help him. God forgive him for this, and so much more.

His anguish was as strong as hers. His guilt and remorse, too. They had sinned together and together they now clung, desperate in their pain.

Another sob choked her and, her chin trembling, she raised her eyes to look at him, silently pleading with him to tell her all would be well.

With both his hands he brushed her hair from her tear-streaked face, the gesture a caress. And then he gathered her into his arms and kissed her with gentle tenderness.

Yet beneath that, there was a deep longing and need that matched her own. Not to be alone. To be with another person, to be loved and cherished.

And from that, desire—hot, and strong, and powerful—surged forth. Another urgency, another need came to the fore.

Seeking, wanting, she pressed her body against Bayard's. He parted his lips and his tongue pushed gently against hers until she allowed him into that intimate warmth of her mouth.

A sound came from his throat—half sigh, half moan— as his hands slid down her back.

More need, more desire, erupted. She forgot where she was, or why, and knew only the passion pulsing through her. Whimpering with longing, she held him tight, and when he moved, pushing her back against one of the pillars, she eagerly went with him as if they were one body.

His knee pushed between hers. Panting, anxious, she clung to him, her breathing fast and shallow, as was his. Her mouth hungry and seeking, as was his. Her hands hot and searching, touching, caressing, as were his.

He broke the kiss to trail his lips down the curve of her jaw and along her neck. Arching, she held on to his shoulders and opened her eyes for one brief instant.

It was enough.

She remembered where she was, and why; the sight of Dunstan's bier reminded her with the force of a blow to her cheek.

She pushed Bayard back. "No!" she whispered, frantic with regret and shame. How could she do this? How could she let her feelings so overrule her again? "Not here! Not now!"

He stepped back and she saw a remorse that matched

her own in his dark eyes. "Oh, God," he whispered. "Gillian, I—"

"No!" she cried again, moving away, afraid of her own weakness. "No, Bayard! Not now—not ever! Go! Leave me! Leave me!"

Without another word, he did.

AS THE CHAPEL DOOR CLOSED, Gillian sank to her knees and covered her face with her cold hands. The candles continued to burn, the scent of incense drifted on the air and the only sound that broke the silence was of a woman weeping.

AS THE FIRST FAINT STREAKS of light dawned in the east, Frederic strode along the outer curtain wall toward the postern gate. Just as Charles had told him, if you walked with purpose, nobody questioned where you were going or why. A very clever fellow, that Charles.

When Frederic reached the postern gate, he was pleased to discover that Tom and Bran, neither of whom was particularly bright, guarded it. "Open the gate."

The men exchanged wary looks. "You're going out?" Tom, the taller of the two, asked.

Charles had assured him a confident man could brave out any guards' questions and so would he, despite the trickle of sweat running down his back. "I'm going to the village on business for Sir Bayard."

"We ain't heard nothing about that," Bran said slowly, his pale blue eyes doubtful. "Bit early, isn't it?"

"I have to return before we go out on patrol this morning. Of course you're welcome to confirm my purpose with Sir Bayard or Lindall if you think I'm lying."

As he'd expected, the guards weren't about to accuse

him of outright deceit. They weren't particularly keen to disturb Sir Bayard or Lindall, either.

"Go ahead, then," Tom said, opening the wicket gate.

Frederic nodded his thanks and hurried on his way. He had to get to the village, meet Charles and return before Bayard realized he was gone. He hoped Tom and Bran would keep their mouths shut and that Charles—

"Here is the young buck himself," a voice said as he passed a farmer's cart full of wood heading for the village, its driver hunched over and wearing a gray woollen cloak and hood.

Startled, Frederic turned and tried to see the driver's face. "Charles? Is that you? What happened to your beard?"

"I cut it off. Damn thing was too itchy."

"Why are you dressed like that?"

"Get up, put on the cloak on the seat, and I'll explain everything."

Confused, but curious as to why the wine merchant was thus attired and the cart full of wood, not wine, and especially why they weren't meeting at the Stag's Head as planned, Frederic climbed aboard the cart and drew on the dark woollen cloak that had been lying on the seat. "God's blood, this stinks."

"Unless you want Bayard to find out you left the castle despite his orders, I suggest you lower your voice. As for that cloak, I borrowed it from a man who doesn't often wash."

"What man?"

"I'll tell you when we're out of the village." Charles reached under the seat and handed Frederic a wineskin. "Have a drink of that."

Frederic pulled out the stopper and took a gulp of very fine wine. "Why aren't you at the Stag's Head?"

"I grew weary of Peg's company and it so happens I can better serve my own master this way."

"Your own master? You work for another wine merchant?"

"Not precisely."

By now they'd passed the green and were nearing the wood through which they'd gone to fetch Dunstan's body.

"So, Frederic, have you decided if you're going to travel west with me and go home to your father, or stay here with the man who treats you like a child?" Charles asked as they entered the forest.

"I'm not sure. My father should know I'm being mistreated, but he's not exactly gentle himself." Frederic studied the yoke of the nag pulling the cart. "You were right about Sir Bayard."

"I was?" Richard d'Artage asked, keeping any hint of triumph from his features. "How so?"

"I saw them last night."

"Lady Gillian and Sir Bayard? They were together?"

Frederic threw back the stinking hood and drew in a deep breath of fresh air. "They were alone in the chapel together."

"Doing what?"

"How should I know? I didn't go inside."

Richard frowned. He certainly would have, if he could be sure he wouldn't be seen. "Then all you know is that they were in the chapel together."

"Alone *at night*. And he was upset when he came out."

"Of course he'd be upset. The steward's been killed."

"Not like that. He came out and closed the door, then laid his hand on it and bowed his head. He whispered her name and then he just stood there for a very long time. I thought my legs would cramp before he left."

"And the lady?"

"She was keeping a vigil for Dunstan, supposedly by herself."

"A guilty conscience, perhaps?"

"She, and Dunstan, and Sir Bayard quarreled after the haying—I'm sure of it. I saw Dunstan ride out that same night and he looked like a man possessed."

"So I was right all along," Richard said. "Bayard wants her, if he hasn't had her already. The steward probably tried to warn her." He cut a glance to his passenger. "And *that's* the sort of immoral scoundrel our king believes is worthy."

"The king should be told about him."

"The king already knows. Consider who else he has in his court—mercenaries like Falkes de Bréauté, men as immoral, greedy, and stupid as himself. John honors those louts while ignoring better, worthier men. And the king's such a dolt, he can't see that even the scoundrels he rewards hate him and will likely sell their loyalty to the highest bidder as soon as they get the chance."

Richard drew the wagon to a halt and turned to look at the youth beside him. "That's why there are many of us who want to put a different, better man upon the throne."

Frederic's brow furrowed. "Such talk is treason."

"True treason would be letting a weak king like John lose our lands here to Philip of France—and he will if he stays on the throne. Unless you want Philip and his court ruling over you, you should help us rid England of John, his child queen and all their allies."

Frederic frowned, for the voice of the man he'd believed to be a wine merchant had changed, along with his formerly deferential manner. He sounded well educated, rich, arrogant—like a courtier. "Who *are* you?"

"I am Lord Richard d'Artage, one of many who seek to end a greedy tyrant's reign."

Gripping the seat of the cart, Frederic stared at him with dismay. "You're a traitor! You were in league with Francis de Farnby. You plotted to kill the Earl of Pembroke and the archbishop!"

The youth began to climb out of the cart, until Richard grabbed his arm to hold him there. "The earl and archbishop support John, so they deserve to die. So do all who help keep that villain on the throne."

"But not all men who support John are evil," Frederic protested. "The de Boisbastons—"

"Seek reward and gain. Didn't John give Armand the lady Adelaide? And Averette is his by rights, too. Why else do you think his brother is here? Surely you don't believe Bayard has come out of the goodness of his heart, or some ideal of chivalry? Good God, Frederic, the evidence of your own eyes—his seduction of Lady Gillian, his shameful treatment of you—prove that he's no honorable nobleman."

Richard saw the youth begin to doubt and pressed on to close the trap. "All those loyal to John are the true traitors. They betray their country and its people by supporting that dog. I'm sure you're clever enough to see that, and that you're the sort of brave, honorable man who should be eager to help our cause. Or am I wrong? Will you go running back to Bayard de Boisbaston and tell him I was here?"

Frederic regarded his companion warily. "Who would you put on the throne in John's stead?"

Richard laughed instead of immediately answering, because he himself didn't know, nor particularly care, as long as he was suitably rewarded by whomever Wimarc chose.

"A better man than John," he replied. "More than that, I will not say until we can be certain of your willingness to join us. Will you?"

"If this rebellion fails, I could lose everything, even my life."

"If this rebellion fails, some peasants and foot soldiers will die, and a few noble fools who don't have sense enough to flee in time. You're not a fool, so *if* our plan looks like it might fail, you'll get safely away to another country. You'll have friends—rich friends—to help you. You won't die or even suffer deprivation.

"But we won't fail," Richard assured him, clapping a hand on Frederic's slender shoulder. "Too many men hate John and will be glad to see him overthrown, even if they lack the stomach to do it themselves. It takes courage to stand up and rid the country of a tyrant. I was sure I saw such courage in you. And when we win, that courage and effort shall be amply rewarded. Lands, titles, a pretty, rich wife, and naturally, a place at court.

"So, my clever young friend, will you join us? Or will you let that Plantagenet destroy England?"

CHAPTER SIXTEEN

As the darkness began to lighten with the first hint of dawn, Bayard rose and went to the washstand. He splashed cold water over his face, but it did little to refresh him. He'd barely slept, too worried and full of turmoil to rest, too wracked with guilt, and dismay, and the knowledge that if he could help in this time of need, he'd also be leaving more ruin in his wake. Gillian was suffering because of him, while he...

He had never imagined heartache could be this wretched. He'd been disappointed and upset before when a woman cast him off as easily as she'd rid herself of an old gown, or failed to respond to his advances. Yet that pain had been fleeting, lasting only until he saw another woman who attracted his attention.

This time, he knew he would never be the same. He would always, forever, measure any woman he met by the standard Gillian set for intelligence, competence, and compassion. He was well aware that few, if any, could ever meet it.

To think he had come here with two clear, simple goals: to deliver Adelaide's letter and to fulfill Armand's request to stay and protect Gillian and Lizette until the conspiracy was no longer a threat. Instead, he'd found himself embroiled in different battles, at first between his mission and an ungrateful woman, and then within himself when he realized the ungrateful woman was so much more than that.

After drying his face, Bayard leaned against the washstand and hung his head. He believed Gillian felt the same desire and affection, given her passionate embrace last night after she'd revealed such anguish and vulnerability. If only they could be together! He would do anything to win her hand in marriage, if the church did not forbid it.

As for any other kind of union… No matter what she felt, or how much he wanted to be with her, Gillian was an honorable woman who needed to be respected if she was to continue as chatelaine of Averette. She would surely never permit herself any intimacy outside of marriage, especially now that they'd already courted scandal and inadvertently caused the death of Dunstan.

Even if she were willing to be with him, he could see more unhappiness for her than joy in such a relationship. If she were forced her to leave her home, she would surely come to resent that—and him.

Sighing, Bayard pushed himself away from the washstand. Glancing out the window, he saw that the sky was now tinged with pink and orange, the few strips of clouds coloring like fingers dipped in paint.

Frederic should be here to help him don his armor.

Wondering what was keeping Frederic, Bayard pulled on his hose, breeches, shirt, and boots and then his gambeson. He managed to get himself into his hauberk and buckled his swordbelt around his waist, forgoing his surcoat. Grabbing his helmet, he strode from the chamber to the hall, looking for his squire.

Frederic wasn't in the hall. To Bayard's increasing chagrin and then dread, no one could say when they'd seen Frederic that morning, or even since they'd gone to sleep in the hall the night before.

As he went to the gate to question the guards, Bayard hoped Frederic's absence was due only to mischief and not something much more sinister. That he'd be found in a loft or storeroom, sleeping. Or even in the arms of a serving wench…as long as he was safe.

"Good day, men," he said to Tom and Bran.

They looked surprised at his greeting, as well they might, but he didn't want to cause any unnecessary alarm or panic. "Have you seen my squire?"

Bran and Tom exchanged wary glances.

"Aye, my lord," Tom stammered, "a while ago. He said he was going to the village on business for you. That's what he told us. Ain't that right, Bran?"

"Aye, my lord, 'tis."

"You didn't think it was odd he'd be going to the village even though it wasn't yet prime?"

Tom stared at the toe of his boots, while Bran looked off into the distance as if expecting to find the answer written on a cloud.

"He didn't say where in the village he was going?"

Both men shook their heads.

"He was on foot?"

"Aye, my lord."

"He carried no pouch or other baggage?"

"No, my lord."

So it wasn't likely Frederic was going home to his father.

Maybe Frederic had simply grown weary of being watched and had gone to the village for sport, although he hoped the lad was smart enough not to wander around after dark, given what had happened to Dunstan. If Frederic weren't in the village, a broader search would have to be made. They didn't have many men to spare, but Frederic should be found, and soon. "I want you two to go to the Stag's Head and see if he's there. If not, question the villagers. If no one there knows where he is, you're to return here at once. Tell Lindall if I'm not back from patrol."

He and his men would also search for Frederic.

The sentries exchanged uncertain glances, and Bayard could guess one cause of their dismay. "I don't care if you've been on watch since matins. You let him leave, you can search for him."

He turned on his heel and returned to the hall. As he'd both hoped and dreaded—for he hated to be the bearer of more bad news—Gillian was there.

When she saw him, she hurried toward him. "What is it?" she asked, an edge of anxiety in her voice.

For her sake, he tried to downplay Frederic's absence. After all, the lad was young, proud, and high-spirited, and there was no sign of foul play. He could well be at the Stag's Head or even somewhere in the castle. "Apparently Frederic decided to make an unauthorized visit to the village this morning. I've sent Tom and Bran to fetch him, but I don't want to delay riding out to wait for him."

She wasn't fooled. "Frederic is missing and you've only got two men looking for him? We should have search parties. He's my guest. I'm responsible—"

"No, you're not responsible for Frederic, at least not more than I am. He's a proud young man and I've kept him on a tight rein these past few days. It's possible he just grew resentful and went to the village for some sport, or perhaps to simply prove he could."

"He had to know his absence would be noticed."

Bayard stopped trying to hide his concern. "That's

what worries me. If he merely wanted to get away for a while, he should have been back by now, before his infraction became serious. I've told Tom and Bran if he's not at the Stag's Head they should question the villagers, then inform Lindall."

"I'll not wait that long. We'll begin a more thorough search at once."

As Bayard looked at her pale, careworn face, at the dark circles under her concerned green eyes, he said, "I'll stay, too, then, and help search for him here. You should rest."

"I'd rather you search for Dunstan's killers. I can lead the search of the castle and village for Frederic." Her eyes pleaded with him to understand. "I must be *doing* something, Bayard."

He did understand. He well recalled the frustration of his days in the Duc d'Ormonde's castle, and when he'd first come here. "Very well, my lady, it shall be as you command."

"I'll talk to Dena. He may have said something to her about family or friends living nearby."

Bayard bowed. "Until later, my lady, when I hope to either see a remorseful Frederic, or bring him here myself."

"Alive and well, please God," she whispered fervently. "Alive and well!"

He hoped so, too, and not just for lad's sake, or his. He didn't want Gillian to feel any more guilt and remorse than she already did. She had suffered enough because of his presence here.

STANDING ON THE DAIS FACING Gillian, Dena's hand went to her stomach as she rapidly shook her head. "No, my lady. I've no idea why he might have gone to the village or anywhere else, unless he went to the Stag's Head."

"He didn't," Gillian said, trying to hide her increasing dismay.

Lindall had returned from the village to tell her that Peg hadn't seen Frederic that morning. Neither had anyone else in Averette.

"You're quite certain he never spoke of a friend or relative living nearby that he might visit?"

"No, he never did, my lady. You don't think he's in danger, do you?"

Whatever hatred or anger Dena might have retained for Frederic, it was clear she was sincerely upset by his disappearance.

"I hope not," Gillian replied, wanting to be as honest as she could while not adding to the girl's fear. Or her own.

But she *was* afraid. She was afraid that, for whatever reason, Frederic had fled Averette and been caught by the same men who'd killed Dunstan. That he, too, would be foully murdered. "You can go now, Dena. The moment I hear news of him, I'll see that you're told."

"Thank you, my lady. I hope…I hope he's all right. I mean, I never wanted him to come to harm, no matter what he did."

"Nor do I."

Gillian watched Dena leave the dais, then turned to the butler, who'd been waiting while she spoke to the young maidservant.

The thin and gray-haired middle-aged man wearing a brown tunic who was in charge of the butts of wine and casks of ale passed a hand over his bearded chin. "I hate to bring you more bad tidings, my lady, but it's about the wine you bought from that Charles de Fenelon. He's cheated you."

Another knot formed in the pit of her stomach. "Cheated? How?"

"More'n half the barrels are full of water, not wine."

"Could they have been switched between the time they arrived and today?" she asked.

"I don't think so, my lady," Edun replied. "There's too many. Maybe if it was two or three, it might have been done that way, but it's fifteen."

He bit his lip and added, "Dunstan didn't check them, my lady. Not like he usually did. He didn't seem to be paying much attention."

He'd been distracted, as had she, and remiss, too. "I'll send some soldiers to the village to see if Charles is still there, although he's probably far away by now. Still, we might be able to find out where he was heading next, provided he was fool enough to say so."

She was the fool for being duped so easily, she silently chided. "In the meantime, empty the butts containing water and try to buy more wine from the vintner in the village."

"Aye, my lady," Edun replied, tugging his forelock before he hurried away, looking both worried and relieved.

She'd waited so long to be in charge of Averette, she thought as she watched him go, and look what her rule had come to. She'd been so sure she could manage the estate, that she could run both it and the household with efficiency, justice and kindness. She and Dunstan had spent hours talking about how things could be done better, and for a few short months, it had been just as they'd hoped and dreamed.

Now, despite her best efforts, she was failing.

There were some things she could not prevent, she knew. She couldn't control the king, or his enemies, or her sisters. She couldn't command the weather, or the growing of the crops, or keep evil from the world.

But she'd failed in other things. She hadn't protected Dena, or Dunstan, or perhaps Frederic, either. She'd allowed a dishonest merchant to cheat her. She'd let her feelings—her desire, her loneliness, her love—take precedence over her duty.

Maybe she wasn't worthy to govern Averette after all. Perhaps men were right and a woman, no matter how clever or determined, simply couldn't run an estate. Maybe she should step aside and allow Armand de Boisbaston to be overlord here.

Would he let her stay? If not, where would she go? What would she do?

She could go to a convent, perhaps, away from the world. From Averette. From Bayard.

She bowed her head and tasted a teardrop as it touched her lips, warm and salty.

Then a resounding crash echoed through the chamber.

Startled, Gillian looked up to see Seltha and Joanna easing a table's top back up against the wall. They must have knocked it over.

"I'm sorry, my lady!" Seltha called. "Didn't mean to…" She hesitated. "Disturb you."

"Maybe you ought to lie down?" Joanna suggested, her genuine concern matching that of Seltha and, Gillian realized, the other servants in the hall who were all watching her.

These people relied on her and counted on her to keep them safe. They loved her, too, in their way.

New vitality surged through her. These were her

people, her friends. This was her home, for now at least, to maintain, and protect, and cherish. To keep safe from any who would bring murder, and mayhem, and anarchy.

She was Lady Gillian of Averette and she would not give up. She would not surrender to doubt and despair. "I'm quite all right," she said firmly, straightening her slender shoulders.

If she had failed in some things, she had succeeded in others. The hall moot, for instance, had left her people satisfied that justice had been done, as it had never been in her father's time. The night of the haying, they'd been genuinely happy and content. She had contributed to that contentment, because they knew she had their best interests at heart.

Regardless of the sacrifices she must make, or her enemies, or anything else that might stand in her way, she would do her duty.

"THIS HAS TO BE THE PLACE where they killed him," Robb said to Bayard and the other soldiers of the patrol as they dismounted in a small valley, where a narrow stream ran between rocky, wooded slopes.

Robb pointed to the blood on the rough trunk of the chestnut tree in front of them and the reddened dirt at its roots. "They tied him to that tree. That's blood soaked into the ground."

Bayard followed Robb's finger as it moved to the blackened stones where a fire had been, the ashes washing away in the rain that bared several glistening coals. The fire wouldn't have been visible unless one was on the rise on either side of the valley.

"That's where they ate, and drank, and slept," Robb said.

And watched. Some of them had surely watched as Dunstan was tortured and killed.

Thank God they hadn't found Frederic's body here or anywhere else as they searched this morning. He could still hope they'd find his squire in some loft or hayrick, sleeping off a night of too much drinking. Or in some peasant girl's arms, sheepish and repentant—or even un-repentant, as long as he was alive. "Still make it twenty men?" he asked Robb.

"Aye, more or less."

"Spread out and search," Bayard ordered the rest of his men. "Robb, I want you to take a good look at any hoofprints, in case there are any nicks or other ways to identify the shoes of the horses those men used. Find the shoe, find the horse, find the men—I hope. The rest of you, tell me of anything unusal, no matter how unimpor-tant it may seem, especially any sign that Frederic—or anyone else—passed this way. We'll go from here back to the meadow where Dunstan's body was found."

The men did as they were told and Bayard did the same, starting at the tree. The lower branches were, un-fortunately, of a perfect height for a man's outstretched arms, and it was clear from the blood on those branches that Dunstan had been tied there as if he were being crucified.

And more. Much more.

The poor man. The poor, poor man. *I'll find them, Dunstan*, he silently vowed. *By God, I'll find them, and they'll suffer for what they did. I give you my word.*

"My lord!"

Alfric waved from the other side of the clearing.

"What is it?" Bayard called out as he ran across the glade, his broadsword slapping against his thigh, his mail jingling.

Alfric pointed at something on the ground. After studying it a moment, Bayard bent and picked it up.

It was hair. Thick, curling, brown hair.

"I thought it might be Dunstan's," Alfric said, his voice rough with suppressed horror. "You know, because of what they did to him."

"The color's wrong," Bayard replied, relieved that it was too dark to be Frederic's, either. I think it was a beard."

He called the other men and showed them the ball of hair. "Any guesses who might have shaved this from his face?"

No answer was forthcoming, and he supposed that had been too much to hope for. It was a common color, after all.

"Has anyone found anything else?" he asked.

The men shook their heads.

"Keep searching," he said grimly.

CHAPTER SEVENTEEN

ARRIVING BACK AT THE CASTLE after dusk, hungry, and cold, and wet, Bayard tossed his reins to Ned, who hurried from the stable to meet the patrol. Lindall came out of the hall, carrying a torch that spluttered in the damp air, although the rain itself had stopped.

"Any word of Frederic?" Bayard asked as he dismounted.

"No, my lord," Lindall replied with a shake of his large head. "I had men search the village and the castle, and nobody saw him. Little Teddy, Hale's son, saw a cart with two men in it going through the village early this morning, though."

Removing his helmet, Bayard raised a brow. "How early?"

"Crack o' dawn. Seems the boy's a light sleeper. He heard a rumble and looked out to see what it was."

"Who was driving the cart?"

"Don't know, my lord, and that's a bit odd. They was wearing hooded cloaks and the cart was full o' wood. Sounds like Ben's cart—he's a charcoal burner—but he don't come to the village except on market days. If the men were talking, Teddy couldn't hear 'em."

"Nobody else saw this cart?"

"No, my lord." Lindall scratched his chin. "I have to tell you, my lord, little Teddy likes to make up stories.

Not that I'm sayin' he's lyin'—might be he dreamed it and thinks it real, especially if he wants to help, see?"

"I want the charcoal burner and his cart found."

"Aye, my lord." Lindall hesitated. "I guess you didn't find nothing, either, my lord?"

"We found the camp where the men who murdered Dunstan did the deed," Bayard replied as they started toward the hall, splashing through the puddles left by the rain that had probably ruined any chance of discovering the murderer's trail.

He related the location to Lindall, who whistled through his teeth. "Clever bastards, eh?"

"We also found this," Bayard said, pulling the wad of damp hair from his belt. "Any clue as to whose beard this might have been?"

"That's a beard?"

"I believe so, yes."

Lindall frowned and scratched his grizzled chin. "Nobody I know's cut off his beard lately."

Bayard sighed and left Lindall to his task. It had been a slim hope to expect that what was left of beard, especially of hair of that color, would be much use.

He considered the two men in a cart. Frederic had left Averette alone, but that didn't mean he had remained alone. Who might have joined him, or whom could he have gone to meet? A woman? Except that Teddy said it was two men. Surely a little boy could tell if it had been a man or a woman in the cart.

The villains who'd killed Dunstan traveled in a pack, like ravening wolves, but that didn't mean they stayed together. Nevertheless, Bayard couldn't believe the squire would be in league with such men. It was much more likely that he'd started to the village on some other purpose and been abducted. Why, then, had he not been struggling, or tied up in the cart? Why, then, would he have left the castle in the first place?

Or it could be that the people in the cart were harmless farmers, or peddlers, or travelers, simply going about their business.

Worried about his squire's fate, angry for not protecting the lad, and for not realizing that he might be upset enough to do something rash or foolhardy, Bayard shoved open the door to the hall. Most of the soldiers and servants had already eaten their evening meal, along with Father Matthew, who was probably now in the chapel saying more prayers for Dunstan's soul.

Bayard hoped he was praying for Frederic's safety, too.

Only a few torches lit the large chamber. Some of the soldiers were already asleep on their pallets on the floor; several more lounged about, tending to their armor or talking quietly or playing drafts. They glanced up when he entered and nodded a greeting as he passed.

There were candles on the table on the dais, and food waiting. There, too, was Gillian, standing with her hands folded and a concerned expression, like a statue of an anxious woman against the colorful backdrop of the tapestry.

As usual she wore the simplest of gowns, this one of light-blue wool. Her girdle of plain leather rested on her hips and her scarf was a white linen square. No cosmetics marred the natural lustre of her skin, and lips, and eyes, although her cheeks lacked the pink blush of good health they'd had the day he first arrived and furrows of concern had left their mark on her forehead.

If only he could bring her good news. That they'd found Frederic alive and well, or that they'd caught the men who'd killed Dunstan. That the conspirators had all been found and there was no immediate danger for her or her tenants, or that her wandering sister was on her way home.

Instead, all he had was a handful of hair.

"You didn't find Frederic," she said when he reached the dais and she gestured for him to sit.

"No," he replied as she poured him some mulled wine. "We didn't find the men who killed Dunstan, either, although we did discover where they did the deed, and something else that might help us."

"What?" she asked as he gratefully drank, the warmth nearly as welcome as her presence.

As she sat beside him, he told her about finding the valley and then the tree, and the blood, and the hair.

"What color was the hair?" she asked.

"Like a doe's hide." He reached into his belt and produced it.

She frowned as she studied it. "That could be Charles de Fenelon's beard."

"Who?"

"A wine merchant who came here recently, supposedly from London. Today I discovered that he cheated me. Several barrels were full of water. But why would a wine…?"

As his suspicions of the man's identity grew, her eyes widened with comprehension. "He wasn't a wine merchant."

"I doubt it, and I think I can guess who it might be. What did this bogus merchant look like, apart from the beard?"

"Shorter than you—about Frederic's height. Slender, well dressed. His hair was long and rather scruffy, which was odd, now that I think of it, for he was very neat otherwise."

"His speech? Educated? Cultured?"

"Educated, but not overly so. But if he'd spoken like a nobleman or courtier, I would have been suspicious, so perhaps he disguised his speech."

If it was the man Bayard believed it might be, he surely had. "Was he handsome?"

She flushed, a hint of color coming to her too-pale cheeks. "Comely, and far too flattering."

Bayard curled a lip. "It was probably Richard d'Artage, the man who was in league with Sir Francis de Farnby at court. He's clever, and sly, and likely quite capable of such a ruse."

"If he *was* this Richard d'Artage, do you think he could have murdered Dunstan?"

"Not by himself, but he could certainly be behind it."

"Sweet Mother," she said softly. "I've been *such* a fool!"

It took a great effort not to touch her hand. "How could you have guessed that one of the king's enemies might disguise himself as a wine merchant and come alone to Averette? If someone had suggested that to me, I would have said he was mad—or ought to be a bard. And if *you* are guilty of being remiss, what am I? I should have kept better watch on Frederic."

Not wanting her to dwell on her mistake, he tore off a piece of bread from a loaf in a basket and nodded at the trencher in front of her. "Have you eaten?"

She gave a little shake of her head. "I was waiting for you," she said, ladling them both some stew made of beef, leeks and beans. "Do you think Frederic could be this d'Artage's confederate?"

That possibility hadn't occurred to him, but there was a chance it was so. Frederic was young, eager, deter-

mined to make a name for himself—much as he had
been before he swore his oath to John.

"It's certainly possible," Bayard admitted. "I thought
that he'd never met Richard, but perhaps I was wrong
and he has. It could be Frederic's been in league with
him all along."

She looked as sick as he felt. If he'd brought a traitor
into Averette—!

"Do you think he was involved in Dunstan's death?"
she whispered.

He forced his mind to function, to consider the like-
lihood. "Frederic might have known what Richard
planned, but he wasn't there when Dunstan was killed.
He couldn't have been. We'd have known he was gone,
and he was so sick when he saw the body, it had to be
a shock to him. Thank God for that, at least. But if he's
with those traitors, I unknowingly brought a viper into
your home and for that, I'm deeply sorry."

Regardless of who might see, she reached out and
took his hand. "You looked for the best in him, not the
worst. I've made serious misjudgements, too."

His gaze met and held hers, and in that moment of
shared dismay, sympathy, and understanding, their bond
strengthened and grew.

Whether they wished it or not.

Then he withdrew his hand and they finished their
meal in silence.

LATER THAT NIGHT, GILLIAN paced in her chamber illuminated by one flickering candle. Outside, a sliver of
a moon hung in the sky, and she could hear the guards
exchanging muffled greetings as they passed. Otherwise,
all was silence.

And loneliness, haunting her as it had so many times

in her life, as if she were a fairy princess locked in a tower.

Often in her childhood, when her anxiety grew too great and she couldn't get away to the village, she'd go up to the roof of the keep and huddle behind a merlon, the raised part of the wall behind which archers would duck after taking their shot. She'd tell herself that an evil witch had put a spell on Averette and she was trapped. But one day, she would find a way to break the spell, and then she would be free.

Not only that, she would find herself beautiful and charming, too, even more than her sisters. She would no longer be grim, gray Gillian, the mouse in the corner.

After their father had died and she'd made her promise with her sisters, it had been as if the spell had lifted. She was free—as free as a noblewoman could be, even if she wasn't beautiful and charming. She had been happy and content, thrilled to finally be mistress of Averette.

And then Bayard had come, at first to frustrate and annoy her, then to make her feel respected and admired and finally, desirable.

So much so, and her own passionate longings had been so roused, that she kept recalling what Lizette had said after she'd made her promise. "We haven't vowed to be celibate." And then, being Lizette, she'd laughed.

They had not promised to be celibate.

She would, of course, be celibate, she'd thought then. Since James had died, who else would want her? Who else would see her as anything other than the lesser of her sisters?

Shoving her hands into the cuffs of her bedrobe, she went to the window and looked out at the night sky, and then at the darkened village.

She knew who *she* wanted, as much as she wanted to stay in Averette. And who, apparently, wanted her.

The 'Gyptian lover, who had his sport and moved on. Who offered and accepted love with no commitments.

If she went to him now, what would he say? What would he do?

Marriage was out of the question and any other union a sin, but her heart demanded that she give in to the fierce yearning within her, that she take what love she could while she had the chance, if he was willing.

And if he was not?

If he was better, stronger, more honorable than she?

How would she know unless she went to him?

Did she dare to do that? Was she bold enough, strong enough, determined enough, to ask for what she wanted with all her heart and take whatever consequences came her way?

Or was there too much to lose?

BAYARD ROSE, SLEEPLESS, from his bed. He couldn't stand another moment staring at the bed curtains, his mind and heart in turmoil.

Outside, rain was falling again, splashing against the stone walls. Where was Frederic? Was he alive or dead? Dry or miserably soaking? Safe, or did he deserve to suffer?

Had that hair belonged to Richard d'Artage? If so, where was that miscreant now? Was he one of the band who'd tortured, killed, and mutilated Dunstan? If Frederic was with them, was he an ally or a prisoner? Would they be able to find some sign of them in the morning, or would any trail be washed away, too hard for even Robb to find?

A soft, familiar sound interrupted Bayard's ruminations and he half turned to see the door to his chamber open slowly. Cautiously.

Grabbing his scabbard, he slid his sword from the sheath.

CHAPTER EIGHTEEN

IT WAS NO ENEMY ASSASSIN who came creeping into Bayard's bedchamber. It was Gillian, clad in a scarlet bedrobe, her hair unbound and falling about her slender figure. She stiffened when she saw him, until he sheathed his sword and put it back on top of the chest.

She closed the door behind her and clasped her hands. Her robe was of soft wool, her feet dressed in fur-lined doeskin slippers, and she looked so vulnerable and lost, he wanted to take her in his arms and hold her close and promise he would always protect her.

Instead, he said, "What are you doing here?"

She came a little closer. "I wanted to…to see you. I was very careful and it's very dark. Please, Bayard, let me stay a little while. I don't want to be alone tonight."

If she'd been stern and commanding, he might have found the strength to make her leave, but at her softly spoken, heartfelt words, his own heart had not the will to make her to go.

He went to the table near the window. He'd brought some wine from the hall, as well as a heel of bread and bit of cheese in case he had more of an appetite in the night. "Are you hungry? You didn't eat much earlier."

"No."

"We'll find Richard and his men if they're anywhere nearby," he assured her, thinking her worries must have propelled her here. "If Frederic's with them, we'll find him, too."

She didn't reply, and he realized that if she stayed here, so vulnerable and so sad, he wouldn't be able to resist touching her. "I'm sorry, Gillian, but I think it might be best…that it's necessary…that it would be better if you were to go."

"I don't want to give you any more guilt or cause for remorse," she said, walking toward him, "but I want to stay, Bayard."

She looked up at him, her eyes glistening not with tears, but…hope? "I want *you*."

Stunned by her declaration, he stood motionless as she put her arms around him, raised herself on her toes, and kissed him.

"I want to love you," she whispered. "I want you to make love with me. I don't ask for marriage, for that would be impossible anyway. I don't ask anything of you at all, except that you let me stay. Take me to your bed tonight."

Bayard's questioning gaze searched her face, seeking… what? Truth? Honesty? He would find it, for she'd just spoken the truth of her heart.

He frowned. "I told you, my lady, I'm not the lascivious cad men think me."

God help her, she hadn't meant to hurt him. "I know that you're an honorable man. I've watched how you treat the women of my household. I've come to see that you're a good and noble man, in the best sense of the word, or I would not be here. I know what I ask is sinful and immoral, but I cannot bear the thought of never being with you, not even once. To never experience pleasure in your arms, loving you and being loved."

She straightened her shoulders and faced him squarely,

resolutely. "If you're reluctant because you think I'm a virgin, I tell you now, I'm not. I loved another once, years ago, and before he died, I gave him my maidenhead."

Surprise flared in his eyes and then something more, something that set the desire dancing in her blood, that told her he was tempted.

"Will you send me away, Bayard? Will you force me to endure the pain of this night alone and lonely, as I have been all my life?" she asked, going closer to him. "Please, Bayard, if you care for me, let me stay. Love me, even just this once."

"God's blood, Gillian, I've never wanted a woman as much as I want you," he said, shaking his head and backing away. "You're temptation itself to me. But what of your reputation? What if you get with child? I've seen the way bastards and the women who bear them are treated, and I won't risk such a fate befalling you, or any child of mine."

She met his gaze steadily. "No one need know we're lovers. No one except you knows about James. And if I should get with child, the people of Averette love me and so do my sisters. I would be safe here, and so would our child."

"While I would be believed to be the cad too many men already think I am."

She realized then how selfish she had been to come here. "I ask too much," she said. "I ask you to dishonor yourself, and that's wrong of me. I'll leave you now, in peace."

With what dignity she could muster, she started for the door—until he took hold of her arm to stop her.

"Peace?" he repeated, his eyes full of longing and anguish. "What peace can there be for me now, without you? You've captured my heart. You have my future hostage in your hands, for what would I not give to be with you, this night and all the rest to come? If you're willing to risk so much for love, can I do less?

"Because I love you, Gillian, as I've never loved a woman, or thought I could. I've never really known love, until I came here and fell in love with you.

"Stay with me," he murmured as he pulled her into his arms. "Because God help us both, I cannot let you go."

Then he kissed her with all the love, all the passion, he felt. The restraints he'd tried to put on his emotions fell away. Instead, the love and longing he'd been trying to deny and keep under fierce control burst free.

He held her close, the sensation of her lithe, strong body against his beyond exhilarating. He wanted her as much as he wanted air and light and happiness. He had done almost nothing to encourage her, and some things to dissuade her. He was innocent of any attempt at seduction. She had come to him. She must love him, as he loved her.

She returned his kiss with fervent passion. Not as a coy woman pretending she was reluctant, like the ladies of the court. Not as a tavern wench, whose mind was calculating what she'd do with the money he would pay. Nor as a woman who thought him only a handsome bauble to do with as she would, to discard when she grew weary, with no thought for his heart.

Excited by her enthusiasm, he slid his mouth from hers, along the soft curve of her cheek, toward the dangling lobe of her ear, while her lips worked their magic on his skin.

"Take me to your bed," she whispered. "Please, Bayard."

"Gladly," he murmured as he swept her into his arms,

the weight of her almost nothing, his blood thrumming
through his body as he carried her to the curtained
bed.

He set her there, then she reached up and pulled him
down beside her. Anxious to feel him within her, to love
and forget the troubles surrounding them, she pulled his
shirt over his head. His body was truly marvelous—more
muscled than James's boyish body had been. His chest
was scarred, his flesh bearing many little marks from
training and battle, like the long thin scar on his face
that did nothing to diminish his appearance.

She captured his mouth with hers and began to undo
the drawstring of his breeches, and when she worked her
hand into inside she realized he was magnificent there,
too.

A rumble between a growl and a groan sounded deep
in his throat and he moved so that he lay between her
legs while his mouth took hers with fierce need.

With his weight on his left forearm and his knees,
his right hand found her breast. He stroked her lightly,
opening her bedrobe to reach inside, the thin fabric of
her shift brushing her sensitive nipples.

Her hands caressed his broad back, his narrow hips,
his ribs and nipples, making him moan with pleasure and
adding to her own. His tongue slipped between her lips
and his hand slid down to the hem of her shift. Slowly,
he pushed it up toward her hips, adding to the building,
exciting expectation within her.

She was moist and ready, fully aware of what was
to come and that this time, there should be none of the
pain or blood that had so upset James. He hadn't been
ignorant, but the sight of the blood upon her thighs had
disturbed him far more than the pain had upset her.

Poor James. So young and so naive, stammering out

his declarations of devotion and trying to love her without really knowing how.

Not like Bayard—mature, certain, admirable, and brave. Kind, generous, and fallible, as she was, and whose hands moved with such delicious, delightful skill.

She stroked his broad shoulders, his back, the muscles beneath his skin moving and shifting, reminding her of the power contained in his virile body.

He pushed her shift up to her belly, and then his hands were below her navel, caressing there, too. She arched, bringing her body hard against his hand, and he laughed, a low deep rumble of joy and delight. "Impatient?" he whispered, raising himself to look at her face.

She shifted and reached for him. "For this," she agreed, placing him at her entrance and then, keeping her eyes on his face, she pushed herself forward, and him inside.

He closed his eyes and groaned, lying still for a moment until he pushed back, filling her more completely, making her moan with pleasure and an unspoken demand for more. Again he took her mouth, urgent and seeking.

More excitement, more need, more urgency followed. She raised and lowered her hips with the rhythm of his thrusts and wrapped her legs about him to bring him closer. She found his nipples and brushed her palms across them, until he was gasping, his neck corded with the growing tension.

She felt him grow harder, larger. His thrusts became more potent and powerful. Soon there was no thought, no consciousness. Only excitement and delight, pleasure and passion.

He gripped her shoulders, and the sinews of his neck tightened with every push, his body tense as the tension grew within her, too. Panting, sighing, moaning, any coherent thought fled. All she knew was the incredible sensation of Bayard loving her, filling her, the power of his body making hers tauten as if she were a bowstring and he the archer drawing her closer and closer until...

Gasping, she rose and fell, bucked and squirmed, her toes curling, her hands gripping his shoulders as she clenched her teeth to keep from screaming with the sheer joy of it.

As she held him in the throes of ecstasy, Bayard stiffened and groaned, and filled her in another way.

James had been tentative, fumbling in the dark, a boy trying to be a man. Bayard was...Bayard was everything a man should be. Everything.

And finally, here in this man's bed and in his arms, she finally, fully understood Adelaide's decision.

And truly realized how much she would lose when Bayard went away.

LATER THAT NIGHT, although still before dawn, Gillian lay with her head on Bayard's chest and twisted a lock of his dark hair around her finger. She couldn't linger much longer; it was time to make her careful, cautious way back to her own chamber and then spend the day pretending she was not in love with Bayard and hadn't lain most of the night in his arms.

Bayard chuckled, the sound deep and delightful. "You're going to pull my hair right out of my head if you're not careful," he said, smiling at her as he slid his hand along the curve of her shoulder.

"Perhaps I should, if you're going to wear it so long," she replied, raising herself on her elbow to look into his face. "Why do you?"

"Because I like the way it looks." He rolled onto his

side, his thigh brushing against her leg in a way that set her blood tingling. "Don't you like the way I look?"

"Peacock, you know I do. But it's so…untidy."

"And my lady likes things tidy."

Gillian reached up to brush his hair back from his face, "Not *always*. I can certainly see the appeal of your hair, and this is rather attractive, too," she noted, tracing his scar with her fingertip. "It makes you look…less civilized."

"And that's attractive?"

"Very. How did you get it? Battle? A melee?"

He tucked a lock of her straight hair behind her ear and ruefully shook his head. "Falling out of a tree."

She stared at him incredulously. "You fell out of a tree?"

"Not recently," he said with apparent gravity. "When I was a boy. Armand used to steal apples from the orchard of a monastery near Lord Raymond's castle. He'd share them with me and our friend Randall. One day, I decided I could steal apples, too, and I climbed up the vines growing on the monastery wall. That was how Armand always got into the orchard.

"I managed that all right enough and I got up in one of the trees. By that time, I was quite proud of myself, I'll admit. Then, when I was reaching out to twist off an apple, I lost my grip and fell. There was a broken branch and it tore my cheek open. I wailed like a stuck pig. And blood? Oh, sweet savior, I bled! The poor monk who ran out to find me nearly swooned at the sight.

"He gathered me up and took me inside, and one of the brothers gave me something to make me sleep. When I woke up, I was home again, my cheek stitched up as neatly as any nun could do."

He leaned down to lightly kiss her bare shoulder. As

always when they kissed, desire blossomed and her body relaxed, warm, and mellow, and welcoming. She slipped her leg over his and inched closer, her naked breasts against the bare flesh of his chest.

"It's late," Bayard cautioned, his breathing none too steady.

A soft knock sounded on the door. "My lady?" Dena called out, her voice muffled by the thick wood.

Gillian grabbed her shift at the foot of the bed. How had Dena known where to find her? What did she want at this hour?

Where could she hide?

Bayard scrambled from the bed and reached for his breeches on the floor. "What do you want?" he called out.

"Is Lady Gillian within? I went to her chamber and she's gone and I thought—"

"No!" he lied.

But Gillian knew something was wrong. She could hear the distress in Dena's weak voice, and the girl's panic. She threw on her shift and pushed past Bayard to throw open the door.

Her face ghastly pale, her skirt bloody, Dena leaned against the wall. "I'm sorry to trouble you my lady, but… but I'm bleeding," she whispered.

"Bayard!" Gillian cried as Dena started to slip to the floor.

He was beside her in an instant. "Help me get her to the bed!"

He gathered Dena up into his arms and carried her to his bed, setting her gently upon it.

Gillian quickly checked to see if Dena had been stabbed or otherwise wounded, but it wasn't that.

"It's the babe," she said to Bayard, who was hovering anxiously nearby. "I fear it's lost."

And she had to get the bleeding stopped or Dena could die, too.

"Go to my chamber," she said to him, "and bring me my box of medicines. You'll find it in the big chest near the door. It's painted blue. Send a servant to the kitchen and have the green jug I use for potions filled with boiling water. Get one of the maids to fetch a bucket of warm water from the kitchen to wash her, and another of cold, as well. I need clean linen—lots of it. And three bundles of straw from the stable. This featherbed will be soon ruined."

As Bayard finished dressing and left the chamber, Gillian went to the washstand and poured what was left of the water in the ewer into the basin. She grabbed every piece of linen there and went back to the bed.

Some of the linen she folded and put beneath Dena. The rest she used to wash and dry Dena as gently and carefully as she could, removing the bloody clothes and the sad confirmation of her loss before she dressed Dena in one of Bayard's clean shirts she got from the chest.

As she took away one square of soaked linen and laid another beneath, Dena's eyes fluttered open. With a pitiable groan, she clutched her belly and drew her knees up to her chest. "I'm dying!" she whimpered. "I've sinned and now I'm dying."

Not if I can save you, Gillian thought, silently praying.

"I'll look after you," she said softly, gently forcing Dena to lower her legs. "I've sent Bayard for my medicines. I know just what you need. Lady's mantle to stop the bleeding and willow bark to take away the pain. You'll be feeling better soon, Dena."

The girl regarded her with stricken eyes. "And my baby?"

Gillian was unfortunately certain of the answer she had to give the poor girl. She leaned down and looked at her with sympathy and regret. "With God in Heaven."

The girl let out a pitiable moan and began to sob.

Gillian rose and went to the door to look for Bayard. He soon appeared at the top of the steps with her blue box in his hands.

"Give that to me, and leave us," she said quietly, fighting to maintain her composure as she took it from his hands. "This is women's business."

He nodded and started to turn, then hesitated. "I was too upset about the girl to be cautious and I fear everyone will realize we were together."

"That can't be helped," Gillian said. She couldn't think about that now. She had to take care of Dena. "I'm just glad Dena came here to find me."

They heard approaching footsteps and the hushed whispers of several women. While Bayard hurried down the corridor to another set of stairs leading to the yard, Gillian hurried back into the chamber.

Seltha arrived, carrying a jug wrapped in a cloth—the boiled water, surely. Others came behind her, crowding into the chamber and trying to see over each others' shoulders.

"Put the jug on the table," Gillian ordered Seltha. "Joanna, the warm and cold water should be by the bed. Linens here on this stool. And then you all can go."

Gillian took one of the clean cloths and a goblet from the table. She wiped the goblet out and poured some of the very hot water from the green jug into it, although this tincture wouldn't be for drinking. She got her medicine box and found the small clay vessel covered with waxed cloth that held the dried lady's mantle. She took a small pouch made of loosely woven linen from the box and put the herbs inside, then dipped it into the goblet of water that, while no longer boiling, was still very hot.

By now, the women had done what she'd told them. "Seltha, find out who's bringing the straw and tell him to hurry. The rest of you, be about your business."

"But my lady, it's not even lauds," Seltha pointed out.

"Then you can all go back to sleep—quietly."

The women did as they were told, but not quietly. They spoke in awed and scandalized whispers. Gillian was quite sure they would be talking and speculating about what they'd seen until the sun rose and their duties really began.

She would deal with that later. For now, she had to tend to Dena, whose life depended on her, the effectiveness of her potion to stop the bleeding, and a merciful God.

CHAPTER NINETEEN

SHORTLY AFTER THE NOON, after having retrieved two horses hidden a short distance from the village and abandoning the wagon and nag that Richard had stolen from a filthy charcoal burner whose corpse had been shoved into his own smoking pyre, Frederic and the rebellious nobleman entered a clearing in the wood on the far eastern border of the estate of Averette.

"We can rest here awhile," Richard said, dismounting. "We'll have to spend a few nights living like outlaws, I'm afraid. A small hardship, sure to be rewarded later."

"Do you really plan to kill Bayard?" Frederic asked, getting down from the saddle and stepping directly into a mud puddle.

"How else to get his brother away from the court and the king?" Richard replied. "We must be rid of those two, and a few others, if our plan is to succeed."

Frederic looped his horse's reins over a hawthorn bush. "What about Lady Gillian and her sisters?"

"They're noblewomen. Of course they'll be treated with all due courtesy."

"And the other women back at Averette? They won't be hurt or killed?"

"If you're worried about that girl you got with child, have no fear. She'll be safe. Perhaps you can ask for her as part of your reward when we triumph."

At the far edge of the glade, leaves rustled although

there was no wind, and men began appearing in the clearing, coming out of the trees like materializing spirits.

Or demons, for they were big, hulking brutes, dressed in a motley collection of mail, armor and leather. They were all bearded and broad-shouldered, and very well armed—and those were only the weapons one could see. Richard didn't doubt they each carried more that he couldn't. Many were scarred and several were missing an eye or an ear or a finger.

"What's the meaning of this?" Frederic demanded, fumbling as he tried to pull out his sword. "Who are these men?"

Richard put his hand on the youth's arm to stop him from drawing his weapon before one of Wimarc's mercenaries killed him. "Confederates of mine," he explained, "so have no fear. They mean *you* no harm."

The youth frowned as Ullric and his men came closer. "They're the ones who killed Dunstan, aren't they?"

"Yes, they are," Richard calmly admitted. "I wanted to learn a few things about Castle Averette, which must have secret passageways and hidden entrances. Unfortunately, my companions got a bit carried away by their enthusiasm for their work. Dunstan died before we learned anything useful."

"I don't know anything about secret passageways or entrances," Frederic declared, looking a little paler.

"I didn't think you did, since you're merely a guest. As it happens, we have another, more knowledgeable source of information about Averette," Richard replied, nodding as another man appeared, one dressed in finer mail and the colors of a soldier of Averette.

"So here's where you got to, young squire," Lindall remarked to the astonished, gaping Frederic. "Shut your gob, boy, before a bug flies in it."

"What…what are you doing here? I thought you were loyal to Lady Gillian."

"And I thought you were loyal to Sir Bayard," Lindall returned.

Frederic drew himself up. "Sir Bayard was not worth my loyalty."

"No man is, or woman, either," the soldier replied, hawking and spitting on the muddy ground. "A man's got to look out for himself in this world, and a loyal man's a dead man—or a poor one," he added, giving Richard a significant look.

The nobleman reached into his belt and produced a leather pouch. Coins clinked within as he offered it to the soldier. "So, what news?"

"Bayard's sending out more patrols, smaller ones. Only ten men each."

That brought a gleam to Richard d'Artage's eyes, and he gestured for Ullric to come closer. "Hear that, Ullric? Only ten."

The Saxon nodded and grinned, exposing what was left of his teeth.

"Bayard and his patrol are going south along the river today, north tomorrow if they don't find anything," Lindall added as he counted the silver coins.

He glanced at Frederic. "Better hope they don't catch you, boy, or it'll be prison and a traitor's death for you."

"It'll be the same for you," Frederic shot back.

"What evidence has anybody got against me? The word of traitors?"

"That money."

"My *earnings* and I'm not so daft to take it to my quarters. They'll find nothing there to say I'm in league with rebels."

"How did you leave the castle? Where do they think you are?"

"I'm second in command. My men don't ask me where I'm going." Lindall snatched the wineskin from Richard's saddle. "God's blood, I'm parched. Next time, I'll be bringing my horse closer."

"Do that and you might have to walk back," Richard said. "I'm not going to get caught because you're too lazy to walk a mile."

Lindall frowned, then took a swig of wine before running a measuring gaze over Frederic. "So, what made you a rebel? Upset over that bit o' skirt?"

"Of course not!"

"Then you won't mind me havin' a taste. I'll tell her I love her, if that's what makes her spread her legs."

He frowned when he saw Frederic's expression. "What, you think now she's had a nobleman, she's too good for the likes o' me?"

The man's jeering laugh was even more disgusting than betraying his lady for money. "Dena's a whore, like all women, and if she's got notions otherwise, she'll find out the truth soon enough, especially now that she's lost the brat you put in her belly."

"What?"

Lindall laughed. "Look at 'im with his long face. Might almost think he cared."

"Is Dena going to be all right?"

"Word is she'll live," Lindall said dismissively after another long swig of wine. He gave Richard a smirk. "Speaking of whores, you were dead right about Lady Gillian, my lord. Dena had to go to Bayard's bedchamber to find Lady Gillian when she started to bleed.

"And her always actin' so high and mighty," he

sneered. "If my lady's father were alive, he'd flay the skin off her back—and rightly, too, the slut."

"Enough!" Richard declared. "Get back to the castle before you're missed. Frederic, take care of our horses. Ullric, with me. We've got some planning to do."

HEARING A SOFT RAP on the door, Gillian rose from the stool beside Bayard's bed. Rubbing her neck and arching her back that ached from leaning over to tend to Dena, she opened the door and found Bayard waiting.

"How is she?" he asked, glancing at the pale figure in the bed.

"She'll be well, I think, thank God. It didn't take as long as I feared it might to stop the bleeding."

"She was lucky you knew what to do."

"And had the medicine to do it. It was fortunate that Dena is young, and strong, and otherwise healthy, although she's upset about losing the baby."

Bayard sighed and leaned against the doorframe. "I thought she might be relieved, given the way Frederic treated her."

"No, she wanted the baby. Very much, I think."

They looked at each other, each thinking about what would happen if Gillian were to get with child. Gillian knew it would cause a scandal and her reputation would be ruined, but she wasn't afraid.

Bayard could easily imagine the children they might have—bold, saucy maidens and strong, stalwart sons—and how much he would love them.

"I don't want to disturb Dena," he said at last, "but I need my armor. We're late riding out as it is."

"Poor Dena's lost so much blood, it would take more than a little noise to wake her," Gillian replied, moving back from the door to let him enter. "Since you have no squire, I'll help you."

Nodding, he went to the wooden chest that held his mail and surcoat and opened the lid, letting it rest against the wall. He pulled out his padded gambeson. He didn't need any help to put on that garment worn beneath his mail. He also didn't need Gillian's assistance to tie the mail hosen that would protect his legs.

"I've decided we have to have more patrols to cover more ground in our search," he said quietly as she helped him with his hauberk. "I'm sending the men out in groups of ten and telling them to stay within the call of a horn. That way, should one patrol be attacked, the others can come to their aid."

She nodded as she lifted the garment of chain mail that covered his torso. It fell to his knees and also had sleeves and coif attached, so it was the heaviest piece of armor he wore.

"It's good you're not a weak woman," Bayard noted as he stuck his arms and head through the appropriate openings. "Otherwise, I'd have to lie down and crawl into this."

"You may yet," she replied.

Fortunately, he didn't have to resort to that. When he had on the hauberk, he raised the coif over his head, then lifted the ventail that protected his neck into place and tied it with the leather thong. She, meanwhile, brought him his helmet, a fine piece of metalwork, albeit marred by a few dents.

"Don't worry, Gillian," he said when he saw her run her finger over the largest in the crown. "I did that myself. I dropped it."

He smiled, although not with any real joy, and she

wondered if that was really true, or if he was saying that in an attempt to cheer her.

It was useless, but she appreciated the effort. "I hope you'll be more careful with both your helmet and your head today, my lord."

"I'll try," he vowed with another smile.

After he had put on his surcoat and buckled his sword belt around his waist and had his long shield over his left arm, she said, "You *will* be careful, won't you? You won't take any foolish chances?"

"With you waiting here for me? No, I've never felt I had more reason to live," he assured her. "But I don't like leaving you here alone."

"You fear an attack?"

"I'm sure if that happens, Lindall can hold it off until the rest of us return. I was thinking that everyone in Castle Averette will know about our liaison. It'll be only a short time before everyone in the village knows, too."

He didn't have to tell her what difficulties she could face then.

"Compared to the risk you face if you encounter the men who killed Dunstan, it seems little enough," she replied, meaning it.

"It still won't be pleasant," he said, reaching for her hands and holding them tight.

She regarded him defiantly. "I can manage the looks and whispers here. Surely no one will dare to cast aspersions to my face."

"When you look like that," he said with a wistful smile as he drew her close for a farewell kiss, "I doubt even the king would try."

CHAPTER TWENTY

As BAYARD FEARED, gossip, and rumor, and speculation ran rampant in Averette before he even rode out
the gate.

It began with the maidservants who'd been summoned
to fetch and carry in the middle of the night. They told
Umbert and the kitchen servants that Dena was dying
in Sir Bayard's bedchamber, and that wasn't the only
shocking thing. Lady Gillian had been there, too—in
her bedrobe and shift!

The significance of that was unmistakable and soon
talk of an illicit liaison between the handsome knight and
the lady of Averette spread through the castle. A farmer
bringing fodder for the cows heard the news from a maid
servant and in short order the village was buzzing with
the story.

Gillian had guessed how bad the gossip would be, but
that didn't make it any easier to accept the difference in
the household's behavior toward her after she left Seltha
to care for Dena and go about her daily duties. Although
no one stared with undisguised scorn or was directly
insolent, she heard the murmurs and whispers after she
passed by. Several of the women didn't meet her gaze
when she spoke to them, and a few openly smirked as
she gave them their orders for the day.

The soldiers, too, didn't regard her with their usual
deference. One or two were barely respectful.

In spite of their manner, she held her head high and went about her business as if nothing were amiss. She pretended she didn't notice anything different and that nothing had changed, even though it had, for her as well as for them.

Not only had she been blissfully happy last night and again this morning with Bayard, she'd felt truly content. She'd believed herself to be so before he came, yet what she felt this morning, nestled in his arms, had been deeper and richer than anything she'd known before, even at her happiest here in Averette.

Nevertheless, it was a long, difficult day. Anxious to know that Bayard had returned safe, she went to wait for him and his patrol in the outer bailey.

When she saw them returning at dusk with Bayard at the head, she realized with even more dismay that they must have had no success. Every man was slumped in the saddle; even the horses seemed exhausted.

Seeing her waiting inside the barbican, Bayard waved a hand before he dismounted, gave his horse's reins to Robb and walked toward her.

"You're a welcome sight, my lady," he said with the ghost of a smile as he removed his helmet and put it in the crook of his arm.

She was too upset to smile back. "As are you," she said as he fell into step beside her. "I was worried about you."

"I can take care of myself, my lady. I've been concerned about you, though. Talk can be more difficult to deal with than a heavily armed opponent in a melee."

She didn't want him to feel any more guilt, so she tried to make light of what had been happening. "It could have been worse," she said as they reached the inner gate.

Elmer and Alfric were on guard. They took their time

coming to attention and regarded Gillian and Bayard in a way that brought the heat of a blush to her face.

And unbridled rage to Bayard's.

"You insolent dogs, have you forgotten who your mistress is?" Bayard exclaimed, fury in every feature as he grabbed the two startled soldiers and threw them into the courtyard. "This is the Lady of Averette and by God you'll give her the respect that is her due or you'll regret it! *Lindall!*"

The second-in-command appeared in the doorway of the barracks, then jogged toward them as Bayard hauled Elmer and Alfric to their feet.

"My lord?" he asked, looking from the frightened men to the enraged knight.

"I want these two impertinent dogs in the stocks tomorrow. All day—and it'll be the same for any lout who dares treat Lady Gillian with anything less than the proper respect. Do you hear me?"

"Aye, my lord," Lindall said, clearly taken aback by Bayard's rage. "The stocks, aye. All day."

Bayard turned to Gillian. "You should have told me it was as bad as this."

"I knew what to expect," she said quietly.

She should have been a model of propriety; by giving in to her desire, she had lost the right to command complete respect.

In time, after Bayard had gone, she would try to regain it. The people liked her, so that was not an impossible hope, she told herself. "Come. You're exhausted and hungry. I have food and drink prepared for you."

She feared he was going to protest. Mercifully, he didn't. And when she led him not into the hall but to his chamber, he only raised a brow.

"Since everyone knows about last night," she said, "there's no need to keep our feelings a secret."

"I suppose not," he agreed, a little spark of relief in his dark eyes, making her glad she'd had food and drink taken to his chamber.

And something else besides.

Bayard's eyes widened when he saw that a tub lined with linen and half full of water had been placed near a brazier, with three bronze jugs of hot water in the coals to keep their contents warm.

"A bath?"

"I thought you might be sore from spending the day in the saddle."

The exhaustion that had been etched upon his features seemed to fall from him like a cloak and his lips curved up in a smile, heating her more than the brazier.

"I'm feeling much better already," he said, his voice low and husky.

"I'm glad," she replied, trying not to let her passion overwhelm her wish to make him comfortable. "Now off with your armor, Sir Knight."

"With pleasure," he said, removing his helmet.

She took it from him and set it in the chest. When she turned back, his smile was gone, replaced with concern as he sat on the end of the bed.

"This is wonderful, but God help me, Gillian," he said, "you must have had a hellish time today. I expected it to be difficult for you when people realized you were with me last night, but seeing those men looking at you that way—"

"I'm not a little girl, Bayard," she said. "I knew what could happen when I went to your chamber, especially if I stayed."

She lightly brushed a kiss across his lips. "It's all right,

Bayard. I have no regrets. I would do it again, without hesitation."

His eyes flared with relief, and desire. "You would?"

"Gladly," she whispered.

As he rose and pulled her into an embrace, she tilted her head and gave him a pert little smile. "Do you think I'm too weak to deal with soldiers' sneers and scornful servants? That I should run away and hide myself? Or wear sackcloth and ashes and moan about my terrible sins, even though you make me happier than I've ever been in my life?"

"I do?"

"You do."

"You've made me happier than I've ever been, too." He sighed and held her close. "I wish with all my heart that you could be my wife and we could always be together."

She tried to laugh. "I wish we could, too, Bayard. Think of the children we would have, with your good looks and my intelligence."

Although she was trying to make light of their situation, she was suddenly filled with an overwhelming longing to bear his children—handsome, merry sons with broad shoulders and quick wits, or pretty, charming daughters with dark curls and brown eyes.

"I'd give anything to be your husband and the father of your children," he murmured, kissing her cheek and then her lips. "I love you, Gillian. I'll always love you."

As she looked into his eyes, she saw the truth of his words and felt an answering truth within her heart. "As I shall always love you."

He gathered her into his arms and kissed her, his mouth moving with slow, wonderful deliberation over hers. Her heartbeat quickened, and she grew aware of his hard male body against hers, remembering their night together.

And yet... "You'd best take your bath before the water gets cold," she felt compelled to say.

Merriment appeared in his eyes. "Are you concerned about the temperature of the water or do I smell?" he asked.

"Both."

"Now you've hurt my feelings," he replied with a pout. "For that, you have to stay and help me out of my armor."

"With pleasure, my lord."

"Brazen wench," he said, grinning.

"Stand still and let me help you."

"I don't want to stand still," he replied, reaching for her.

She danced out of his reach. "If you don't cooperate, my lord, the water will be freezing by the time you're naked."

"Very well," he muttered, standing motionless long enough for her to lift the hauberk off him.

"I believe, my lady," he remarked as he put it in the chest, "that you simply want me naked as quickly as possible."

"Perhaps I do," she said as she started to unbuckle his gambeson, although he was quite capable of doing that himself.

"Shameless hussy," he growled as he removed the padded jacket.

She sat on the end of the bed.

"What are you doing?" he asked as he took off the mail hosen and added it to the chest.

"Watching, since you seem quite capable of disrobing without any further assistance from me."

"I believe that, as chatelaine, it's your duty to assist me."

"Some duties are much more pleasant than others," she noted as she went to him.

He tugged her into his arms and pressed a kiss upon her neck.

"I can't untie your breeches if you hold me so close," she chided, and then she realized he was doing a little untying of his own. "What are you doing?"

"I don't wish to insult you, my lady, but it seems to me you could use a bath yourself."

"In the same tub?"

He tugged off her scarf and threw it aside, then ran his fingers through her unbound hair. "You have some objections to sharing a tub with me?" he asked as his hand slipped into the back of her loosened bodice to caress her.

"I simply hadn't considered the possibility."

"Does it not appeal to you?" he asked, stepping back to take off his breeches, while she held her gaping bodice to her breasts.

"I must confess I find it very appealing," she admitted.

Especially when he stood naked before her.

"Then take off your gown, and slip off your shift, and join me," he said as he climbed into the tub and eased himself down.

Her blood racing, her heart pounding with anticipation, she wiggled out of her gown. He made her feel so desired, so wanted, so womanly. And wanton.

"Now that's a sight for tired eyes," Bayard said, his voice low and enticing.

Giving him an alluring smile, she slowly lowered one

shoulder of her shift. "Would you like to see more, my lord?"

His eyes dark with yearning, he nodded.

She lowered the other shoulder. "Still more, my lord?"

Another nod.

She took hold of the end of the drawstring at the neck of her shift and pulled the knot undone. Very, very slowly.

He groaned. "Have mercy, Gillian!"

"Mercy, my lord? After you drove me to distraction for days with your handsome face and virile body?"

"I didn't mean to."

"But you did nonetheless," she said as she lowered her shift.

His eyes eagerly followed her garment's progress. "Come here, Gillian," he said in a husky rasp when it fell to the floor.

"We need more hot water."

"My blood's surely heated this water nearly to boiling."

Ignoring him, she walked over to the hearth and brought back another of the ewers. She glanced below the water. "Anxious, are you? I suggest you move to the side. I don't want to burn…anything."

He slid over as she poured the contents of the ewer into the tub. She'd no sooner set the ewer on the floor beside the tub than she heard a sloshing sound and Bayard's hands grabbed her around the waist and lifted her into the tub.

"Bayard!" she cried as she landed on his lap.

"Gillian!" he returned, laughing and moving her so that she was facing him. There was something rather difficult to ignore between them that was not a lump of soap.

He traced the trail of a droplet of water down her cheek from her eye to her lip while a little smile played about his perfect lips. "I'm sorry if I surprised you. I got impatient."

"You're not a bit sorry."

"In truth? No." He leaned forward and brushed his lips across hers, warm and wet. "I want you."

She reached for him and stroked him lightly. "So I see."

He closed his eyes and moaned softly. "You are a very immodest woman, Gillian d'Averette."

"And you're a very insolent man," she replied as his hands began to meander over her body.

"Insolent? I prefer to call it…interested," he said as he leaned forward so that his lips and mouth and tongue went where his hands had been.

She gasped when he sucked her nipple between his lips, then inched closer, her hands slipping around his neck.

"I'm still impatient," he whispered.

"So am I," she gasped, raising herself enough so that he could enter her, then lowering herself slowly. His groan told her he felt the same passionate pleasure when they joined.

Keeping her arms around his neck, she rose and fell as desire overtook her, not insensible to the realization that her breasts were close to his mouth. Neither was he, and as he pleasured them, her need and longing grew and flourished.

It became stronger and more potent. Tense and ardent.

Their breathing quickened to gasps and sighs. Water

splashed over the sides of the tub onto the floor and Gillian's shift left lying there, but they didn't notice. The water cooled but they didn't care, too caught up in their own passion.

And then the glorious release, powerful and overwhelming. Their cries filled the chamber until they stilled, sated and complete in each other's arms.

A SHORT TIME LATER, GILLIAN rose, shivering, from the tub.

"I suggest you get out of there, Bayard, or you'll catch cold," she said as she reached for her shift, to discover it was soaking wet.

"Or be permanently shrivelled," he agreed as he climbed out. "Put your shift over the stool near the brazier and get into bed."

"Then I won't have a shift to wear."

His eyes gleamed. "So I see."

Blushing, she hurried to get under the covers. He followed and put his arms around her, rubbing her arms to warm her.

He realized at once something was wrong—something more than the troubles they already faced. "What is it? Are you unwell?"

She blushed again and didn't meet his gaze. "If I'm upset, it's for a foolish reason."

He cupped her chin and gave her an encouraging smile. It was hard to imagine Gillian being foolish, about anything. "What foolish reason?"

Lowering her eyes, her thick lashes fanned across her cheeks. "I wish I were more beautiful for you."

Any trace of amusement fled. "You're the most beautiful woman I've ever known."

She regarded him wistfully. "That's a lovely thing for you to say, Bayard, but it's not true."

"It is," he insisted, fervent sincerity in his voice and eyes and heart. "Other women may possess outward beauty that all the world can see, but you have a better, finer beauty that won't fade or change with age because it lives inside you. It's your strength and determination, your concern for your people, your love, that makes you truly beautiful, Gillian, and it always will."

She turned her head against his naked chest, so that he wouldn't see the tears that came to her eyes.

"You're not crying, are you?"

"No." Not exactly, because she was trying not to.

"Good, because I like a woman with spirit, one who isn't afraid to speak her mind to me."

That made her smile.

He levered himself up onto his elbow and caressed the swell of her breasts and her flat belly. "You're still shivering, my Gillian."

"Then warm me."

He did.

As Gillian and Bayard slumbered in each other's arms, Frederic untied one of the horses' leads from the rope tethering the mercenaries' mounts. The moon was a sliver in the night sky, and Richard and most of his men were asleep. Frederic had been careful and quiet and gotten the saddle on without difficulty, or disturbing the other horses so that they did little more than whicker and refoot.

Slowly, cautiously, he led his horse down a narrow path through the trees. He'd kept a careful eye on the route they'd taken here. D'Artage had tried to confuse him, but you couldn't move the sun. He was to the north and west of Averette, probably about twenty miles from the castle as the crow flew. It would take some hard riding, but this horse was a fine one—probably stolen from a knight—and he should be able to get back to Averette before—

"Where are you going, my fine young gentleman?" a rough voice demanded from the shadows.

"Lord Richard asked me to take a message for him."

A huge, balding man who smelled even worse than Ullric stepped out of the shadows. "Where? To who?"

Frederic drew himself up. "I don't answer to you."

The mercenary drew his sword. He had another stuck in his belt, and a dagger, too. He wore no mail, only a boiled leather tunic, and there was a smirk on his face. Frederic was sure that, like the other mercenaries, this fellow believed he was a soft, spoiled boy too craven to kill a man, too afraid to strike with his full strength, and lacking cold-blooded determination.

As the stinking lout came toward him, Frederic waited, just as Sir Bayard had taught him. Wait so you don't waste your chance. Wait until you see the best, most vulnerable spot. Wait so that your opponent thinks you're afraid. Wait, especially if you are.

Then strike, and strike hard. You may not get another chance.

So Frederic waited, and soon the stinking lout discovered how much he'd underestimated Frederic de Sere.

CHAPTER TWENTY-ONE

"IS YOUR SHIFT DRY?" Bayard asked shortly before dawn as he pulled on his breeches.

The tub, now full of cold water, still stood in the middle of the room. They hadn't left the chamber since he'd returned from patrol. Nobody had come seeking them and they had seen no need to leave.

"It's not too damp to wear," Gillian replied, glancing at him over her shoulder as she picked up her shift and put it on.

"I don't want you to catch a chill. Maybe you should wait here and I can tell Seltha to bring you another one," he suggested.

"Certainly not! I can tell when a shift is dry enough to wear. I'm not a child prone to take silly risks, as you should know by now."

His arms came around her and he pulled her back against his chest. "I'm very well aware that you're a woman, my lady."

"And not a silly one?"

"God's blood, no!" he cried with mock horror. "Indeed, you're about the least silly person I've ever met. You make *Armand* look like a jester."

He felt her stiffen, so he turned her in his arms so that she was facing him. "What's wrong?" he asked when he saw her face.

She shrugged. "I'm not serious *all* the time."

He kissed her forehead and then her delectable lips. "I know. Have I told you that I adore your laugh?"

She raised her eyes to look at him with wonder. "You do?"

"Very much. And your dancing. I recall you were very far from serious the night of the haying."

She laid her head against his chest. "I was so worried that I'd acted without proper decorum. Considering what I've done since…"

"A waste of worry," he agreed.

"But enough of this dallying, wench!" he cried, trying to lighten her mood as he reluctantly stepped away. "I have a patrol to lead, and you have a gown to put on, because if you don't, I'm not going to be able to leave and I'll want you to stay with me to keep me company. I can be very persuasive, my lady—how much so, you have yet to learn—so you probably would stay and then you would be seriously remiss in your duty to your household."

Despite his efforts, she didn't smile as she went to put on her gown. "We can't have that."

He regretted referring to her duty, even in jest. "I didn't mean to upset you."

"It's not what you said, Bayard," she replied. "It's just…we have so much to trouble us—Dunstan's death and traitors and Frederic."

He remembered that, of course. He was aware they'd only managed to forget for a little while in each other's arms.

His beloved regarded him with haunted eyes. "Do you think your squire's dead?"

She was too intelligent to accept a comforting lie, and he wouldn't treat her like a feeble woman incapable of dealing with the truth. "It's possible, but I think we would have found his body. I'm hoping he decided to go home to his father and paid someone to take him there. A cart wouldn't have been his preferred way to get there, but he didn't have a lot of money."

"What about Dunstan's killers and Richard d'Artage? Do you think they've fled?"

"Perhaps. I'm going to keep searching," Bayard said as he buckled his swordbelt around his waist.

"Where are you going today?" she asked.

"North, along the river."

RICHARD GLARED AT THE IDIOT who'd been guarding the horses. "What do you mean, his horse is gone and you didn't see or hear him take it?"

"It's as I say," the Dane replied, spittle forming at the edges of his lips that were almost covered by his heavy beard, terror in his pig-like eyes. "I think he put something in my wine last night to make me sleep."

"You think he hid a sleeping potion in his clothes and carried it around with him?" Richard demanded, his grip tightening on the hilt of his sword.

Even as he derided the man who was supposed to guard the horse, he wondered if it could be so. Had that idiot boy been scheming to desert him all along? If so, where had he gone?

Home to his father, afraid of what he'd gotten involved in? Or back to Averette to warn Bayard and ruin all their plans? Maybe Bayard himself had sent Frederic to find out what he could about the men who'd killed that fool of a steward.

Ullric burst out of the trees nearby, running faster than Richard ever thought he could. "Juan's dead! His body's in the woods!"

Richard cursed under his breath. "Where?"

Panting and sweating and stinking even more than usual, Ullric pointed in the direction of Averette.

Another curse burst from Richard's lip. "I'll kill that mewling little whelp myself!"

"What, that *boy?*" Ullric panted with disbelief. "You think *he* killed Juan?"

"Fool! Dolt! Who else? If it were Bayard or his men, we'd be under attack. The boy is missing and he's taken a horse."

"What do we—?"

"Shut up and let me think!"

How long would it take Frederic to get back to Averette and tell Bayard where to find them? How much time would Bayard and his men need to get here?

He'd led Frederic on a circuitous route to this place. The lad would get lost trying to find his way back to Averette and then return here, or at least ride around confused. That would give them some time. Frederic might yet be close by, close enough to catch before he could get back to Averette and betray him.

Just as his mother had abandoned him to run off with a common soldier and left him with his bitter, angry father, who'd betrayed his son by taking a new, younger bride and siring more sons to steal his inheritance. His first lover had deceived him, taking his money and his heart, then selling herself to another richer man as soon as the sheets were cool. The king had also betrayed him, rewarding lesser men and overlooking him.

And now, despite his offer of riches and rewards, he'd been tricked by a stripling and betrayed to a handsome knight who'd had everything given to him. Who hadn't endured the slightest hardship during his captivity in France. Whose brother had been rewarded with the hand of the most beautiful woman at court, Adelaide d'Averette, who'd looked at *him* as if he were dirt beneath her haughty heels.

A roar burst from Richard's throat and he lunged, shoving his dagger into the Dane's throat. The man didn't even have time to gasp before he died.

Breathing hard, Richard let the body drop and only then remembered that Ullric and his mercenaries were watching.

"He failed me," he said in explanation as he bent down to wipe his blade on the Dane's tunic. "That's what I do to men who fail me."

He pointed at two men staring. "You and you, bury him, and be quick about it. Then catch up to the rest of us. Ullric, come with me."

ONCE AGAIN, GILLIAN TRIED to maintain an aura of calm serenity as she went about her daily duties. As before, she noted a curiosity and lack of deference on the part of her household. And attempted to ignore it. Then Father Matthew waylaid her after mass.

She had to admit, at least inwardly, that she'd expected him to speak to her sooner.

Now he stood before her in the chapel where she'd been so memorably—and sinfully—with Bayard the night she'd kept vigil for Dunstan.

"I've heard some very disturbing news, my lady," Father Matthew began, "regarding you and Sir Bayard de Boisbaston."

She saw no point to dissembling. "If you've heard I spent the night in his bedchamber, Father, that's true. I did."

"To discuss estate business?" he hopefully replied.

She was touched he didn't immediately condemn her,

but she wouldn't hide her sin. "No, we were not discussing estate business."

Father Matthew's face reddened and he looked slightly ill. "I'm shocked, my lady. Shocked and disappointed."

"I realize I've not behaved properly and will duly make my confession and seek God's forgiveness, but we're in love."

"That doesn't matter!" the priest returned, his shock changing to disgust. "You aren't married—and you cannot marry. The church forbids such unions."

"Which is why we didn't wait for a wedding." She clasped her hands together and spoke with force and resolve. "We love each other, Father Matthew."

The priest held up his hand to silence her, more imperious than he'd ever been before. "This is what comes of your unwomanly conduct. I have warned your elder sister time and time again that all you ladies would come to grief if you didn't marry, and just as I predicted, you have.

"If only your parents had instilled more maidenly virtues in you! Now we are witness to the result of their neglect—your elder sister weds with most unseemly haste, you marry not at all, and God only knows what will become of your younger sister. It wouldn't surprise me if that worldly creature ends her days in a brothel!"

If Father Matthew had spoken only of her and her sin, Gillian might have been able to remain composed. But when he dared to cast aspersions on her sisters, he had gone too far.

"I accept that it's wrong to make love without benefit of marriage," she replied, her voice low. "And my father did try to instill *maidenly virtues* in his daughters—by beating us for any perceived wrong, including simply talking. We were to be meek and mild like our poor mother, who suffered more cruelly at his hands than you, or any man, could ever imagine, trying time after time to give him a son after he'd forced himself upon her, until she was too weak to get up from her bed. He as good as *murdered* her because his daughters were not good enough and never would be."

Her hands on her hips, her whole body shook with the force of her anger. "If I were a lord standing before you now, if I had taken a woman into my bed with no plan of marriage, would you speak to me as you have? Would you dare to chastise me as if I were an errant child? No! You do so because I'm a woman and therefore expected to resist a man's advances, although at the same time, you believe women weak, frail vessels. How is it, Father, that we are to be so strong and yet so weak at once? Why is it you will blame Eve for her sin, but not Adam for being fool enough to listen to her?"

The priest raised a trembling finger and pointed at her. "Be quiet, you foul, unnatural creature with the tongue of the serpent! Evil, unrepentant woman! You'll surely burn in hell!"

"Perhaps I will, if God is not the forgiving, loving Father you have always said he is. But I believe He is, and He'll forgive Bayard and me for our love."

With that, she turned on her heel and hurried from the chapel.

As she strode across the yard to the hall, she was sorry for losing her temper and more sorry to sin, but she truly did believe God would understand and forgive them, since they acted out of love.

A shout came from the wall walk.

Hoping it wasn't more trouble, Gillian hurried toward the gate. Before she got there, however, the inner gates swung open to admit a sizeable party, with a knight and lady at their head.

Joy rushed through Gillian. "Adelaide!" she cried as she dashed to meet them.

Her sister dismounted without waiting for the help of Ned, who came to stand by her horse. Gillian supposed the knight must be Adelaide's husband, Armand de Boisbaston, although his arrival was much less important to her than Adelaide's.

She fell on her sister's neck and hugged her tightly. "Oh, Adelaide! I'm so glad you've come!"

"It's good to be home!" Adelaide said as they embraced. "I told Armand we had to leave court as soon as I got your message about poor Dunstan."

Adelaide turned to the mail-clad knight waiting patiently beside her.

Like Bayard, he was dark-haired, except that his hair fell uncut past his broad shoulders. He had brown eyes like Bayard, but darker and flecked with gold. His nose and jaw were similar, too.

"Gillian, this is my husband, Lord Armand de Boisbaston," Adelaide said, regarding the man beside her with affection and admiration.

"Lady Gillian," her brother-in-law said, his voice as deep, but not nearly as attractive, as Bayard's. "A pleasure. I've been anxious to meet both of my sisters-in-law."

Gillian's happiness diminished and she dreaded revealing that Lizette hadn't yet returned, although she must. "Lizette isn't—"

"Here. I know," Adelaide said with a comforting smile. "A message from her reached us before we left the court. It seems she's fallen ill on the road, although not seriously, thank God. Iain's with her."

Relief washed over Gillian and she felt some of the weight of fear and responsibility fall away. If Iain was with Lizette, she would be safe, and soon she would be home.

"Where's Bayard?" Armand asked.

"On patrol. Something else has happened," Gillian replied. "Come into the hall and I'll explain."

As best I can.

AFTER ADELAIDE TOOK some time to admire the tapestry now hanging on the dais, Gillian suggested they retreat to the solar for privacy. Many of the servants, happy to have Lady Adelaide back at Averette and understandably curious about her husband, came into the hall pretending to have work to do, or that they had to pass through.

Once in the solar, Gillian and Adelaide sat in chairs, while Armand leaned against the window sill, his arms crossed over a chest as broad as Bayard's.

Quickly and succinctly, Gillian told them what had happened since Dunstan's death. Adelaide and Armand were quite understandably shocked when they heard Richard d'Artage might be with the men who'd killed Dunstan and that Frederic de Sere was missing.

"I always thought Richard too cowardly to do anything on his own," Adelaide said, anxiously fiddling with the emerald-and-gold crucifix around her neck. "I never would have guessed he'd come here alone, though, even in disguise."

"Nor I," Armand grimly agreed. "But all the skill with disguise in the world won't save Richard. We'll find him."

"We've been worried Frederic might not be as trustworthy as we believed," Gillian said. "We fear he may have joined the rebels. Unfortunately, we have cause to believe he's not as honorable as Bayard thought."

She told them about Dena's seduction and Frederic's behavior when it was discovered.

"Poor girl," Adelaide said with pity and compassion. "How is she now?"

"She should be well soon," Gillian replied. "I've assured her she can stay at Averette."

Gillian glanced at Armand, wondering what he made of that decision, but he didn't seem dismayed. If anything, he looked satisfied.

"Quite right," Adelaide said firmly. "And you needn't fear that Armand would object. You're in charge of Averette, just as we promised."

Gillian wondered what they would think when they heard that she and Bayard were lovers.

If they heard, for who would tell them? The servants? She doubted they would dare, nor would they be eager to bring bad tidings. The soldiers? They would be more likely to tell Iain and he wasn't here. Father Matthew? That seemed most likely, but perhaps her outburst of temper would make him hesitate.

Gillian got to her feet. "You both must be tired and hungry. Come, let's return to the hall and have some refreshment." She smiled at her sister and brother-in-law. "If we don't let the servants have a look at your husband soon, Adelaide, nothing will get done."

"I am to be on display?" Lord Armand de Boisbaston inquired.

"I get to show you off," his wife replied, giving him a little kiss that made Gillian want to weep.

"THAT'S THE TRUTH, my lord! I swear on my life!" Frederic cried as he grovelled on the ground in front of

Bayard. His left cheek was bruising from the fall from his horse, and an arrow protruded from his right shoulder where one of Averette's Welsh archers had shot him after he hadn't heeded Bayard's command to halt and identify himself.

Frederic could still move his arm and there wasn't much blood, so Bayard was fairly certain the wound wasn't mortal. The lad's pleading voice was strong, too, although that could be desperation. Or it could be conviction, he inwardly conceded.

"You were with Richard to discover his plans, and *not* to betray me?" Bayard said, repeating what Frederic had told them and making no effort to hide his skepticism, even though he hoped that, however implausible, Frederic spoke the truth.

"I wanted to prove myself to you and when Charles—Richard—kept trying to get me to agree that John was a bad king, I got suspicious. He also kept telling me what a terrible man you were and offering to take me home to my father. But when he was drinking, he seemed too well-spoken to be a merchant. He'd forget, I think, that he was playing a part.

"He suggested that if I wanted to leave your service, I meet him at the Stag's Head. He had something better I could do, he said. I wasn't sure what it might be, or if he was a rebel, or just didn't like John or you, so I decided to take him up on his offer and try to find out one way or the other. He told me who he really was and I pretended that he'd convinced me to join them. And then I met his men. They're terrible, Bayard! Brutal and mean and rough. *They* killed Dunstan. I came back to tell you. Richard d'Artage is a foul traitor and must be stopped!"

Bayard reached down and pulled Frederic to his feet. "You're sure he said his name was Richard d'Artage?"

"Yes, although there's another nobleman who leads the rebels. Ullric—one of the mercenaries—told me that *he* paid the mercenaries who are with Richard now."

"What's this nobleman's name?"

"I don't know. Richard never said and neither did Ullric. Ullric only talked about him after he was drunk. He kept saying Richard shouldn't act like he was God Almighty when he was just a rich man's lackey. The rebels plan to kill you, Bayard, and your brother, and every nobleman who might help John continue his reign."

Bayard's jaw clenched. That was the conspiracy as Armand had described it.

Neither he nor Armand had any love for John, who was too greedy, too immoral, too stupid and selfish to be a good king, but the alternative was anarchy and possibly another ruler who would be worse. And he had given his sworn oath he would protect his king.

"Lindall's betrayed you, too," Frederic continued, panting. "He's sold Richard information about you and the patrols—where you'll be, and when."

"Lindall?" Bayard repeated, as taken aback as the soldiers around them who muttered in disbelief and exchanged skeptical looks.

"That's a lie!" Alfric declared, dismounting and approaching. "Lindall was born at Averette. He's second only to Iain, and Iain trusts him. We *all* do."

"That's Iain's mistake—and yours—if you think a fellow'll be loyal simply because he was born in a place," Frederic retorted. "Richard paid him a lot of money—I saw it myself."

"A likely story. When did this happen, eh?" Bran demanded.

"Yesterday morning. He said nobody would question him if he left the castle."

Alfric and Bran's confidence ebbed and the other men suddenly looked doubtful, as well.

"Has he done that often, leave the castle with no explanation?" Bayard asked.

"Aye, a few times," Alfric grudgingly admitted. "I thought…*we* all thought…he had a woman in the village. Not Peg, 'cause that wouldn't have been a secret, but, um, the miller's wife's always been friendly to him and we thought…"

Bayard cursed himself for not being more diligent. He shouldn't have trusted anyone at Averette except Gillian.

"I swear to you, Bayard, on my life, that I'm loyal to God's anointed king and to you," Frederic said fervently, regarding Bayard with pleading eyes. "You're a decent, honorable knight, no matter what lies Richard tells about you. I want to be like you, my lord, and not a deceitful coward like Richard who hires such monstrous men to do his bidding. I want to go back to Averette, to be your squire and serve you."

Frederic straightened his slender shoulders and spoke with more resolve. "I want to tell Dena I'm sorry, too. If you throw me in the dungeon, so be it, but I want to see her and tell her that I'm sorry I was so cruel to her and try to make it right somehow."

Believing him and pleased by the lad's contrition, Bayard nevertheless had to focus on the present and what needed to be done. "Robb, you and Alfric take Frederic back to Averette. We'll continue the patrol try to find Richard."

"But you need me!" Frederic protested. "I can show you where they are!"

"Even if I believed you—and I'll admit I'm inclined to do so—they aren't going to be there now," Bayard replied. "Once they realize you've gone, they'll either flee or attack. I hope they—"

An arrow hissed through the air and thudded at Bayard's feet.

With a curse, Bayard grabbed Frederic by the shoulder to pull him out of harm's way.

"Off the road," he ordered his men as another arrow fell, and then several more. "Make for the trees!"

Before he could get to his horse, Frederic cried out. He fell to the ground, an arrow in his side.

As arrows started to rain down like a storm of barbed thorns, Bayard threw Frederic over his shoulder and carried him to Danceur. He got Frederic on the horse and mounted behind him, then wheeled Danceur sharply, his horse whinnying in protest as more arrows stuck in the mud beside them. He spurred Danceur to a gallop and rode toward the elms and oaks beyond the grassy verge.

An arrow hit his horse's flank. Danceur screamed in pain and stumbled, sending both Bayard and Frederic tumbling to the ground.

Realizing what had happened, Bayard rolled away before his legs got caught beneath his horse. Dizzy, but still conscious, he rose and saw Frederic lying in a crumpled heap nearby.

Then, hoofbeats. Coming closer.

Grabbing his shield from the back of his saddle, Bayard turned to face a column of men riding toward them. At their head was a knight wearing a brilliant blue surcoat trimmed with scarlet and green.

Richard d'Artage.

There was no time to get to the trees before Richard

and his men would be upon them. Bayard had faith in the soldiers he'd trained. They would surely beat any band of mercenaries Richard could bring against them.

But d'Artage was his.

"Come to me, Richard," he sang under his breath as he planted his feet, drew his sword and prepared to meet his foe. "Come to me, and go to God."

CHAPTER TWENTY-TWO

HAD THE MAN GONE MAD? Richard wondered when he realized it was Bayard de Boisbaston himself standing on the road like a simpleton, with only his sword and shield to defend himself. Richard had seen the mounted knight go down, but hadn't dared to hope it was de Bois-baston himself.

"He's mine!" Richard shouted to the mercenaries charging beside him, raising his sword to strike. He was going to take Bayard's head. Maybe he'd send it to Armand as a gift...

Something moved at the edge of his vision, behind Bayard's horse with its helplessly flailing hooves.

Some...*one!*

Just as Bayard moved out of the way and lifted his sword with both hands, that someone flew over the fallen horse and grabbed Richard's ankle, pulling him from the saddle.

Cursing, Richard got to his feet and struck so hard at his assailant, he nearly cut him in two, barely noticing it was Frederic as he shoved the bloody body away with his shield. He heard Bayard's war cry above the other sounds of battle—shouts, screams, the clash of sword on sword—as his mercenaries met Bayard's men.

His blood pounding, Richard took his stance while Bayard de Boisbaston strode toward him, sword upraised, left side protected by his shield, and a look of such malevolent anger, and hate, and resolve that Richard knew one of them was going to die that day.

So did Bayard—and it was going to be Richard. If he didn't hate the rebel already for what he planned to do, watching him strike down poor Frederic would have been enough to make him kill the cur without compunction or remorse.

"You're a dead man, d'Artage," he shouted, putting away the sorrow he felt at Frederic's ill-fated attempt to save him. The boy should have left him to face d'Artage, who was no great fighter. Never once, in all Bayard's recollection, had d'Artage participated in a melee or practice session at court.

"It's too bad killing you is going to be too quick and easy a death for you," Bayard called out as he prepared to attack. "If any man deserves a traitor's death—!"

"Spoken like the arrogant, braying ass every son of Raymond de Boisbaston is!" Richard jeered as they circled. "You and that brother of yours think you're the only men who know how to fight—because I let you think it! Why show you what I can do until I need to? But if you ever go to Italy, look up Carlo del Ponti. He's very skilled and he taught me well—certainly better than that cretin of a father could ever teach you. Your father was no more than a lumbering ox, a lout, a blackguard, and you're just like him!"

"We'll see who's the better man," Bayard said, noticing that every time Richard sidestepped with his right leg, his right shoulder dropped a little and he twisted slightly, so that his body was more protected by his shield.

A good, protective move. Yet there was a risk in that move, for it meant Richard had to go a little extra distance when it came time to strike.

"You and Armand are doomed," Richard sneered,

keeping his eyes on Bayard's blade. "Not his wife, though. Not Adelaide—and not right away. Not till I've enjoyed her and taught her some humility."

Bayard laughed with scorn. "Now I *know* you're a fool. You couldn't teach the ladies of Averette anything."

"And you could, I suppose. I'm sure Lady Gillian required some instruction in how to be a woman. Tell me, Bayard, what was it like, bedding such an unnatural creature? Or did that make it better for you?"

Rage filled Bayard, but he controlled it. Let the man say what he would; he wasn't going to see another dawn, especially since Bayard noticed something else.

Richard was already tiring. His movements were getting slower, and he was starting to pant. That's what happened if a man didn't keep limber and practice. He grew as rusty as a neglected sword, as slow and ungainly as a horse fed too many oats and rarely exercised.

Wanting to tire him more, Bayard made as if to strike. As Bayard had intended, Richard easily avoided the blow, yet it made him jump and then hurry to regain his position. Bayard didn't give him that chance; he struck again, this time with more purpose.

Richard parried the blow rather easily, Bayard had to admit. He *had* been well trained, if not by some Italian, by someone who knew what he was about.

In the distance, the sounds of fighting continued, although with fewer shouts and clashing weapons, and those that reached Bayard's ears seemed more distant. He hoped his men were winning and the mercenaries fleeing.

He only let his attention wander for a moment. He had to concentrate on defeating Richard—who suddenly rushed him. His sword connected with Bayard's shield, the wood nearly shattering as Bayard shoved him back.

That was close. *Too close*. Another moment and—

Richard moved in and swung again. Bayard's blade caught his, pushing it down and away from his knee and foot.

Richard didn't hesitate. He struck again, backhanded this time, twisting like a snake, more quick and deadly than Bayard ever would have given him credit for.

Fortunately, Bayard was agile and he leapt out of the way. He didn't retreat, though. He attacked, raining blow after blow on Richard's shield, making the man duck and sway and step back, and back again as he moved inexorably forward.

Sweat dripped down Richard's face and from the end of his nose. His chest rose and fell with the effort to breathe, the sound rapid and rasping. He was definitely wearying, so Bayard kept up the attack, moving as deliberately as if he were cutting grain.

And then came the familiar sound of an arrow through the air. It struck Bayard in the back, jabbing into his mail just below his left shoulder blade. He stumbled forward.

Mercifully, Richard was too surprised himself to take advantage. By the time he realized Bayard had been hit, Bayard had recovered and gotten out of reach. Pain radiated from his back and he could feel warm, wet blood on his skin and dampening his gambeson. In spite of that, his garments moved independently of his flesh, telling him the arrow had pierced his armor enough to cut him, but not to lodge in flesh and bone.

If he let Richard think the blow was mortal, he could lure him closer.

"You're doomed, Bayard," Richard sneered, obviously

sure he had the upper hand. "All I have to do is knock you down."

"Then do it," Bayard said, his jaw clenched and lowering his shield as if he was too weak to hold it.

"Perhaps I'll just stay here and watch you fall. Then my men and I will find your other patrols and take them one by one, until there are only the men who remained at Averette. We'll lay siege to it, and I'll tell Lady Gillian that either she surrenders to me or I'll fire the village and kill everyone in it. I seem to recall your brother finally gave up Marchant when Philip threatened to do that. *She* will agree, don't you think? She cares so much for her peasants and the villagers."

Bayard was sure Gillian would surrender if so forced and, seeing his face, Richard realized he did. "She's as foolish as your brother. I'll have her and through her, Armand, and Adelaide. They'll come to rescue her and catch your killer, you see, and that will be the end of them."

"You sound very certain," Bayard said, taking a few steps to the right so that Richard, still with sword raised, followed. Then he went to the left, keeping the man moving, keeping him active, exhausting him more.

"Oh, I'm sure that's what they'll do. After I've killed Armand, I'll join our forces in the north and soon I'll be in Westminster, close to the new king."

"And who might that be?"

Richard laughed. "I don't know, but anyone would be better than John."

"Better for you, at any rate, or at least that's what you hope, isn't it?" Bayard suggested. "You couldn't succeed with John despite your toadying. What makes you think you'll have better luck with his successor, who'll already know you can't be trusted?"

Bayard heard the hiss of another arrow and instinctively shied to the right, to see it stick in the ground nearby.

"Leave him to me!" Richard shouted, looking back over his shoulder at the lone archer dressed in a motley assortment of armor. "He's mine!"

As the archer retreated back into the trees, another man with an ax came running from the forest as if all the fiends of hell were after him. He spotted Bayard, stumbled to a halt, then turned and ran in the opposite direction.

With a shout of triumph, Bayard confronted Richard. "Your men are running away!"

"Just one," Richard retorted. "Every army has its cowards."

"And every court its traitors," Bayard said, lifting his shield and again pressing his attack, the arrow's cut forgotten.

"I'm not a traitor!" Richard cried, moving backward. "John's not fit to rule. You know we're right, Bayard. Any man of sense sees John for the grasping, greedy buffoon he is, one who'll lead this country to ruin and the rule of Philip. Join us! Join us in overthrowing that leech and I promise you'll be richly rewarded."

Richard wasn't moving as quickly, nor was he holding his sword steady.

Soon, Bayard told himself, *soon.* All he had to do was keep Richard talking and moving, and bide his time. "Even if I agreed John's a terrible king, trying to overthrow him will lead to anarchy and civil war."

"Clever men can rise in the world during anarchy and civil war."

"Or fall, which is what you obviously intend for Armand, and me, and the ladies of Averette."

"I can overlook past wrongs if you'll join us."

"And make Armand my enemy?"

Richard shook his head to keep the sweat from dripping in his eyes. "Convince him to join us. You would be valued allies."

"What reward can you offer me? Or is only your master able to make such promises? Perhaps I should go join him."

"Kill me and you'll never know who he is."

"Frederic told me," Bayard lied.

"He couldn't have. I never said."

"We know more than you think, Richard."

As he'd planned, he saw the confusion in d'Artage's eyes, noted the slowness of his feet—and with blinding speed, raised his sword and struck.

He was so swift, Richard couldn't block the blow, and using all his strength, Bayard drove his weapon forward, only to feel it blocked by Richard's mail and turned aside.

Richard struck back, hitting Bayard's arm with more strength than he'd expected. The blow didn't pierce his mail, but Bayard heard a bone crack and agonizing pain forced him to drop his weapon.

Richard stepped on it and raised his own. Using his shield like a battering ram, Bayard dove at Richard, shoving him onto the ground, driving him down and landing atop him, sending Richard's sword skittering along the ground away from them.

Mouth gaping, Richard gasped for breath, while Bayard reached for the sword. Richard grabbed Bayard's shield by the upper edge and tugged it to and fro. With a cry of pain and frustration, Bayard pulled his arm from the shield straps. When he did, Richard shoved the shield up, striking Bayard hard on the jaw.

As Bayard struggled to recover from the pain and dizziness, Richard reached for his sword. Realizing Richard was armed again, Bayard rolled away, then scrambled onto his hands and knees, searching for his own weapon.

Richard staggered toward him. He raised his sword again, up over his head—just as Bayard grabbed the hilt of his blade. He turned and raised it, intending to shove it into Richard's chest, but Richard saw what he planned and staggered back out of reach. His wheezing breath sounded worse than if from mere exhaustion.

Richard must be wounded. How? He'd not penetrated Richard's mail. Nevertheless, d'Artage was definitely hurt and leaning to the left, trying to protect that side of his body....

His ribs. When he'd tackled Richard with his shield, he must have broken the man's ribs.

Energized by that conclusion, Bayard hauled himself upright. His back was on fire and the pain from his broken arm excruciating. He couldn't hold his sword in his right hand; that was useless to him now.

But he could still use his left and he gripped his sword tightly. "Want to surrender, Richard?"

"My blows must have addled your wits," the courtier replied through thinned, pale lips as he raised his sword and prepared to attack once more.

Bayard easily avoided the downswing of Richard's blade. "My wits are well enough. How are your ribs?"

"Excellent," Richard retorted. "And your arm? Can you feel the broken bones rubbing together? Quite painful, that, I understand."

It was, but Bayard made himself laugh. "Lord Raymond gave me worse pain."

"Ah, yes, your father," Richard panted. His skin had

gone from white to clammy gray and he now held his sword with both hands. "There's an honorable fellow for you. No wonder there's not a woman you see you don't try to take, even the homely ones like Gillian. God's blood, man, how desperate are you that you'd creep between that bitch's legs? Or was it that she's your relative? Excited by the sinfulness of it, were you?"

"If there's a sinner here," Bayard replied, "it's not me."

As Richard stepped once more to the right and dipped his shoulder, Bayard took his chance. With a roar, he ran at his enemy and knocked him flat again. This time, though, he put one foot on Richard's broken chest and pressed down until Richard screamed in pain.

"I don't want to kill you, Richard," he said. "I want to know who gives you your orders."

"Better…to die…than tell…"

"If you aren't the man behind the conspiracy, you could live."

"You'll put me…in a cell…a traitor's…death."

Bayard hesitated. What could he offer a traitor? Banishment? Exile? Would a man like Richard truly be content to flee the country never to return? To live without money or power? Would he not come back to seek revenge, if nothing else, as he'd come to Averette?

A horse burst from the trees carrying one of the mercenaries, running hell-bent away from the battle.

Straight at Bayard.

CHAPTER TWENTY-THREE

WITH ADELAIDE AND ARMAND behind her, Gillian ran to the gates as what remained of Bayard's patrol entered the courtyard. She frantically searched for Bayard among the mounted men, several of whom were obviously wounded.

"I'll fetch your medicines," Adelaide said from somewhere close by as Gillian spotted a body covered by a cloak laid over the back of one of the horses.

It *couldn't* be Bayard. She would know if he was dead. She would feel it in her heart. Her soul.

"Where's Bayard?" she demanded of Robb, who was bleeding from a deep gash in his forehead and dismounting slowly from his horse.

"Isn't he here?" he replied, looking around with confusion.

Perhaps he was just dazed from the wound, which she hoped wasn't serious. She would know better once he had his helmet off. "You're the first ones to return."

"God save him then," Robb murmured as he wiped the blood from his face. "He's not with us."

"What happened?" Armand's deep voice demanded behind her.

Robb looked at him, then back at Gillian with even more confusion. "Who's he?"

"This is Lord Armand de Boisbaston."

She remembered her duty as chatelaine of Averette,

which she still was by solemn vow, even if Adelaide was here. "Come to the hall and tell us what happened while I tend to your wound." She raised her voice. "All the wounded to the hall!"

Robb took a step, then wavered, and Armand hurried forward to help him. Instead of questioning Robb more, she stopped Alfric as he limped toward the hall. "Who died?"

"Frederic de Sere, my lady. That son of a bitch who said he was a wine merchant sliced him open from neck to gut."

A wail such as Gillian had never heard cut the air. Dena leaned against the door of the hall, near enough to have heard what Alfric said.

Sobbing, she began to slip down to the ground. Gillian started toward her until Robb shook off Armand's supporting arm and trotted to her. He put his arm around her and, whispering tenderly, raised her to her feet. Despite his own wound, he helped her back inside.

"Frederic died valiantly, my lady," Alfric said, "trying to save Sir Bayard's life."

Trying?

"He got that Charles de Fenelon off his horse before the man struck him down."

"And then?"

"And then, my lady, I was too busy fighting some hulking German brute to see what happened next. I got separated from everybody and only met up with them when the fighting was done. Robb told us to come back here."

"Without Sir Bayard?"

Alfric frowned. "Robb said he'd gone after that wine merchant. More'n that, I don't know."

"I see," she said, summoning her courage. Until she

saw Bayard's body, she would believe—she *must* believe—he was alive and well. "Go to the hall and I'll take a look at that leg."

Through the crowd of horses and soldiers, grooms and stable boys, she spotted several household servants hovering anxiously at the door of the kitchen and more by the well.

"You women, fetch water!" she called out. "We'll need plenty in the hall for the wounded. Seltha, bring me all the linens you can find. You stable boys bring fresh straw for bedding. Make stew, Umbert, and soft bread. And have Edun tap two kegs of ale for those who aren't wounded. They've earned it."

Trying to concentrate on what must be done immediately, Gillian gathered up her skirts and hurried into the hall, which was now full of wounded and exhausted men.

Adelaide waited for her on the dais with her box of medicines. She'd rolled back her long cuffs, exposing her slender arms, and wrapped a sheet of linen around her waist to protect her gown. She had another sheet over her arm for Gillian. "Tell me what to do," she said as Gillian rolled back her own sleeves.

"Help me decide who's the most badly injured. And ask if anyone knows where Bayard is. Where's Armand?"

"Seeing to the horses and making sure we're prepared for an attack."

"Our enemies must have suffered more than our own men. There can't be enough of them left to attack the castle."

"*If* that was the only force our enemies had," Adelaide said, her expression full of an anguish and dread that mirrored Gillian's own.

If this was but a preliminary attack...if there was

another, stronger force prepared to move against them...

Gillian spotted one of the stable boys who'd arrived with his arms full of straw. "Leave that and go to Lord Armand," she said to him. "Tell him to expect farmers and villagers to come to the castle for safety. I'm sure several must have seen the patrol returning and are already gathering their things to seek sanctuary here. Then find Lindall and tell him to come to me."

She addressed Adelaide as the boy ran off to do as she commanded. "Some of the villagers are going to need help, and the peasants on outlying farms are going to have to be told and brought here. I'll have Lindall send men to fetch them."

Hoping the villagers would come quickly, she turned her attention to the wounded. Fortunately, there was nothing more serious than deep cuts and flesh wounds, easily tended, and by the time she was finished, Armand had joined them in the hall.

She could tell by the look on his face that something else had happened, and it wasn't good.

He didn't wait for her to pose a question, but spoke to both the ladies of Averette, although his gaze flicked most often to his wife. "Lindall's nowhere to be found. Apparently nobody's seen him since the patrols rode out this morning and he announced he was going to the village."

His words seemed to suck the air from Gillian's lungs. That sounded just like Frederic. Oh, God help them, like Frederic!

But Armand didn't look dismayed; he looked...angry. "Forgive me, Gillian, but I have to ask you—how much do you trust Lindall?"

She stared at him, baffled. Lindall had been here since she was a girl. "I'd trust him with my life."

"As would I," Adelaide said, equally taken aback by her husband's question.

"One of your men told me that Frederic claimed Lindall had betrayed us to Richard. That he sold information about where Bayard would be. I went to the man's quarters myself, and it appears that he packed all his belongings before he rode out the gates this morning."

Gillian reached for her sister's hand and grasped it tightly. God help her, not another mistake! Not another failure.

Armand's dark eyes filled with sympathy. "Treachery comes in many forms. It can be difficult to see and even more difficult to accept."

"I won't accept it yet," she said, unwilling to lose faith in a man who'd been in the household for so long. "There may yet be an explanation. First, though, we have to find out what happened to Bayard."

Armand said nothing and neither did Adelaide, but her eyes spoke volumes to her husband as they followed Gillian to one of the pallets of straw in the hall. Dena sat beside it, holding Robb's hand.

Robb struggled to sit up when he saw Gillian and the others approaching. His wound had bled freely, as head wounds do; fortunately, the cut on his forehead hadn't been deep, nor had his skull been damaged. "Any news of Sir Bayard?"

"Not yet," Gillian said, gesturing for Dena to sit back down after she rose to offer Gillian a seat on her stool. "What happened today?"

"Start at the beginning," Armand added.

Robb nodded, took a deep breath and glanced at Dena before answering. "We were attacked. That young

Frederic come riding toward us and Ianto, thinking he meant to attack, shot him in the shoulder with an arrow. That Welshman's always too quick with his bow."

Ianto was sitting nearby drinking some ale and he grunted in protest.

"Well, you *are*," Robb said. "Anyway, Frederic fell off his horse and Sir Bayard dismounted and went to him. Some of us tried to stop him, thinking it might be some kind of trap, but he didn't listen. Frederic said he was coming to lead us to the men who killed Dunstan. They were led by a traitor, he said, Richard something."

"D'Artage?" Adelaide asked.

"Aye, that was it!" Robb confirmed with another glance at Dena, his voice and manner growing more confident. "Sir Bayard wasn't ready to believe him, I can tell you, no more than any o' us. And when Frederic accused Lindall o' selling information to this Richard, I was sure he was lying."

Robb frowned when he saw their faces. "What? You believe that?"

"We have some cause to," Gillian replied. "Go on."

"Well, my lady, then we were attacked. I thought I'd been right about Frederic, until he got hit with another arrow, so if he betrayed us, them mercenaries betrayed *him*."

"Alfric told us he was killed trying to help Bayard," Gillian said.

"I knew he wasn't evil," Dena whispered with tears in her eyes.

"What did you see before that?" Armand prompted.

"Before that, my lord, Sir Bayard ordered us back into the trees. He'd got Frederic onto Danceur when these mounted men appeared, looking like devils on horses. Sir Bayard's own was struck and fell. Sir Bayard got up, though, and he was standin' waitin' for the one leading the men to attack him."

"Sweet Mother of God," Gillian murmured, horrified.

"He wasn't ridden down, my lady," Robb said with an encouraging, if not entirely reassuring, smile. "I seen that much. Last I saw him, he was fighting that Richard—looked to be winning, too."

Gillian was relieved to hear that, but if Bayard had defeated his opponent, why hadn't he returned to Averette?

She addressed the other wounded men. "Did anybody else see Bayard during the skirmish?"

"I seen him, my lady!" Ianto announced. "Sir Bayard had his man down and I thought that was going to be the end of it, until a rider came charging out of the woods, straight at him. He got out of the way, all right—a little slow for him, I thought—and next thing I know, the man on the ground—Charles or Richard or whoever he was—was back on his feet. As the rider went by, the fellow got hold of his leg and dragged him right off the saddle.

"Then he got the horse between him and Sir Bayard and managed to mount. I tell you, my lady, he could hardly move but he climbed on the beast, probably because he knew if he didn't, he'd be dead.

"So then another man come riding out of the woods—the cowards were all running away by then, you see—and Sir Bayard got one of them off his horse and took it. Thought he was going to fall off, I did, but he didn't. He rode after the other fellow, chasing him down the road toward London.

"I ran after him, calling for him to wait for me to get a horse, but he didn't stop. I don't know if he heard me or not."

"He wasn't going to risk Richard getting away, especially if he thought the man had important information," Armand said, confirming what Gillian thought—and feared. "At least we know which way they went."

"If they stayed on the road," Gillian murmured with dismay.

She looked at the window and realized, to her further dismay, that dusk had fallen.

Armand, Adelaide, and Ianto followed her gaze.

"We can't go after him tonight," Armand said. "There's not even a quarter moon to see by."

Gillian envisioned Bayard lying wounded and alone in the dark. Ianto had said he'd moved slowly. Perhaps he was hurt, and if his injury was serious, time was of the essence. If he was losing blood, if the night was cold and it started to rain, he could be dead by morning.

If he wasn't already.

Her mind and heart simply refused to accept that possibility. He must and would be found. "Search parties can go out now. They can carry torches."

Armand regarded her with sorrow and regret. "As much as I'd like to find him—and God knows I do— it's too much of a risk. Even with torches, we wouldn't be able to see his trail clearly, especially if they left the road. If Richard's got an ounce of sense—and he does— he won't stay on the road, precisely because it'll be too easy to follow him. I'm sorry, Gillian, but we must wait until morning, and in the meantime, pray that God keeps Bayard safe."

Gillian's rational mind recognized that Armand was right. They might even make things worse by destroying important clues as to Bayard's whereabouts in the dark. Nevertheless, her heart rebelled against doing nothing except waiting.

Adelaide put her hand on her arm. "He's right, Gillian. I know it's hard, but he's right."

She had to be strong and brave, as Bayard was. "Very well," she reluctantly agreed, "but I'm joining the search in the morning."

Armand looked about to protest, until Adelaide said, "He might be hurt, and if so, Gillian should be with you."

The image of Bayard's body bloody and in a ditch in the dark came to her and a cry of anguish built in her throat.

She willed it away. She had to be strong, to show Armand that she could cope with whatever they found, so that he would let her go with him. And because the people of Averette needed her to be strong, a pillar of confidence in a terrible time.

"So be it," Armand agreed. "We'll leave at dawn."

He gave Gillian a smile that was meant to be hopeful. "Try not to worry. Richard d'Artage is more courtier than warrior. I wouldn't be surprised if we find my brother sitting under a tree somewhere, with Richard d'Artage trussed up like a fowl beside him."

Gillian wanted to believe him, but until she saw Bayard again, her fears kept hope at bay.

It was the pain that woke Bayard in the darkness. Sharp pain in his arm and back. Dull aches everywhere else. He could see nothing in the pitch darkness. He'd laid down in the shelter of the hawthorn bush, huddled beneath it like the wounded creature he was after he'd fallen from the horse into a patch of gorse, too dizzy to continue the chase.

After he was on the ground and the horse had wandered off, he told himself he'd rest a moment, then try to make his way back to Averette on foot.

Richard was still riding through the wood and across meadows, skirting the farms and the riverbank where people might see him.

Richard was wounded, too, his ribs broken. Of that Bayard was certain. How, then, could he stay on his horse?

He had…hadn't he? Or had he been chasing a riderless gelding and Richard was somewhere behind him…?

Please God, surely not!

Shivering, his teeth chattering, Bayard licked his dry and chapped lips. He could taste blood where they'd cracked.

He had to get up. He had to keep moving. He had to find water. He couldn't stay here and risk falling into a sleep from which he wouldn't wake. He had to make himself move; otherwise, he'd die for sure.

Holding his broken arm against his chest, he staggered to his feet. Above, stars filled the night sky, pinpricks of brightness that might illuminate heaven, but provided little light for mere mortals below. Where was the moon?

There, or part of it. Not much to light his way. And it would be colder still before dawn. If he lived that long…

He *must* live that long, he thought as he stumbled forward. Gillian was waiting for him. Gillian needed him. He needed her. He couldn't die now, not when he had found a woman whose love made him feel worthy and respected and good. No matter what the future held for them, he had to see her again, to tell her one more time that he loved her.

His knees felt too weak to support him. But they must, they *must!* He had to get back to Gillian.

How many times had he stood for hours in the yard of Boisbaston Castle, certain he was going to collapse, exhausted, hungry, thirsty, and wet if it was raining. He'd never given up then. He wouldn't give his father the satisfaction. He would stand there until he died, he'd thought.

Tonight, he would keep walking until he died.

What if Richard had also lost his horse? What if he encountered that traitor? He still had his sword; did he have the strength to wield it?

Feeling sick and in pain, Bayard leaned against a tree, the branches brushing his face. He rested his body against the rough bark, grateful for its support. He would stay here a moment.

Just a moment.

His legs began to buckle, but he forced them straight. He was Bayard de Boisbaston and he would not give up.

CHAPTER TWENTY-FOUR

Robb and a pack of leashed hounds led the search for Bayard the next morning, accompanied by Gillian, Armand, and several mounted soldiers.

Robb had claimed his head was perfectly fine. Since he seemed to be well and he was their best man for such a task, Gillian had agreed that he should come. She'd also noted the farewell kiss Dena bestowed on him before they rode out, happy for Dena even if the sight made her own heart ache with dread.

Despite Robb's expertise, every one of them scanned the trees and bushes as they went along the trail that the two horses had made away from the site of the battle. A few of the men remained behind to see to the bodies. None, mercifully, had been men of Averette. Iain and Bayard had trained them well, so although there had been wounds, none had died.

The same could not be said of their attackers. Gillian had been told five had been killed, and there had been at least one more body under a tree when they'd returned this morning. It had been a terrible scene; and the crows and scavenging animals had already been at their awful work.

She turned her attention to the hoofprints on the grassy verge her father had cut along the sides of the road. Unfortunately, it seemed the horses had soon left the road and gone into the wood, then across a pasture and into another wood, one that continued all the way to the border of the estate and beyond.

As they now made their way through the dim forest, their horses' footfalls muffled by the age-old detritus of dead leaves, no one spoke. The only noises to break the stillness were the squeak of leather, the sound of horses breathing and the soft little sounds of collision from the clay vessels, well wrapped to prevent breakage, in the bag Gillian had tied to her saddle. She'd brought sicklewort ointment to stop bleeding, a potion of poppy to dull pain and clean linens for bandages.

Even though she was exhausted after a sleepless night, every sense was alert for any sign of horse or man, any clue that Bayard and Richard had passed this way.

Occasionally she glanced ahead at Armand de Boisbaston, riding with such authority at the head of her soldiers. It was clear they respected him as much as they did Bayard or Iain.

It was also obvious that Armand was very worried about his brother, even though he'd been as comforting as Adelaide last night when they'd sat in the hall long after everyone else had retired.

"Bayard's tougher than any man I ever met," he'd said, stretching out his long legs. "When our father made us hold up buckets of water or sand by the hour for punishment, Bayard always lasted longer than anyone."

"He made one of my men hold up buckets of water after he got drunk," she told Armand. "He said it was less humiliating than the stocks."

"I suppose it is, but it makes you think your arms are going to drop off."

Armand had reached out for Adelaide's hand then, almost as if he needed her touch. As Gillian craved Bayard's.

"I well remember the first time Bayard truly lost his temper," Armand said. "Have you ever seen him really angry?"

"Yes, I have," she replied.

Adelaide and Armand exchanged looks.

"When Dunstan was killed."

"Ah, of course," Armand murmured. "An awful thing, and I didn't even know the man."

"I think you would have liked him," Adelaide said, squeezing his hand. "He was a bit like Randall."

The friend Bayard had mentioned when he spoke of stealing apples. "You were going to tell me about the first time Bayard lost his temper."

Armand gave her a rueful little smile. "Frankly, I was beginning to doubt he had one which, considering his mother's fierce rages, was rather surprising. Then one day, he tried to steal some apples from a nearby monastery."

"He told me about falling out of the tree."

"He did?"

"Yes. When I asked him how he got the scar on his face," she replied. "He didn't say he lost his temper, though."

"Well, he did. My stepmother blamed me for his mischief, although I'd been at my studies. She was shouting at me—not something unusual for my stepmother—and she raised her hand to hit me."

Armand lifted his hand as if to strike a blow. "And suddenly, there was Bayard, his cheek sewn up as neatly as that tapestry behind us, looking fit to burst the stitches. He said that if she laid a hand on me, she'd be sorry.

"I don't quite know what he intended to do if she did and I don't think she knew, either—whether he was going to strike her in return, or go to our father. But he looked capable of anything at that moment.

"She called him an ungrateful whelp, then lowered her hand." Armand did the same. "She never hit him—or me—again."

Gillian recalled the way Bayard had looked when he was standing behind her in the courtyard during the hall moot, and when they'd heard about Dunstan's death, and as they retrieved his body. Capable of anything? If someone he loved was threatened, she didn't doubt it.

But he was capable of great gentleness and kindness, too. Of loving….

Ahead, Robb paused a moment, looking this way and that as he stopped on what seemed to be the brink of a small gully. She almost expected him to start sniffing like one of the hounds that were yelping and lunging against their restraints with excitement.

Robb raised his arm to point. "There, down by the brook!"

Hope soared through Gillian as she and Armand kicked their horses to a trot, getting as close as they could to the rocky slope leading to a small, bracken-bordered stream that trickled over rocks and stones and pebbles.

Beside it lay a man, facedown, clad in mail and a helmet.

The surcoat he wore didn't belong to Bayard. God be praised, it wasn't Bayard.

"D'Artage," Armand muttered.

He looked at Gillian, then dismounted and held out his hand to her. "If he's alive he might be able to tell us where Bayard is."

Nodding, she accepted Armand's help to dismount, then gathered her skirts in her hands and started down the slope, skittering and sliding, keeping her eyes on the man below. His hand was close to the clear trickle of water; he'd probably been trying to drink before he'd slipped into unconsciousness.

Armand reached the man first and, kneeling, gently turned him over.

It was the man she knew as Charles de Fenelon. The chest of his surcoat was bloody and damp, his eyes closed, his face pale.

"He's alive, but barely," Armand said as she knelt opposite him. He raised his eyes. "This is Richard d'Artage."

What breath the injured man drew was rasping and uneven, telling her his lungs must be damaged, perhaps by a blow or a fall from his horse. His face was more gray than white and his lips were blue. Despite the coldness of the morning, he didn't shiver, which told her just how weak he was; his body didn't possess the vitality to do even that.

If ever she'd seen a man on the brink of death, she was looking at him now. She doubted there was anything she could do except ease his passing—after trying to find out where Bayard might be.

"Have someone bring me my bag," she called back to Robb, who was trying to keep the dogs under control.

As she waited for her medicines, she scooped up some water in her hands and put it to Richard's bloody lips. He coughed and spluttered, and his eyes fluttered open. His breathing quickened, and she could hear a sound that told her air was leaking from his lungs beneath his bloody mail, like bellows with a hole.

"Hel...met..." he said, raising his arm ever so slightly.

She slowly eased the heavy helmet from his head, leaving the coif because she would have to move him more to lower it. "Where's Bayard?" she asked as she gently took his face in her hands.

"Dead."

She sat back on her heels, numb. Disbelieving.

"Where's his body, then?" Armand demanded with no sympathy and no pity.

"I...don't..."

"Tell me where you left him or by God, I'll kill you right now."

She took her bag from Tom, who'd brought it, and held it close to Richard so he could see it. "I have medicine in here that will take away your pain. I'll give it to you if you'll tell us where Bayard is."

Maybe Richard wanted to trick them one more time. Perhaps Richard had lost or left his horse and crawled into this little gully and Bayard had ridden past. Maybe he wanted them to believe he was dead so they'd stop looking.

"He's...dead."

"Then *where is his body?*" Armand demanded.

Pain twisted Richard's features and his breathing grew more shallow, the horrible sound from his chest worse. "Maybe...not..." he whispered. "Pain..."

"If they got separated in the dark, he may be telling the truth," Armand grudgingly conceded. "He may not know where Bayard is—or if he's alive or dead."

"Will that potion prolong his life?" Armand asked. "Even if we could find out where Richard last saw Bayard that would help."

"I'll give you the medicine if you'll tell me where you last saw Bayard," Gillian offered.

Richard closed his eyes. "Please...help me...."

Unable to resist his plea, she pulled open the leather pouch and got out the clay jar that held the poppy mixture and an empty copper cup. She filled it with a little water from the stream and added the poppy mixture, stirring it with her finger. Then she held the cup to Richard's lips. She didn't dare to raise him higher, in case broken ribs had done the damage. That would do more. He coughed and spluttered, but most went past his lips.

It took a little while to work, and more than once she feared that he was going to stop breathing before it could ease his pain, or that she'd given him too much, or they'd come too late, until his eyes opened again. They were dulled from the potion, but he seemed more peaceful and his breathing sounded a little easier.

"Where did you last see Bayard?" Armand repeated.

"Don't...remember." Richard's face twisted with a scowl and he spoke with all that remained of his energy. "Bastard! She...should... I wanted... You bloody bastard."

"Richard, if you want any hope of heaven, you'll tell me where you last saw my brother."

Richard turned away and grabbed Gillian's hand with unexpected strength. "There's another... Not me. He's the one you want. He's the one..."

"Who?" Gillian desperately demanded. "Does he have Bayard?"

Richard didn't answer. His eyes closed and his body relaxed and his hand slipped from Gillian's. He grimaced as the last of the air seeped from his lungs.

And then he was still.

Gillian sat back on her haunches, too stunned to move except to look at Armand. "Who's he talking about? Lindall? Or somebody else?"

Armand rose and with a savage kick sent Richard's helmet flying up the bank. "Those damned treasonous bastards! I was afraid this conspiracy is more extensive than we assumed. I'd heard something before we left court—a rumor that a lord in the Midlands might be behind it."

"What lord?"

"We don't know—yet. But we'll find out. By God, we will!"

As she looked at Armand with stricken eyes, his expression softened. He came around Richard's body and offered her his hand to help her to her feet. "If you'd like to go back to Averette, we'll keep—"

"No, no," she protested as she found her balance and her resolve. "I want to keep looking for Bayard."

He nodded, then gestured for Tom and another soldier to approach. "Take the body back to Averette. Tell my lady—"

"Lady Gillian! Lord Armand!"

A short distance away, up on the other side of the stream, Robb waved frantically. "He's here! Sir Bayard—he's here!"

Gillian cried out with joy. Thank God, thank God!

But was he alive or dead?

Alive, she told herself, reaching for her bag of medicines and praying with fervent hope. He *must* be alive. Please God, alive!

She started forward so quickly, she nearly tripped over the stones and fell into the icy water of the stream. Armand grabbed her arm in his powerful grasp and pulled her along with him. They ran as fast as her stupid, cumbersome skirts would allow.

They soon reached Robb, who was standing beside Bayard. He sat with his back against a tree, his right arm cradled in his left. He was nearly as pale as Richard had been, and there was blood smeared on the tree. He'd obviously been leaning against it until he'd slid down to sit.

"Bayard!" she cried, dropping her bag as she went down on her knees beside him. "Oh, Bayard!"

She took his face gently between her hands and kissed him. His skin was warm to her touch, but not fiery. No fever. *Alive and praise God, no fever*, she thought, as she pressed more light kisses upon his forehead and cheeks. "Thank God you're alive. Never leave me again! I won't leave you. Never! I promise!"

His left hand came up to cup her face and bring her lips back to his. "Good. I won't leave you, either. I promise. I want us to be together. Always."

Armand cleared his throat, but they ignored him, kissing until she leaned too close, and he gasped in pain.

She drew back at once, to find his lips twisted into a grimace. "As much as I enjoy your embraces, my arm's broken."

Guilty but still elated, Gillian reached for her bag. "Are you hurt anywhere else?"

"My back—an arrow."

Of course. She'd seen the blood. "Was it in deep?"

"No. Hurts like the devil, though, and I've lost a little blood, I think. Not too bad," he murmured, the weakness of his voice belying his words. "Get me back to Averette and I'll be fine."

He looked up at Armand. "Richard's still out there," he said, his voice seeming to lose vitality with every word. "You've got to find him. He can tell us who's leading the traitors."

"Never mind Richard," Gillian said. "We're going to take you home to Averette."

"Yes," he whispered as his eyes closed. "I want to go home. To Averette."

CHAPTER TWENTY-FIVE

SOMETIME LATER, BAYARD opened his eyes and realized that although his back hurt and his arm ached, he was lying on clean sheets, staring at the familiar canopy of his bed in Averette. He was also warm and dry, and as thirsty as if he'd traversed a desert.

The chamber was illuminated by a flickering beeswax candle, and for the first time since he'd fallen from that horse, he believed he wasn't going to die.

He couldn't quite remember getting here, though. He *could* recall the fight with Richard, the chase, losing him, slipping from his horse…the struggle through the dark…the certainty he was going to die alone…and then Gillian kissing him.

Wonderful, marvelous Gillian, who'd promised never to leave him. Who'd brought him home.

Whatever might happen and wherever he might go, *home* would always, forever, be where Gillian was.

She must have found him somehow. He could just imagine her resolutely leading a search party and refusing to give up.

Had Armand been there, or had he dreamed that? What had happened to Richard and the rest of the mercenaries?

An arm slipped around his shoulders to help him sit up and a familiar voice said, "Sip this slowly and don't try to talk yet."

"Gillian!" he croaked, looking up into her lovely face, happiness washing over him like warm water.

"Yes. Now please, my love, lie still and drink this. It'll help you."

He'd rather kiss her, but he lacked the strength to raise himself any higher, so instead he did as he was told. He tried not to gulp the beverage she held to his lips. It tasted a little strange—water, with something added.

"It'll take away the pain and help you rest," she explained as she lowered him back onto the pillows.

Her arm slid out from behind him and he moved his left arm to grab her hand.

"Don't go," he whispered, his throat sore, as he held her tight despite the waves of pain rippling through his body.

She set the goblet on the wooden table near the bed, gently disengaged his fingers, then sat on the stool beside him, close enough to see but not to touch. "You have to rest, Bayard. You lost a lot of blood and your bones need to mend. It was a clean break, thank God, and you managed not to do much extra damage. Still, you must take care if it's to heal properly. Fortunately, I'm fairly certain the wound in your back's not going to fester and get worse, although you'll have a scar."

"How long since the battle?"

"Two days…well, nights, now," she amended. "It's nearly dawn."

He studied her face, seeing how weary she was, how pale. "You should rest, too."

"Soon." She gave him a pert little Gillian smile. "I assure you I've not been martyring myself at your bedside. Dena's been tending to you when I've been looking after the other wounded. You'll be happy to hear none of our men died in the fighting."

He was, but he was curious about a vague memory. "Is Armand here?"

"Yes, and Adelaide, as well. They arrived after you rode out. Adelaide's been helping me run the household, and Armand's been trying to find any of the men who attacked you, to learn who sent them."

He was glad, very glad, to know Armand was here. "No luck?"

She shook her head. "The men we found were all dead. If any survived, they've fled without leaving a trail."

She gave him a softer smile. "Enough talk of battle. We're safe now. And Armand's told me some very interesting things about you."

Bayard's cheeks colored with a blush. "I can imagine. I told you, I was young and foolish once."

"He's told me *good* things," she assured him. "Things that make me love you even more, although I would have said that was impossible."

That brought him a little relief as he caressed her hand. "What about Richard?" he asked. "Did he get away?"

She lifted Bayard's hand and kissed the back of his bruised knuckles. "He's dead."

His eyelids were starting to feel heavy, although his pain seemed to be dissipating. He also had the oddest sensation that he was floating. "Lindall?"

She laid his hand on his chest. "We'll talk more when you're feeling better. Sleep now, my love, and later I'll bring you something to eat. Armand should have returned by then, too."

THE NEXT TIME BAYARD awoke, it was daylight and the afternoon sunlight streamed in through the window. His back wasn't quite so sore, and his arm ached a little less. He heard someone moving about and raised his head slightly to see Gillian tidying up what appeared to be soiled bandages. There was an open clay jar on the table, and something smelled a bit minty.

It was him, he realized. Well, not him, exactly. Gillian must have put some kind of salve on his wounds.

Whatever she'd done, he felt stronger and in less pain, so he contented himself with watching her move about the chamber with her usual brisk efficiency.

Until she turned and caught him looking at her.

"No need to stop," he said, realizing his throat felt better, too. "I enjoy watching you work while I rest."

"And I enjoy watching you rest," she replied, coming toward him with a smile that made him feel better still. "You look very innocent in your sleep."

"And when I'm awake?"

"Not nearly so innocent."

"Have you slept?"

"Yes, once I was sure you were going to be all right," she replied, sitting on the stool beside the bed and brushing a lock of hair from his forehead. "You've no fever and no infection. As soon as your arm heals, you should be as healthy as you ever were."

"Thanks to you."

"And Robb, who found you. And Armand, who held you in front of him on his saddle all the way back here. He'll be here shortly. I told him you might wake soon. Would you like something to eat? There's bread, and some cider, and cheese. And Umbert's been making beef stew every day since you returned so it would be ready for you."

"Gillian, I—"

"Of course you can't eat lying down. Here, let me help you up."

Before he could speak, she was beside him, helping him to a sitting position. That hurt more than he'd expected.

"I'm sorry. I tried to be gentle," she said, sitting again on the stool. "I've been wondering if you think Frederic sincerely tried to warn you, or if you think he meant to lead you into a trap? I know he was shot with an arrow, but I can believe that once he'd served Richard's purpose, Richard would want him dead."

"I truly think the lad meant to help us," he replied, believing it.

"I'm sorry he's dead, but I'm happy to know he died honorably." She sighed. "They found the charcoal burner's remains. Richard must have killed him and taken his cart."

"God save us, I hope that's the last!" he said. "Perhaps, our enemies will think twice before moving against us now."

"I hope so, too, and we don't have to be worried about Lizette. Adelaide's had a letter from her. She's been ill, but Iain's with her and she's on her way home. She should be here in a few days."

"That's a relief."

Bayard reached for her hand and grasped it tightly. "So here we are, Gillian, safe and sound. The question is, what's to become of us? What are we going to do?"

Gillian had wondered, too, and through the long, terrible ordeal of uncertainty, not knowing if he was alive or dead, she'd made a decision. Some would say it was wrong—even sinful—but in her heart, she believed it was right.

"I was so afraid I'd lost you, Bayard," she said with

all the intensity of her resolute nature. "I feared I was never going to see you again. I can't bear that thought, Bayard. I want to be with you always—whatever you do, wherever you go. If I can't be your wife, I don't care. All that matters is that I'm with you…if you want me."

"I remember what you promised when you found me, and what I promised, too," he said, his own heart aching to hear her heartfelt words, and a different kind of pain—worse and more terrible—assailed him, because she deserved nothing less than an honorable marriage with the best of men, and he could not give her that. "Gillian, I can't ask such a sacrifice from you. You should have—"

"You, or no one," she said staunchly. And then her steadfast gaze faltered. "Unless you no longer want me."

"Want you? God's blood, I *need* you, like I need air to breathe or water to drink. But we can't marry. The church—"

"I will live with you anyway. I'll go wherever you go," she said, for her love for Bayard was stronger, more powerful, deeper and more fulfilling than even her love for Averette.

He stared at her with both hope and disbelief. "You'd leave Averette to be with me?"

"I'd do anything to be with you, Bayard," she averred. And then she smiled gloriously. "After all, I love you."

"As I love you—with all my heart."

He brought her hand to his lips and kissed it. "My life would be barren without you," he whispered as she leaned down.

Just as their lips were about to meet, a sharp rap sounded on the door. Bayard cursed under his breath and Gillian blushed as Armand came striding into the room, accompanied by his wife.

Marching up to the bed, Armand smiled as Bayard rarely saw him smile. Then he frowned as if seriously displeased. "You gave us quite a scare, you big oaf. Why the devil didn't you wait for help? Foolish bravado to go haring off after Richard that way."

"Obviously, I didn't want him to get away."

"*Obviously*, you weren't thinking at all. You could have died."

Bayard smiled. "I didn't, though."

"Thanks to Gillian."

Bayard's hand gripped hers. "Yes, thanks to Gillian."

Adelaide came to stand beside her husband. To be sure, Adelaide was lovely and other men would look at the sisters and think Bayard had won the heart of the lesser woman, but he knew better—although he'd never say so to Armand.

Adelaide glanced at their joined hands and delicately cleared her throat. "As delighted as I am that you're going to recover, I have to ask…" She hesitated a moment. "That is, I'm concerned…"

Armand looked at their joined hands and sudden understanding dawned in his eyes. He glanced uneasily at his wife.

Gillian's joyous smile took Bayard's breath away. "Armand, you can have Averette. Bayard and I are in love and I'm going with him, wherever he chooses to go."

"You're in love? And you'd leave Averette?" Adelaide exclaimed with disbelief, more for the latter than the former.

"If I must to be with Bayard," Gillian declared. "I

love him and he loves me, and we want to be together even if we can't marry."

Armand's staring regard went from Gillian to Bayard and back again. "God's blood, Bayard. I never thought... imagined..."

Adelaide's alabaster brow furrowed with concern. "You would live in sin?"

"Gladly," they both replied at once, and with equal determination.

Adelaide sat on the end of the bed. "Canon law forbids your marriage for now," she said slowly, "but perhaps not forever. I've heard that several nobles and clergymen are seeking a change. There are so many restrictions that in some villages, nobody's free to marry anyone, and several familial alliances have collapsed when either the bride or groom died young. The nobles want more ways to unite their families. I've heard the pope's amenable, but until—if—that law is changed..."

"Whether the law permits it or not, Gillian and I are going to stay together. If not here, somewhere else," Bayard said. "Nothing would make me happier than to marry Gillian, especially if we're so fortunate to have children. And I'm sorry her reputation must suffer. Mine was never much to begin with—'Gyptian's child, 'Gyptian lover—"

"That's it!" Gillian cried, leaping to her feet as a way to give their children legitimacy and their proper rights in the world burst into her mind. "Although it means saying you're a bastard, Bayard, and might cost you your estate."

"What do you mean?" Adelaide asked, clearly baffled.

"Say he's a bastard?" Armand repeated, equally puzzled. "I know full well he's not. I was there when he was born.

"Not in the room," he clarified, "but I know for certain there was no switching of babes, whatever people say."

They might be confused, but Bayard had already realized what she was suggesting. "But if I *say* I am—that my mother really did buy or steal a baby to replace her own dead offspring—then I'm not really your half brother. We're no relation at all, and then Gillian and I can marry!"

"That's ridiculous!" Armand cried. "Claim you've been impersonating a nobleman all these years? John will throw you in prison at the very least, and take your estates in forfeit to the crown."

"Not necessarily," Adelaide said, her eyes shining with excitement. "Not if Bayard *offers* him the estates, as compensation for a ruse he only just discovered and knew nothing about. We can say Bayard only recently found a confession among his mother's documents. It was hidden somewhere."

"Adelaide could write it—she's very clever," Gillian suggested.

"God's blood, I think it could work," Bayard said, smiling with delight.

"I believe it could, too," Adelaide agreed, "especially if Bayard becomes castellan of Averette by the marriage. Then John will be sure of having one dependable stronghold in Kent. That should be worth a good deal to him, since he's losing the loyalty of more barons every day.

"It would also offer John a chance to look magnanimous without costing him anything, while providing him with even more lands with which to increase his income or reward his supporters. That should appeal to John."

Armand stroked his chin. "By God, I believe you're

right. It just might work—if you don't mind being a bastard, Bayard, and losing your mother's estates."

Bayard had never been so happy to be called a disparaging name. As for the estates he rarely visited, he would gladly trade them all for the chance to stay at Averette, and without regret. "Not if it means Gillian and I can marry and live together here. Heaven knows I've been called worse things in my life. It would be worth that, and more, to be Gillian's husband."

Armand de Boisbaston finally smiled. "Then I suppose my wife had better start composing a confession."

BAYARD HAD JUST DROPPED off into a light doze when the door to his bedchamber opened. He heard the sound and snapped awake, wondering who it could be, hoping it was....

Gillian, just like that first night they spent together, except this time he felt no guilt, and shame, and worry about the desire they shared.

She wore her bedrobe over her shift and peered at him in the dim light, the candlelight flickering on her pretty face.

"I'm awake," he said, answering her unspoken question. "Have you come to bid me good night?"

"Are you feeling any worse?" she asked, coming a little closer.

Her hair was unbound, falling about her slender shoulders, and her green eyes were shadowed in the darkness so he couldn't quite make out her expression.

"No. In fact, I'm feeling much better." That wasn't precisely a lie. Just seeing her made him feel better. "And much stronger since I've eaten, and much happier since you and your sister thought of a way that will likely allow us to marry, God and John willing."

"Adelaide seems quite confident John will agree, and Armand says if anybody can persuade John, it's Adelaide."

"I think he's right, although while I don't deny Adelaide's a worthy advocate, I suspect *you* could convince John to agree simply by looking at him with those eyes of yours."

"I'm not sure if that's a compliment or not."

"It's a compliment, I assure you."

She caressed his cheek. "I think I would be more likely to argue with the king if he tried to deny us. I'd probably wind up in prison."

Bayard took hold of her hand and kissed her knuckles, making her heart race. "Then it's just as well Adelaide and Armand don't want us to go to court with them."

He sighed with mock dismay. "I also think Armand's completely besotted. No wonder he believes his wife is capable of anything. It seems to be a family failing, at least of this generation—thinking the women we love are the most wonderful, competent women in the world."

She sat beside him on the bed. "I think it's a failing in this generation of *my* family, too. I do believe I'm as besotted with you as my sister is of Armand—perhaps even more.

"Adelaide's already told the servants that you're not really related to Armand, and she sent for Hale, so that he could tell the villagers. He was quite relieved to hear we weren't as sinful as he feared. He said little Teddy's been very upset that you were hurt. I told him he could bring his son to see you tomorrow."

"I'd like that, but not as much as I'm enjoying seeing you now," Bayard replied, his eyes darkening with desire. "In fact, I'd like to see more of you, my lady."

"If I were thinking of your welfare," she said, her

voice low and seductive as she slipped off her bedrobe, "I'd let you sleep alone tonight."

"Let *me* worry about my welfare," he said. "I feel that I would be best served by some company. Yours, at any rate. If you'd sent Robb or even Armand, I would have preferred to be alone."

"Shall I get in beside you?" she asked, her voice a sultry whisper.

"Unless you'd rather stand there and tease and tempt me all night."

"Do you think I'm teasing and tempting you?"

"I *know* you are."

"Sweet saints, how cruel of me," she said without an ounce of contrition as she wiggled out of her shift. "Tell me, sir knight, how does it feel to be the one being tempted?"

Even though he was still in some pain, his excitement and anticipation grew with every wiggle. "Terrible…and wonderful."

"You've teased and tempted plenty of women, I'm sure," she replied, her soft, smooth flesh bronze in the candlelight.

"If I weren't injured, my lady," he murmured, reaching out for her with his good arm, "I'd be leaping out of this bed and taking you right there on the floor."

"Truly?" she said, stepping back out of reach. "Is that a promise?"

"Come here, Gillian."

"Is that an order?"

"Call it a very fervent request. And if you don't— wounds or no wounds—I'm coming after you." He threw back the bedclothes as if determined to do what he said.

"No, stay there!" she cried, quickly joining him

beneath the covers. "You mustn't exert yourself too much."

"Then I shan't," he said easing himself onto his left side, so that he was facing her. "Although my shoulder and arm hurt much less with you beside me."

She inched closer to him, until her naked body nestled against his and she could feel his warm breath on her cheek. "You must be careful of your arm most of all, Bayard."

"I will," he said, gingerly moving his left arm around her. "This will have to content me tonight."

"I love you, Bayard de Boisbaston," she murmured, lightly kissing his cheek. "I love you for everything you do and are, and if the king won't let us wed, I'll live with you anyway. Anywhere."

"You would really give up Averette to be with me?"

"I've said it, haven't I? *You're* willing to give up everything—your title, your estate—so that we can be together." She levered herself up on her elbow and gave him her haughtiest, most imperious look. "Are you doubting that a mere woman is capable of equal sacrifice in the name of love?"

"No. I'm wondering what I've done to be so blessed."

She slid back down beside him. "You are yourself, Bayard, and that is more than enough."

"When you say such things, I can believe it."

"Then I shall keep saying such things until you know it for yourself."

"And I shall tell you every day of my life how much I love you and need you and cherish you, Lady Gillian d'Averette. Always of Averette, God willing."

"As you'll be the lord of Averette." She gave a melodramatic sigh. "I suppose I've presided over my last hall moot."

"Oh, no," he assured her. "That's one responsibility I'll gladly leave in your capable hands."

"But your presence might keep Geoffrey and Felton from squabbling. That would be no small thing."

"I propose we *share* such a duty. You know the people far better than I, and I can intimidate those who bring frivolous suits so that they think better of it."

She laughed merrily, joyfully, the delightful sound filling the chamber and making him laugh, too.

"Oh, I do love you, Bayard de Boisbaston!"

"And I love you, Lady Gillian of Averette. Now and always," he said as she nestled against him.

Where she belonged.

EPILOGUE

IN THE SOLAR OF HIS CASTLE, Lord Wimarc de Werre crumpled the small piece of parchment in his elegant hand and tossed it into the brazier. The sheepskin curled, then the edges caught and soon the scent of smoldering parchment filled his nostrils while the message was reduced to ash.

The scowl on his face disappeared when the man he'd sent for appeared at the door.

"You wanted to see me, my lord?" Lindall asked, his eyes darting about like those of a ferret caught in a trap.

"Yes, I do. Come in. Sit."

Still anxious, the former second-in-command of Averette sidled into the room, then perched gingerly on the edge of the delicate ebony chair as if he feared it would break beneath him. Wimarc could have told him not to worry; that, like him, the chair's outward appearance gave no indication of its true strength.

Instead, he steepled his long, bejewelled fingers and regarded the traitorous soldier over the tips. "It may interest you to know, Lindall, that those rumors about Bayard de Boisbaston's birth are true. He's not Raymond de Boisbaston's son."

Lindall's eyes widened. "He's a bastard?"

"Yes. According to a friend at court, Bayard's just

admitted his mother's child died at birth and she obtained another infant to take its place—Bayard."

Lindall relaxed and a wide grin split his homely face. "Confessed under torture?"

"No. It seems that since Bayard claims he only recently learned the secret of his birth, our magnanimous sovereign has decided not to imprison him," Wimarc said, his description of the king dripping with sarcasm. "John's also *graciously* decided that, since he requires a loyal lord in Kent, Bayard should marry Gillian d'Averette and become castellan there. No doubt the offer of Bayard's estates in compensation played a part in that decision, as well as the fact that Armand de Boisbaston and his beautiful wife spoke on the bastard's behalf."

"Sir Bayard's going to marry Lady Gillian?" Lindall repeated incredulously.

"Apparently."

Lindall scowled and shook his head. "I don't believe it."

"Alas, the marriage doesn't require your approval, or mine. Only the king's. It's most unfortunate Bayard was left alive and Richard died."

Beads of perspiration appeared on Lindall's upper lip. "I did what I could, my lord. They disappeared after the battle—Bayard and Richard both. I killed what wounded men of yours I could find, though, so they couldn't say who paid 'em."

"A service I greatly appreciate and have compensated you for accordingly," Wimarc noted. "However, the fact remains that the de Boisbastons are still alive to serve our idiot of a king. If my plans are to succeed, I need them dead. Which brings me to you, Lindall."

"You…you want me to kill them? I ain't no assassin,

my lord. Killing in battle, I'm your man, but sneaking up on somebody all by myself—"

"Fortunately, that isn't the task I had in mind for you."

The soldier once again relaxed and he ran his hand over his lip.

"Gillian and Adelaide's youngest sister, Elizabeth, is on her way back to Averette. I want you to take twenty of my men, find her and bring her here."

Lindall gulped. "That isn't going to be easy, my lord. Iain Mac Kendren's gone after her and—"

"And found her, or so I'm told," Wimarc said, cutting off the man's whining. "I understand their progress back to Averette has been slow because the lady's been ill."

He untied the heavy purse at his belt and tossed it to the soldier. Lindell missed and it fell to the floor with a heavy clinking sound. "Fifty marks. There'll be another fifty for you when you deliver Lizette to me."

As Lindall bent down to retrieve the payment, Lord Wimarc's thin lips curved up in a malicious smile. "I understand she has a charming voice. I would hear her sing for me."

AUTHOR'S NOTE

SOME OF YOU MAY BE scratching your heads and thinking, "Hold on! There's no reason Bayard can't marry Gillian. He's not *her* brother-in-law."

If I were writing a story set after 1215, you'd be right—there would be no problem for brothers from one family to marry sisters from another family if their sibling had married into the same family. That is, if Fred from Family A married Alice from Family B, and Fred's brother, Frank, wanted to marry Alice's sister, Anna, that would be fine.

However, after about 300 A.D. the church began to create more restrictions as to who could marry whom, until by the early thirteenth century, when this book is set, if Fred married Alice, their families would be considered joined as if by blood. That is, under canon law, Fred's brother Frank became the brother of Alice's sister Anna as if they were born of the same parents.

However, the prohibitions against marriages of people related by affinity to the second and third degree—siblings and cousins, among others—caused some problems, as Adelaide mentions in the story. In some places, it meant that everybody in the village was related either by blood or affinity to everybody else, so nobody could find anybody to (legally) marry.

Especially among the nobility, marriage was about alliances, both political and economic. If one of the members of the first couple died, the alliance between their families could be in jeopardy. By allowing marriages between more family members, that was less likely to occur.

So in 1215, the Fourth Lateran Council abolished the restrictions against marriages between people related to the second and third degree of affinity. However, at the time of my story, such a marriage would still have been prohibited by canon law.

You may also be wondering about my use of the term "'Gyptian" to describe Bayard's alleged origin. I do mean the modern equivalent of "Gypsy," a term first recorded much later than my story. The name was based on the belief that the Gypsies, or Roma, originated in Egypt.

Actually, there have been many places suggested as the origin of the Roma, including Babylon, Nubia, and Abyssinia.

Some people also believed they were descended from Celtic Druids, or Noah, or the Biblical Abraham and Sarah. Some stories claimed they were doomed to wander the earth because their ancestors refused to help Joseph and Mary when they fled to Egypt, or because they forged the nails that held Jesus to the cross.

One of the more interesting suggestions is that they are the descendants of the Euxians, who lived near Persia and were famous for being able to foresee the future.

It's also unfortunately true that the Roma were thought to steal or buy children. I employed this prejudice as something Bayard's enemies tried to use against him, but that he was able to turn to the good. Playing on that mistaken belief allows Bayard and Gillian to avoid the restriction to their marriage imposed by the soon-to-be-changed canon law.

HISTORICAL

Regency

REAWAKENING MISS CALVERLEY
by Sylvia Andrew

One stormy night Lord Aldhurst rescues a cold, dazed
lady and intends to shelter her until she remembers where
she comes from. James wants her to stay as mistress of
his mansion, but the nameless beauty on his doorstep is
London's most sought-after debutante!

THE ACCIDENTAL PRINCESS
by Michelle Willingham

Etiquette demands Lady Hannah Chesterfield ignore the
shivers of desire Lieutenant Michael Thorpe's wicked gaze
provokes, but her unawakened body clamours for his touch...
So she joins Michael on an adventure to uncover the secret
of his birth—is this common soldier really a prince?

Regency

THE UNMASKING OF A LADY
by Emily May

It's common knowledge that Lady Arabella Knightley spent
her early years in London's gutters. But what the Ton
doesn't know is that she helps the poor – by stealing
jewels from the rich! Adam St Just determines to
unbutton Lady Arabella...or unmask her!

On sale from 5th November 2010
Don't miss out!

*Available at WHSmith, Tesco, ASDA, Eason
and all good bookshops*

www.millsandboon.co.uk

HISTORICAL

CAPTURED BY THE WARRIOR
by Meriel Fuller

With the country on the brink of anarchy, soldier Bastien de la Roche will do what it takes to restore calm. He captures spirited Alice Matravers, a servant to the royal court, and uses his charm to blackmail her into gaining an audience with the King. Only Alice uses her fieriness to melt his hardened heart.

KLONDIKE FEVER
by Kate Bridges

Disguised as a drifter, Mountie Dylan Wayburn finds himself riding in the same stagecoach as Lily Cromwell. The beautiful redhead was once his family's servant and she could blow his cover sky-high, not least because her full lips beg to be kissed...

Regency
WICKED WAGER
by Julia Justiss

Anthony, Lord Nelthorpe has committed many sins— including his attempt to seduce well-bred Jenna Montague Fairchild. But now Anthony's injuries from the Waterloo battlefield are being nursed by the very woman he wronged...

On sale from 5th November 2010
Don't miss out!

2 FREE BOOKS
AND A SURPRISE GIFT

We would like to take this opportunity to thank you for reading this
Mills & Boon® book by offering you the chance to take TWO more
specially selected books from the Historical series absolutely FREE!
We're also making this offer to introduce you to the benefits of the
Mills & Boon® Book Club™—

- **FREE home delivery**
- **FREE gifts and competitions**
- **FREE monthly Newsletter**
- **Exclusive Mills & Boon Book Club offers**
- **Books available before they're in the shops**

Accepting these FREE books and gift places you under no obligation to buy, you may cancel at any time, even after receiving your free
books. Simply complete your details below and return the entire page
to the address below. You don't even need a stamp!

YES Please send me 2 free Historical books and a surprise gift. I
understand that unless you hear from me, I will receive 4 superb new
books every month for just £3.99 each, postage and packing free. I
am under no obligation to purchase any books and may cancel my
subscription at any time. The free books and gift will be mine to keep
in any case.

Ms/Mrs/Miss/Mr ——————— Initials ———————

Surname —————————————————————
Address —————————————————————
——————————————— Postcode ———————
E-mail —————————————————————

Send this whole page to: Mills & Boon Book Club, Free Book Offer,
FREEPOST NAT 10298, Richmond, TW9 1BR